IMPROPER INFLUENCE

BY USA TODAY BESTSELLING AUTHOR

MELISSA F. MILLER

BROWN STREET BOOKS

Three things shine before the world and cannot be hidden.

They are the moon, the sun, and the truth[.]

Pokala Lakshmi Narasu

The Essence of Buddhism (1907)

1

Bodhi King stared down at the cold, rigid body of Jasmine Courtland. She had a tangle of red curls, long dancer's legs, and a smattering of freckles on her pale skin. No wounds, no evidence of disease, nothing to suggest she was anything other than a perfectly healthy twenty-two year old. Aside from the obvious fact that she was dead.

According to the report from the EMTs, the recent college graduate had complained of a fever and fatigue for two days. She'd been reading a novel beside her parents' swimming pool earlier in the day. When her father came out to see if she wanted to join him for lunch, he found her unresponsive body on the ground next to her lounge chair.

By rights it should have presented to Bodhi, the forensic pathologist who caught the case, as a puzzling and bizarre death. Unfortunately, it did not.

He already knew what he'd find when he autopsied her heart: the cause of death would be myocarditis, an infection of the heart.

Myocarditis was rarely contracted by people living in the United States and was even more rarely fatal. Yet it had been the cause of death in two more otherwise healthy young women in Allegheny County in the past week and a half. Once he finished his exam and signed her death certificate, Jasmine Courtland would officially become the third woman in Pittsburgh to die as a result of myocarditis in the past ten days, joining Nina Penrose and Christa Taylor.

The media would decry her death as inexplicable, a statistical anomaly.

But was it?

He turned away from the corpse toward the laptop sitting on the stainless steel table behind him. It was his practice to type up contemporaneous notes during the autopsies he performed. He typed a few lines into the file labeled 'Courtland, Jasmine,' and then clicked on his directory of notes to cross-reference the Penrose and

Taylor files, hoping some common fact would jump out at him, connecting the three apparently unrelated deaths.

Bodhi blinked. He scanned the list of files, and his pulse quickened. 'Penrose, Nina' and 'Taylor, Christa' were not there.

"Not possible," he muttered to himself.

He pulled up the search feature and searched his entire hard drive for each of the files in turn. The search box informed him "*No files found.*"

His heart thumped in his chest. He hovered his fingers over the keyboard, but they shook. So he took a moment to slow his breathing and steady his hands before he repeated the search—this time tapping into the official database of cases maintained on the network.

Although he kept a local copy of each of his active cases on his laptop because the network was notoriously slow, he was meticulous about always saving to both his hard drive and the network, just in case his laptop died. He could always pull the files down from the network.

He waited patiently as the hourglass spun lazily on his screen, letting him know the computer was working on his request. It spun for a long time. So long, in fact, that his anxiety fizzled into boredom. At last, the network coughed up the results of his search.

No files found.

~ ~ ~ ~ ~ ~ ~ ~ ~ ~

HE RACED from the exam room to his small, uncluttered office. Every horizontal surface was clear. The only personal touch was a square, wooden box filled with smooth rocks and white sand that he raked when he needed to clear his mind.

He crouched and pulled open the lowest drawer of the metal filing cabinet on which the rock garden sat. He removed the top notebook from a stack of composition notebooks. Squatting beside the cabinet, he opened it and thumbed through the pages.

A frown creased his lips, and he turned the pages faster, running each sheet between his finger and thumb. He reached the last page and closed the notebook then turned it over to examine the back cover: "August 3, 2012—March

18, 2013" was written across the back in black
marker.

Wrong notebook. The current one should have
been on the top.

He removed the entire stack from the drawer
and flipped through it, consciously slowing his
breathing. The rest of the notebooks were in
reverse chronological order. None was out of
place or missing. But his current notebook was
gone, and with it, the entries he'd made when
he'd autopsied Nina Penrose and Christa Taylor.

Although he maintained his official records in
electronic format, he also kept handwritten journals, where he recorded his personal thoughts and
feelings about his cases. The entries were his way of
honoring the lives of the dead who passed through
his hands. He jotted down the thoughts that flitted
through his consciousness during autopsies,
capturing details that suggested the intimacies and
intricacies of life, like a tribal tattoo, stretch marks
lining a mother's stomach, old surgical scars, or
calloused fingertips—were they the result of
manual labor or hours of guitar playing?

He doubted the passages he'd written about
the dead young women would hold any forensic
value, anyway, but with his electronic files lost in

the ether, he'd wanted to check. The fact that his computer records were missing was strange and inconvenient, but he imagined they could be reconstructed by the information technology specialists. But the loss—no, call it what it was, the *theft*—of his private journals felt like a very personal violation.

He replaced the notebooks and rocked back on his heels.

Saul David passed by his open door.

"Hey, Bodhi, what did the Buddhist coroner write down for the cause of death?"

"Life," he responded automatically, providing the punch line to his colleague's favorite joke and closing the drawer.

Saul's chuckle floated down the hallway behind him.

Bodhi stood and reached for the small wooden rake resting against the corner of the wooden box. As he raked curved lines around the rocks and through the sand, he took note of two unfamiliar feelings coursing through his body: burning anger and queasy fear.

2

Sasha McCandless smiled patiently at the attorney sitting on the other side of the highly polished conference room table. She waited while he pawed through his pile of manila folders, each neatly labeled and containing a single exhibit.

He cleared his throat but kept his eyes down on the papers in front of him. Finally, he said, "Let's go off the record."

The court reporter's fingers stopped moving. She rolled her neck and picked up her copy of sports section of the *Pittsburgh Post-Gazette*. She folded it in half lengthwise and turned her attention from the attorney squabbling to local hockey coverage.

Chip Clark cleared his throat again and

steepled his fingers. He kept his voice even but gave Sasha puppy dog eyes, pleading with her not to embarrass him.

"If your client would just answer the questions, Sasha. These subjects are within his knowledge—"

Sasha cut him off right there. "Chip, come on. You noticed his deposition in his personal capacity. If you wanted to depose a corporate representative, you should have issued a 30(b)(6) notice. You know it, and I know it. Mr. Nelson is here to answer questions regarding his personal knowledge about the contract between VitaMight and Greenway Pharmacies, and nothing further." She flashed her adversary a tight smile and watched his face turn purple.

"Sasha, be reasonable."

"I *am* being reasonable. You don't get to choose the corporate representative; VitaMight does. And I'll tell you right now, they wouldn't have sent Mr. Nelson. So, if you have any more questions for Mr. Nelson, ask them. If you're going to keep asking questions that can only be answered by a corporate representative, we'll shut this deposition down and call it a day. I'm sure Mr. Nelson would like to get home in time to catch the start of the Penguins' game, right, Alex?"

"Hmm?" Sasha's witness, apparently bored by the back and forth between the lawyers was craning his neck to read the front page of the court reporter's newspaper upside down on the table. He turned to face her. "Sorry. What did you say?"

She gave him a long, meaningful look that said *pay attention*.

Chip squared his shoulders and took one last shot at bullying her. "I guess we'll have to call the judge then."

Sasha stopped herself from laughing aloud at the empty threat, but just barely.

"Be my guest. Here, do you want me to get an outside line for you?" She pulled the star-shaped phone toward her. "I'm sure Judge Sawyer would be delighted to address this issue on a Friday afternoon."

Chip stared at her.

She stared back.

The court reporter yawned, and Alex Nelson kept reading her newspaper.

"Back on the record," Chip said, finally.

Alex looked up from the paper and folded his

hands in front of him—the very picture of an attentive, dutiful witness.

The court reporter dropped the sports section and hovered her fingers over her keys, ready to resume her silent, rapid keystrokes whenever Chip resumed his idiotic line of questioning.

The room was still for a long moment.

"I have no further questions," Chip said.

He opened his briefcase, snapping the clasps with unnecessary force, and shoved his meticulous piles of papers into it in a haphazard heap.

"Are you gonna want both minuscript and full?" the court reporter asked, unperturbed by the awkward end to the deposition.

"Yes," Chip said. Then he snapped his briefcase closed and walked out of the room without another word.

"Friendly guy," the court reporter observed. "What about you?"

"Just an electronic copy, expedited, please," Sasha said, swallowing a laugh at Chip's hurried exit.

The electronic version of the deposition transcript would contain both the full-sized version and the minuscript, condensed to fit four pages on a single sheet of paper. It would give her everything she needed and help her in her ongoing quest to avoid dying in an avalanche of paper someday.

"Sure thing."

Sasha gathered her own papers into a stack while the court reporter and Alex exchanged views about the Penguins' latest acquisition—a hot new goaltender.

"You did great," she lied, walking Alex to the door.

He was a nervous witness and she'd spent two full days preparing him not to volunteer information, not to guess, and to pay attention. But he seemed to be almost uncoachable. Chip's error had been their saving grace. If he'd properly noticed the deposition of corporate representative and the company had produced Alex, she would have had a mess on her hands. As it was, Alex mangled the handful of questions that she'd allowed Chip to ask.

Alex stopped in the doorway and beamed at her. The tension left his shoulders, and she felt a bit of sympathy for him. Everyone hated being deposed, and most people were bad at it. He was a business guy, not a lawyer.

"Make sure you tell Harper that, now," he said, shaking her hand.

"Oh, I'll definitely be giving the General Counsel a report," she said.

Sasha's assessment would be more honest than the glad-handing Alex had just received, but she'd be sure to focus on the positives. Harper Roberts was a worrier. It wouldn't do to feed that worry—not over a case that she'd almost certainly win on summary judgment, especially now that discovery was closed and old Chip had neglected to depose a corporate representative.

Alex smiled. "Thanks. You take care."

"I'll walk you out," she said.

"Oh, no need. I'm going to pop in and get a brownie downstairs," he said.

Ordinarily, she would have insisted, but walking beside Alex made Sasha feel like she was part of a circus act.

He was six-feet, seven-inches tall. She was not quite five feet. Her neck would be sore from peering up at him before they reached the coffee shop on the first floor.

"Okay, then have a good weekend."

He raised a hand in salute and pushed through the door.

She turned back to the court reporter, who had packed up her equipment and was shoving her newspaper into her large, vinyl purse.

"Are you all set?" Sasha asked.

"Yep." The woman gave Sasha a friendly smile. "Go, Pens!"

Sasha smiled back and held the door open for her.

~ ~ ~ ~ ~ ~ ~ ~ ~ ~ ~

AFTER THE COURT REPORTER LEFT, Sasha poked her head into Naya's office, but her legal assistant was nowhere to be seen. She pulled Naya's door shut and returned to her own office to check her messages and see whether her email in-box had exploded during the deposition.

She was composing an email to Harper, when Naya appeared in her doorway, holding a mug of coffee in her hand.

"How'd it go?" she asked, crossing the room and depositing the mug on Sasha's desk.

"For me?" Sasha asked, distracted by the smell of Jake's dark roast.

Naya nodded, a wry smile on her lips. "Who

else? I know you must've been jonesing in there. What's it been—four hours?"

"At least," Sasha agreed. "Bless your cranky heart," she said, raising the mug in Naya's direction before taking a drink.

"You need to try Champion Fuel," Naya said.

"Who what now?"

"Champion Fuel. Seriously, Mac, do you live under a rock? Hot new energy drink? Official fuel of the Pittsburgh Penguins? Brand-new bottling facility on the South Side? Ringing any bells?"

Sasha shook her head. "Sorry. Does it taste like coffee?"

"No."

"Then what use would I have for it?"

"Point taken," Naya said, dropping herself into Sasha's guest chair. "So, the deposition—how'd it go?"

Sasha shrugged and sipped her coffee.

"Alex was shaping up to be a disaster, but I held Clark's feet to the fire and told him no 30(b)(6) notice, no questions outside Alex's personal knowledge."

Naya laughed. "And Alex's personal knowledge regarding sub-paragraph 16(g)(iii) of the distribution agreement would be … exactly nothing?"

"Exactly. He didn't negotiate that agreement. He didn't even work for VitaMight when it was signed. The sales to Greenway just happened to get shuffled into his department after VitaMight sold off the herbal side of the business. So, despite his best efforts to help the other side, we should be able to get the case kicked on summary judgment."

A slow, satisfied smile spread across Naya's lips. "Sweet."

Sasha had noticed Naya's interest in the strategy underlying their cases—already strong—had grown since she'd been accepted to law school.

Naya was going to excel, Sasha knew. The question was how Sasha was going to run the office without her.

She realized Naya was staring at her.

"What are you thinking?" Naya asked.

"Nothing."

She shook off her unproductive worry. She'd run the office single-handedly before Naya had joined her; she could do it again if need be.

"Okay. It's almost five. Do you have time to grab a drink?"

The desk phone rang before Sasha could

answer. Naya craned her neck and leaned across the desk to read the display.

"It's the Prescott switchboard. Want me to get it?"

Sasha shook her head and hit the speaker button.

"Sasha McCandless."

"Sasha, Garrett English here. How've you been?"

The overly jovial voice on the other end of the phone triggered an unfortunate image of her former coworker. It was the summer of 2006, and Sasha and Garrett—along with a handful of other rising stars—had been invited to a sailing party on the head of the litigation department's boat. The party was for the benefit of that summer's year's crop of summer associates—law students who were paid an obscene amount of money and given a sanitized glimpse of what life as a Prescott & Talbott attorney could be. High-profile cases for Fortune 100 clients. Gourmet meals. Black tie parties. Intimate dinners in part-ner-owned mansions. And sailing on yachts. Sasha called them TCBY events: This. Could. Be. Yours!

Of course, none of it would be theirs. Not

unless and until the new recruits survived a solid decade or more of mind-numbing abuse.

But, that day, on Noah Peterson's yacht, Sasha and Garrett's job was to act like they spent all their weekends sailing down the Allegheny River with multi-millionaire partners, and not chained to their desks from sunrise until the Downtown restaurants closed and Pittsburgh rolled up its sidewalks.

Garrett, unfortunately, had gotten progressively greener the longer they'd bobbed along the river. And, then, as Noah regaled them with a story about challenging counsel to a fistfight during a deposition, and Sasha widened her eyes as if she hadn't heard this embellished story at least two dozen times, Garrett turned to the summer associate nursing a Corona next to him and said, "You don't want to mess with Noah!" in that same cheerful voice.

Just then, the boat lurched and, apparently so did Garrett's stomach, because he turned and vomited on Noah's shoes.

And, Sasha thought now, it was that poor aim that had landed Garrett in 'of counsel' purgatory —the holding pen for attorneys who had aged out of the associate ranks but either had chosen personal lives over partnership or, as in Garrett's case, were delusively waiting to get called up.

"I'm great. What can I do for you?" she said.

"I'm calling to ask you to put up a Chinese wall on your VitaMight breach of contract case."

"Newsflash: I'm a sole practitioner. Whom exactly am I supposed to wall off?"

"Your legal assistant."

Sasha glanced across the desk and met Naya's surprised eyes.

"And I would do that why?"

The false cheer faded from his voice.

"Because Prescott represents the supplement company that purchased your client's herbal division, and Naya may be assigned to that file when she joins us in September."

Sasha was silent for a moment, allowing her flash of anger to fade before she responded.

"First, VitaMight isn't just *my* client. It's your former client, remember? You can't tell me the firm's representing a client whose interests are adverse to VitaMight, especially when I know for a fact the business and finance guys represented VitaMight in the sale of the herbal division that's at issue in my case."

"VitaMight understood when we represented them in that sale that we'd be representing

Herbal Attitudes on a going forward basis with regard to the herbal business," he said.

She continued as if he hadn't spoken.

"Second, you're asking me to bench Naya because you *might* assign her to do work for this client some day in the future when—excuse me, *if*—she comes to work there? That's crazy. She could decide not to go to law school and turn down your scholarship and job offer. Herbal Attitudes could fire you before September. There are multiple contingencies that may or may not happen, Garrett. This case could settle—or more likely, I'll win on summary judgment. Not to mention, Naya works *here* now. If she's conflicted out from working on something when she gets there, it'll be Prescott's obligation to wall her off from the representation. I don't have any duty to prevent that from happening."

"Look—"

"Don't interrupt me. I let you speak. Now, you show me the same courtesy."

He was immediately cowed.

"I'm sorry. Go ahead."

"Third, your client isn't even in the case. Neither party has named Herbal Attitudes."

After a beat to make sure she was finished, he

said, "That's true. But you served it with a third-party subpoena *duces tecum*."

She closed her eyes. He was right, of course. She had sent a subpoena *duces tecum*—a request for things, in this case, documents—to the herbal company seeking any files it had related to the dispute over the distribution of the memory supplement at issue in the case.

"That's right. I did. You're representing the company on that?"

"I am."

"Your discovery responses were due today, Garrett. Let me guess, you called about this conflict issue, but while you have me, you just happen to want me to talk about an extension to respond to the subpoena."

It was a maneuver straight out of the Prescott & Talbott playbook: First make an overreaching demand, guaranteed to be denied out of hand; then, ask for what you really want. The idea was to back your opponent into a corner: an attorney who had denied not one, but two, requests for an accommodation from opposing counsel ran the risk of looking unreasonable if the issue ever came up in front of the judge.

From the way Naya twisted her mouth into a

knowing grin, Sasha knew she recognized the move for what it was, too.

Their eyes met, and Naya twisted her lips into a sneer, leaving no doubt as to how she felt about the manipulation.

Sasha was inclined to agree. She was gearing up to tell Garrett there would be no extension when he chuckled.

"Oh, no, I don't need an extension. Our production is being hand-delivered to your office as we speak. Have a good weekend, Sasha. And, think about what I said. You don't want to be responsible for tanking Naya's career before it even starts, do you?"

Before she could answer, he disconnected the call, still laughing.

The reason for Garrett's amusement became clear about twenty minutes later when three sheepish-looking mailroom employees from Prescott & Talbott wheeled litigation carts holding a total of eighteen bankers' boxes full of documents into her office.

Garrett wasn't relying on the overreaching demand. No, he'd chosen a different tried and true Prescott play: bury the sole practitioner in paper.

3

—————

Mackenzie Lane slowly removed the wireless headset and placed it on her desk next to her phone. Then she raked her fingers through her hair, massaging her scalp, as she processed the situation and sketched out her next move.

First, she knew her source—correction, *sources*—had reliable information. She had learned early on to always have at least two independent sources in place in every possible piece of any hierarchy.

Sometimes when she thought about all the people she relied on, a mounting panic rose in her chest, making it difficult to breathe. Each person she cajoled, bribed, or threatened was a potential point of weakness. Any one of them could turn from ally to enemy at any moment. But it was the way the political machine worked.

She comforted herself by reciting a list of powerful men—and they were almost all men—who'd risen to national prominence on the strength of networks like hers. Her goals were equally lofty. A deputy director position in a mid-sized city was a career ambition for lots of people, but for her it was a mere stepping stone. She had her eye on a senatorship. At a minimum.

So she forged ahead, cultivating sources in the various departments of city government. Despite the fact that it carried almost no political juice of its own, the Medical Examiner's Office was no exception. Mackenzie adhered to the belief that one never knew which relationships would pay off, so it made sense to nurture as many as possible.

And in the case of the Medical Examiner's Office, it looked like her friendships were becoming very valuable. One of her sources was well-placed and well-paid; the other had no idea she was harvesting information every time they spoke. The news she received from both was the same. So, there was no denying she had a problem.

Second, she knew she had to share the latest

development with Barry, but the trick would be to do it in a way that wouldn't spook him. Spooking him would undo all the good she'd accomplished in the past six months. And, she reminded herself, she'd done a lot of good.

She turned and walked over to the window. She pressed her forehead against the glass and stared down at Grant Street. It was after five, and the worker bees were flowing along the sidewalk in a swarm that led to parking lots, cars, and suburban homes. A significant number of them would stop off at taverns or bars to celebrate the end of another workweek. They'd pick up pizzas to take home to their families. Run into the grocery store for a few essentials and a lottery ticket. Maybe fill their cars' gas tanks for the weekend ahead. Their thousands of small transactions would pile up in the coffers, adding to Pittsburgh's recovering economy.

And the economy *was* recovering—thanks in no small part to her efforts.

Sure, Barry was the mayor, and he took the credit, held the press conferences, and posed for the publicity shots. But he knew as well as she did that he couldn't have done it without his Deputy Director of Economic Development for the City of Pittsburgh.

She was the one who wooed the corporations to relocate, to expand, to hire workers and pump money into the city. She was the one who pushed the tax breaks through City Council, wore down the unions on their demands, and strong-armed the zoning boards. She was the one who single-handedly created the South Side waterfront revitalization district.

And she was the one who was going to have to tell Barry that they had a problem. A serious problem. In fact, she was hard pressed to think of a worse problem than a spate of dead women who all traced back to a single, very high-profile source of the city's newfound riches, which, in turn, had her fingerprints all over it. A public relations disaster would end her career—not to mention Barry's.

She felt her heartbeat begin to slow as her initial panic faded, and her natural determination rose to the foreground.

It wasn't as if she'd never delivered bad news before. In her previous life, as a corporate management consultant, she often found herself in the delicate position of explaining to the very person who had hired her that, in her expert opinion, it would be in the company's best interest to eliminate his position—or maybe his entire department. She'd comforted more than one sobbing vice president in her day.

But, in the end, business people were easy to persuade. Numbers, preferably preceded by dollar signs and followed by zeroes, always worked. Politicians were also swayed by numbers —voting percentages, usually. But sometimes donation amounts. Either way, she always managed to get everyone to fall into line and adhere to her script.

She'd turned down a shot at partnership in the management consultant world—and the million-dollar incomes it could provide— because she'd discovered power and influence mattered more to her than money. She got a jolt of pure adrenaline every time she convinced someone to yield to her will, vote the way she wanted, or pull out a checkbook to fund a project. And, as convincing as she could be when she wanted something, she could be downright ruthless when it came to protecting that some-thing once she got it.

Mackenzie rolled her shoulders then reached into her desk drawer. She removed a pocket mirror and a lipstick and carefully lined her lips, applying the deep red stain with the care and precision of a soldier oiling his rifle.

4

Sasha pushed open the door to her condo and hoisted the six-pack of assorted craft beers in greeting to her fiancé.

"I stopped at The Sharp Edge."

She rested the cardboard carrier on the kitchen island and shed her suit jacket then slid her feet out of her pumps.

Connelly looked up from a mound of dough that he was stretching into a disc and smiled his slow, crooked smile. "Great, I'm thirsty."

To Sasha, pizza and beer at the end of the workweek meant picking up a six pack and a large pie from Village Pizza on her way home from work. She should have known when Connelly said he'd take care of the pizza that it would involve something more complex than placing a takeout order.

She leaned against the counter and watched him work the dough. A sweep of black hair fell over his eye.

Since leaving his last position as the chief security officer for a pharmaceutical company, he'd let his hair grow out from the regulation cut he'd sported ever since she'd met him while he was still working for the Department of Homeland Security. The slightly shaggy style made him seem relaxed and approachable.

But he was still the same Connelly. Serious. Disciplined. And surprisingly busy for someone who officially had taken very early retirement. Unofficially, though, he was quietly doing something for one or more of the federal law enforcement agencies. He fielded the occasional cell phone call that prompted him to walk outside to talk and was careful to always password-protect his laptop when he left it open.

She didn't ask, and he didn't tell. Between her clients' confidential information and his national security secrets, there was plenty they couldn't talk about. As long as they both understood the reason for their shared silence, she figured it wouldn't have to drive a wedge between them.

He wiped his hands on a striped kitchen towel and handed her a bottle opener. She pried the caps off two lagers and passed one across the island to him.

"Thanks."

He leaned toward her and brushed his lips against her ear. A shiver ran along her spine, and, as usual, the strength of her reaction surprised her. She pressed her head against his warm chest for a moment.

She nodded toward the pizza dough. "Does that have to rest or anything?"

"Five minutes. How was your day?"

Something soft and furry wrapped itself around her ankle. She bent and scooped up Java one handed. He began to purr instantly and rubbed his face against her hand.

"Fine—until I got a call from Prescott."

Connelly narrowed his gray eyes and peered at her through a lock of hair. "Another attempt by Will to lure you back?"

"Not this time." She released the wriggling cat and sipped her beer. "They hit me with a document dump."

"Document dump?"

"Prescott represents a third party who has to provide discovery in one of my cases for Vita-

Might. In typical Prescott fashion, they waited until the end of the day today—the deadline for the close of discovery—to deliver a stack of boxes full of documents. It's a classic move. The big firm overwhelms the sole practitioner with paper. Anything relevant is buried within hundreds of thousands of pages of paper."

"Why? What's the point of that?" Connelly asked.

She smiled at his naivety. "The point is to work me to death and hope I miss the important stuff hidden in all the dross they just dumped on me. And, they're taking the position that Naya can't work on the case because she's going to be joining them at the end of the summer.

He turned his attention to a small glass bowl and began to whisk together olive oil and tomato paste.

"Do you want some help with dinner?"

"Nope. Can they do that?"

"Do what? Bury me in paper or make me bench Naya?"

"Both. Either."

She considered her answer. Could they? Sure, they just had. The document production was standard operating procedure. It wasn't particu- larly courteous, but it wasn't improper. The attempt to strong-arm her into removing Naya from the case was ... weird. It made no sense that she could see, and she was fairly certain the state ethics committee would agree with her that there was no live conflict. But, the reality was she wasn't going to put Naya's position with Prescott at risk to test her belief.

"I guess so," she finally answered in a defeated voice.

"What does that mean for your workload?"

He kept his eyes on the sauce that he was spreading across the dough in neat, concentric circles. His tone was casual, too casual.

"I'm going to have to work. Probably all weekend. If there *is* anything hidden in those boxes that's going to require me to notice a deposition or take more discovery, I'll have to file papers with the court on Monday. I mean, discovery officially closed today."

As she said the words, her stomach dropped. There were two possibilities: one, Garrett hadn't focused on the subpoena and the eleventh-hour production was simply a function of his lack of attention; two, there was something in the production that he wanted her to miss. Knowing Garrett, her money was on door number two.

"Oh."

The note of disappointment that crept into his voice puzzled her. She searched her memory for plans they'd made and drew a blank.

"Am I forgetting something?"

"No. I just hoped we could tackle some wedding planning this weekend." He flashed a small smile. "It's okay, though."

But she knew it was very much not okay. He'd proposed back in February, and, since then, they hadn't so much as set a wedding date.

A *wedding date.* The phrase weighed on her, like a brief she needed to draft or an impending deadline. She couldn't wait to marry Connelly; in fact, she'd suggested they elope right away. But, he'd dug in his heels and insisted on a proper wedding, with all the work that entailed.

Not only that, he'd enlisted his future mother-in-law as backup. Just thinking about it, Sasha groaned inwardly. Valentina McCandless had very definite ideas about what qualified as a proper wedding, and, as far as Sasha could tell, meeting her mother's standards would involve at least as much work as opposing class certification. Maybe more. Which would have been fine if Connelly and her mother had taken on the planning, but Valentina was too busy cooing over not one, but two, new grandchildren to help.

Sasha placed her beer on the counter and slipped her arms around Connelly's midsection.

"It's not okay. I want to make an honest man of you. I want to call myself your wife. I just ... I can't spare the time this weekend. I'm sorry, Connelly."

He finished covering the pizza with fresh mozzarella and carefully sprinkled chopped basil over the top, then he turned around and took her hands in his.

"I know. But at some point we need to start making decisions—officiant, venue, music, flowers, menu, all that stuff. You know that right?"

We could go to Ohio tomorrow and come back married, she thought. She'd done a quick Internet search of all the jurisdictions that didn't impose a waiting period before issuing a marriage license and committed them to memory—just in case he changed his mind about eloping.

But, she didn't say anything. Instead, she stretched onto her tiptoes and covered his warm mouth with hers, driving away thoughts of both Garrett English's document production and her mother's guest list and color scheme preferences.

5

Early Saturday morning, Mia Martinez traipsed out of the nightclub still dancing and laughing, even though her buzz had worn off hours ago.

"Woo, am I hot!"

She lifted her glossy, dark curls from her sweaty neck and fanned herself.

"Yeah, you sure were *hot*. I didn't see you pay for a drink all night," Raina told her, deliberately misunderstanding Mia's point.

"Or sit down even once," Chelsea added.

Mia just laughed. It had been a long week between studying for finals, sending out resumes for summer internships, and working her shifts for the campus catering company. She should have been dragging. But she'd been bouncing off the walls, moving and dancing for hours, flitting between the girls she'd come with and friends she'd run into at the club.

In fact, she realized, she wasn't ready to call it a night.

"Hey, anybody wanna hit Nico's? Some greasy eggs and bacon would hit the spot!"

"Sister, you're crazy. It's almost two o'clock. Go home and get some sleep," Chelsea said.

No one else seemed interested in prolonging the fun either.

Mia walked with the group to their cars. Everyone was set for a ride home, so, after a flurry of hugs, she slid behind the wheel of her red Miata, started the engine, and cranked the music.

A short beep of the horn goodbye at Raina, who'd pulled out of the lot behind her, and Mia was cruising down the mostly deserted street, with the window down so the breeze could cool her down. She was still sticky from dancing.

By the time she'd navigated from the South Side to the one-bedroom apartment she rented on the top floor of an Oakland row house, her skin was clammy, and she was feeling tired and queasy.

She tripped up the staircase, clinging to the

handrail, suddenly dizzy and breathing hard.

In her apartment, she grabbed a bottled water from the refrigerator and headed straight for the bedroom.

The evening's fun forgotten, she just wanted to get out of her clothes and get to sleep. She realized she must've hit a wall. She was exhausted and out of breath. And now she was shivering.

Mia gulped the water and curled up under her comforter, still wearing her skirt and tank top. She didn't even bother to take off her jewelry or wash her makeup off her face, even though she could hear her mother clucking disapprovingly in her mind.

She fell into a restless, fatigued sleep, wondering if she'd caught some kind of bug—she felt so crappy out of the blue. Her iPhone fell from her slack hand and bounced off the hardwood floor. She didn't stir.

FORTY MINUTES BEFORE SUNRISE, her racing heart stuttered to a stop.

~ ~ ~ ~ ~ ~ ~ ~ ~ ~

As Mia Martinez drew her last, gasping breaths in her walk-up apartment in South Oakland, four miles away, Bodhi stood on his porch in Highland Park, shivering in his blue-and-white striped pajama bottoms and a thin white t-shirt.

He sipped his hot tea and stared out at the gray predawn sky. He had slept fitfully, unable to quiet his mind. Finally, at four-thirty, he'd admitted to himself that rest was out of his grasp and had started his day.

He couldn't stop thinking about the dead girls whose bodies had passed through his hands. He had recorded his thoughts about their fleeting lives, and now those thoughts were gone, too, along with his official files. His mind and spirit were jangling, unsettled. And he didn't know what to do.

When people expressed surprise at his chosen vocation, he understood. People would ask why he didn't become a doctor who helped the living rather than deal in death? And when he was younger, he would have tried to explain that he didn't fear or revile death, death held no surprises, and he considered it an honor to provide dignity to a life that was passing out of this world and into its next phase. That was all true, and vaguely Zen enough to satisfy most questioners.

But it wasn't the only reason: he'd gone to medical school with the dream of ministering to the needs of the sick and diseased in countries that the United States had written off as "third world." But, he'd quickly learned, through clinical work and classes, that the emotions of his patients and his colleagues overwhelmed him. Their worry and distress would wash over his body in a physical wave and he would feel their anxiety as if it were his own.

The dead had no such concerns. They had left their bodies behind as empty vessels, devoid of fear, or anger, or sorrow. And he had found peace working for and with them. Until now.

A rustling next door jarred him from his thoughts. His neighbor stepped out onto her porch clutching her robe to her chest and stooped to pick up her newspaper.

"Good morning, Mrs. Willham."

She turned and squinted in his direction. "Bodhi, you startled me." She shook her *Tribune-Review* out of its biodegradable wrapper and went on, "You'll catch your death of cold standing out here like that."

He smiled at her scolding. Cora Willham had raised five children; the admonition was second nature to her. With her husband dead and her kids scattered around the tri-state area, she had turned her mother hen attentions to him.

She was halfway back into her house, her head bent over the front page, when she stopped in the doorway and jabbed a finger at him.

"These deaths are shameful. All these pretty young girls. What are you doing about it? Says here the medical examiner's office attributes the deaths to natural causes."

He was surprised by the anger in her tone.

"Yes, ma'am. The official finding is myocarditis—that's an infection of the heart. Did you know one of the girls, Mrs. Willham?"

"No, but I know a load of malarkey when I hear it."

The door banged shut behind her, and Bodhi was alone with his thoughts. The principal one being that he, too, believed the official statement sounded—as Mrs. Willham so colorfully put it—like malarkey.

The question, he knew, was what was he going to do about it?

Bodhi sipped his tea and stared at the sky.

6

Mackenzie ignored the knot in her stomach and smiled encouragingly across the breakfast table at Barry, hoping he'd get the hint. But, being Barry, he missed the signal entirely, and focused on smearing entirely too much cream cheese onto his bagel.

She ratcheted her smile up a notch and turned to Stone "Fred" Fredericks, the chief executive officer of Better Life Beverages, Limited. "Mr. Fredericks, let me assure you that the mayor and our entire team remain committed to our partnership."

Fredericks smiled back at her, letting his gaze linger just a second or two too long for a business meeting, and then turned to Barry. "Z'at true, Mayor Closky?"

Barry spoke around a mouthful of bagel. "Absolutely, Fred. Mackenzie speaks for everyone on my economic development task force. We're not worried about any fallout, and you shouldn't be either. As I understand it, there's not even a definite link to the dead young ladies, isn't that right?"

Mackenzie winced. When Barry made the argument, he sounded like a tobacco executive pretending the science wasn't settled on lung cancer. She'd have to work with him on his delivery.

Stone, Junior—called Stone by everyone except his father, who referred to him as "S.J.," as if he were still a child—cleared his throat and spoke before Fred had a chance. "Well, it's true that there's no conclusive link, Mr. Mayor, but from what Ms. Lane tells us, the medical examiner's office found *withania somnifera* in the stomach contents of all three dead girls. That's a pretty big coincidence."

Stone turned his serious brown eyes to Mackenzie. "Isn't that right?"

She pushed the scrambled egg around her

plate with her fork while she formulated an answer.

"Yes. From what my source tells me, the medical examiner's office is trial testing some sort of software that looks for patterns across cases. The software hit on a link. There's no evidence, though, that your product was the source of that ingredient. And, from what your father's told us, Champion Fuel actually features a proprietary blend of four herbs, and there was no reference to the other three herbs in the reports. Plus, I understand there's no evidence that *withania somnifera* causes myocarditis. So, while it's not a great scenario, I don't think it's a crisis." *Yet*, she added silently.

Stone turned his mouth down into a slight frown. "Well," he said slowly, "that's partially true. There is no known causal connection between *withania somnifera* and myocarditis, but let's be frank, those girls probably drank Champion Fuel if that stuff was found in their systems."

"Why do you say that?" Barry demanded, finally worried enough to focus on the conversation.

"Well, the drink is exploding in popularity— especially among women in the eighteen- to twenty-five-year-old demographic. It's wildly popular with college-aged women, so it wouldn't be at all surprising if the deceased women drank our product. They're our target market. And, while *withania somnifera* is available in other formats, it tastes ... for lack of a better word ... disgusting. So most products contain trace amounts only. Our selling point is that we've been able to mask the flavor to a large extent but deliver the benefits of a larger dose. By the way, that also explains why the other three ingredients in Champion Fuel may not have shown up —our drink is mainly *withania somnifera* and caffeine. The other ingredients are present in much smaller—probably undetectable—quantities," Stone explained.

"Bah," Fred said. He slapped a hand against the table. "Conjecture and bellyaching. That's what this is. Like S.J. said, other people sell it. Hell, you can buy it as a pill supplement, loose tea, and in energy bars. No reason we have to get tagged with this issue—if it even is an issue."

Relief washed over Barry's face and he nodded his agreement. He looked meaningfully at Mackenzie. "This supposed link, it won't become public?"

Mackenzie's source had taken a significant

risk to ensure no one learned about the link that software had identified. She knew Barry didn't want to know any details, though, so she simply said, "Yes."

That settled the issue for Barry and Fred. They moved on to talk about the hockey playoffs and their plans to catch a game together in Fred's luxury box.

Mackenzie tuned them out and watched Stone, who was shredding his paper napkin into narrow strips. A nervous habit, she imagined. He'd bear keeping an eye on: there was no room for nerves in business.

He felt her eyes on him and looked up. She gave him a reassuring smile.

7

Sasha's vision blurred, and the type on the page she held seemed to swim in front of her eyes. *Time for a break.* She blinked hard a few times, finished skimming the report, and placed it face down in the growing pile to her right. Unfortunately, the mountain of boxes containing unread documents to her left had barely shrunk in the four hours she'd been reviewing them.

She wished Garrett had pulled another big firm stunt and made the documents available for review rather than copying them. The rules required the former; attorneys usually went ahead and did the latter as a matter of mutual courtesy. By exchanging copy sets, both sides avoided having to camp out in a warehouse somewhere and review originals. Lawyers griped about that like it was a fate worse than jury duty, and she could attest that it was grueling, uncomfortable, and boring to park yourself in a chair on someone else's territory and paw through documents.

But at least boxes of originals had staples and paper clips and folders, all of which provided some sense of order and recognizable flow to the documents. Plus there was always the possibility of finding a crackerjacks prize of sorts—a fancy, jeweled paper clip; a Post-it note doodle of stick figures stuck to the back of a redweld; a neon orange folder; anything to inject a little liveliness into the review. In contrast, straight copy files like these were just sheet after sheet after sheet of paper with no natural breaks between documents. Monotonous pages crammed into as few boxes as possible, banded with giant over-stretched elastic bands, made an already-disheartening task worse somehow.

She stood and stretched. She was trying to decide whether to go for a quick run or settle for some yoga postures on the office floor when Naya poked her head into the room.

"What are you doing here?" Sasha asked.

"I was in the neighborhood," Naya said.

They both knew she was lying.

"Naya, you can't help. You heard English. One document review isn't worth risking your scholarship with Prescott. I'll get through the boxes."

Naya walked into the room and eyed the stack of boxes beside Sasha's desk.

"You sure about that?"

Sasha rubbed her eyes. "It's just going to take some time." She checked the time. "Want to grab a bite with me? I'm going to need sustenance soon."

"Sure. How about the Thai place?"

"Perfect."

Sasha grabbed her sweater and purse and shut out the lights. She confirmed that the door locked behind her, and they headed downstairs.

As they walked along Walnut Street, dodging Saturday morning shoppers laden with bags and packs of preteens with their heads bent over their phones, Naya returned to the subject of the call from Prescott.

"Mac, it doesn't sit right with me—Prescott calling and pushing you around."

It didn't sit right with Sasha either; but she wasn't willing to go toe to toe with Prescott when the outcome could affect Naya's future.

"Naya, seriously, it's fine. You might as well

get used to it now. Once you're a Prescott lawyer, they're going to own you in a way they never did before."

They stopped at the corner to wait for a break in traffic. Naya turned toward Sasha. Her signature eyebrow arch indicated she didn't like what she'd just heard.

"*Own* me? Nobody owns me."

Naya's voice was loud and angry. The man standing to Sasha's right, glanced over in surprise then quickly looked away when Sasha held his gaze.

"Shh. Calm down. We'll talk about it over lunch." She patted Naya's arm in what she hoped was a soothing manner.

Naya glared at her but held her tongue. They crossed the street in silence, and the eavesdropper trotted ahead of them, eager to get away from the brewing conflict.

Sasha used the time to formulate her thoughts. Naya was possibly the least sentimental person she knew. The older woman prided herself on being realistic, resilient, and resourceful—all traits that had served her well as a legal assistant and would, Sasha knew, be helpful to her in law school and beyond. Sasha also knew that some small part of her friend harbored an idealistic vision of her future life as a Prescott & Talbott lawyer. That piece of Naya was perhaps so minuscule that it was invisible to the naked eye, but it was there. And it was Sasha's job to gently disabuse her friend of her fairytale dream, but to do it in such a way that she didn't destroy Naya's excitement and anticipation about her new career.

They settled into seats near the window. The restaurant was not quite half full. The weekend lunch crowd was more boisterous than the office workers who frequented the place during the workweek, and Sasha was glad for the noise.

Naya was likely to yell at her at least once. The din in the background would help to cover any of the shouting that Sasha anticipated.

She didn't have long to wait.

As soon as the smiling waitress filled their glasses with ice water and left with their orders, Naya lit into her.

"Mac, you know you can't go telling a black woman someone *owns* her, right? I mean, you do know that, don't you? Tell me you know that."

Sasha put a hand up and gestured for Naya to lower the volume a bit.

"Naya, I'm not trying to compare a professional position with a six-figure salary to an existence as a slave in the American South—"

"But?"

"But," she continued, "it's not all that different from indentured servitude."

Naya stared at her, her almond eyes full of disbelief.

Sasha took a sip of water then tried to explain. "Look, I know you worked at Prescott for a long time. Answer me a question: who do you think had more autonomy—you or the junior associates?"

Naya laughed so hard she nearly choked.

"C'mon, Mac. The lawyers. I was support staff."

"Right. And if you wanted to turn down an assignment, could you?"

Naya cocked her head at the question. "Like, if I were too busy to take on additional work?"

"Sure."

"You know I could have. I rarely did, though. The overtime was sweet—"

"We'll get to that next. But, you could say 'sorry, my plate's full,' right?"

"Yeah."

"With what repercussions?"

"None. An attorney couldn't ...?" She trailed

off and traced a small circle on the tablecloth with one fingertip.

"Oh, an attorney *could* turn down work. And some people have done it. Once. No one who plans to stay at Prescott does it twice."

"Come on. Really?"

"Really. It's a guaranteed ticket to a bad annual review. And an associate might be able to recover from one bad review, but two? Forget it."

Naya looked closely at her. "Is that what happened to Hannah?"

Hannah. Sasha had almost forgotten about poor Hannah Marsden-Smythe. That was exactly what happened to Hannah, who had the audacity to ask not to be assigned to a trial on the other side of the country when her twins were three months old. Then she compounded that error in judgment by asking for unpaid leave to care for her father-in-law when he was dying.

"Yes," Sasha said simply.

Naya chewed her lower lip.

The waitress appeared with spring rolls and jasmine tea.

Naya stopped her before she could leave again. "We'll have a bottle of the house wine, too. White."

Naya turned back to Sasha. "None of this is a

surprise, you know. But, come on, it's not *that* bad."

Sasha snagged a spring roll with her chopsticks and swirled it around in the small dish of plum sauce while she considered her answer.

"It's not all bad. Prescott's one of the top firms in the city—if not the top. You'll get excellent experience; it'll open a lot of doors for you. But, on a per hour basis? You'll make less than you did as a legal assistant there. There's no overtime for attorneys. And there's no end to the work. You'll spend vacations, holidays, and weekends in the office—"

"I know all that, Mac. I've done all that." Naya combed her fingers through her hair and shook her head.

The waitress returned with the bottle of wine and two glasses. After the pouring/sniffing ritual, Sasha took a long swallow of the crisp, dry wine and leveled her gaze at Naya.

"You've done all that and been compensated, thanked, and appreciated for it. It'll be different when it's expected and taken for granted. I think that'll be the biggest change for you. You'll be treated like a professional, like your brain is an asset. But, you won't be treated particularly kindly. You're going to have to bite your tongue a fair amount. And, I love you for it, but let's face it —you aren't exactly a shrinking violet."

Naya laughed at that, a long, loud chuckle. Then she picked up her glass and her smile faded.

"That's the truth. Well, maybe things are different now with Will in charge."

Sasha shrugged. It was possible. Anything was possible.

"Maybe," she allowed.

Naya drained her glass.

The smiling waitress returned with two steaming, fragrant plates piled high with food. Sasha's stomach leapt at the sight. She'd skipped breakfast—something she rarely did—in her effort to get a jump on tackling the mountain of documents that waited for her in her office.

They ate in silence for a few moments. Then Naya put down her chopsticks and said, "I'm going to talk to him."

"To whom?" Sasha asked around a mouthful of pad Thai.

"Will."

"About?"

"VitaMight." Naya put up a hand to forestall the objection she must have known was coming. "Say whatever you want about Prescott, Will's a decent human being. If he knew what Garrett's up to, I think he'd put a stop to it."

Sasha agreed that Will was a good egg—or as close to one as a person would likely find in the rarified environs of Prescott & Talbott. But she wasn't so sure that he was unaware of Garrett's machinations. Or that he'd disapprove of them if he knew. Business, after all, was business. And lawyers were notoriously flinty-eyed about such things. She left room for the possibility that she could be wrong. After all, Will had stood by her on more than one occasion during the past year and a half. And she considered him something of a friend, if not a mentor. But still, it would be a mistake for Naya to march—and march she would—into Will's office and demand that he call off the dogs.

"You don't want to do that. Let me talk to him."

Naya eyed her over her bowl of noodles.

"I don't need you to carry my water, Mac. And you need help. You can't review all those documents alone."

Sasha bit back a frustrated sigh. Lord, was Naya ever stubborn.

"That's not what this is, Naya. You can't begin your career as a Prescott attorney by demanding concessions before you even start working there. This is an issue between Prescott and me. I can't let you burn goodwill on it. I'll reach out to Will, okay?"

Naya pursed her lips and considered this. "When?"

"Soon. Early next week."

"Monday," Naya said.

"Fine. Monday," Sasha agreed.

Placated, Naya returned her attention to her curry. "How are the wedding plans coming along?"

Sasha groaned and reached for the wine.

8

Allegheny County's Chief Medical Examiner spent every Saturday morning from seven until noon in his office, catching up on all administrative nonsense that inevitably piled up during the week. Although he no longer performed autopsies—unless a celebrity was involved or there was heavy media interest in a case—he never seemed to have time to get through the stacks of requests that needed his approval, reports that needed his signature, and backs that needed his scratching each week.

Jefferson Anderson Jackson (the name his parents proudly wrote on his birth certificate and promptly discarded in favor of "Sonny") was trained as both a lawyer and a doctor. But he functioned principally as a politician these days. While he didn't exactly miss being in the trenches, he did not enjoy the paperwork that came along with his current position. As a result, he was usually not in the best of moods during his Saturday morning work sessions, and his staff had learned to steer clear of his office during that block of time.

Or so he thought.

But notwithstanding the conventional wisdom that Sonny was best avoided on weekend mornings, Bodhi King was lurking around his door, wearing a path in the carpet from the kitchenette to the small library and back.

Sonny knew two things: One, Bodhi was a health nut and, therefore, unlikely to find anything appealing in the kitchen's offerings, which ran toward the stale doughnut and burnt coffee end of the culinary spectrum. Two, Bodhi, like most of the forensic pathologists under the age of fifty, had electronic subscriptions to all the research journals.

It was theoretically possible that there was some mildewing tome in the library that he needed to consult. But it was more likely that he was working up his nerve to interrupt the boss.

Sonny leaned to his side to peer through his

partially open door. Bodhi passed by again on another circuit to the kitchen.

Sonny put down his pen and scratched his neck—a gesture his wife jokingly claimed activated his brain. Bodhi was the least labor-intensive employee Sonny had ever known. He didn't seem to have the arrogance or ego that sometimes came along with a medical degree. He didn't get emotional about grisly cases. He worked all the Christian holidays, kept his head down, and avoided the back-stabbing office politics that permeated the building worse than the constant odor of formaldehyde. In short, he was a dream employee, and Sonny had been on the lookout for more Buddhist coroner candidates, hoping to someday have a staff full of Bodhis.

So, if Bodhi needed to talk to him, it was probably important enough to listen to. At a minimum, it was unlikely to be a complaint along the lines of the last employee issue Sonny had been subject to on a Saturday morning. One of the forensic pathologists had measured his office and discovered that it was a full two square feet smaller than everybody else's. But Bodhi was no Wally Stewart, and Sonny was willing to wager Bodhi had never noticed the size of his office, let alone compared it to a colleague's space.

He grabbed his travel mug, crossed the room, and opened the door wide. At the end of the hall, the door to the kitchen swung closed.

In the kitchen, Sonny headed for the sink and began rinsing out his mug. As the water ran, he turned toward the small electric stove, where Bodhi paced back and forth in front of a tea kettle.

"Morning, Bodhi," he said over his shoulder. "You coulda heated that water quicker than greased lightning in the microwave an 'at, you know?"

Sonny was Pittsburgh born and bred. He'd left Pittsburgh at eighteen to attend college in Boston and had stayed in New England for medical school and beyond. As a result, his Pittsburgh accent had long since had its rough edges filed down to the polished, neutral cadence of an academician. After he'd been lured home to head up the Medical Examiner's Office, he'd found it handy to resurrect his Pittsburghese. It distanced him from the former, almost universally reviled, Chief Medical Examiner, who had relocated from Northern California for the job. And it seemed to disarm people and get them to lower their guards. Sometimes he applied it thicker than others.

Bodhi just smiled. Sonny figured it was some kind of religious thing, the food preparation, and left it at that.

"What're you doin' in here on a Saturday anyway? It's a beautiful day. Hope you aren't catching up on paperwork like me." He placed his mug upside down in the drainer and then turned to face Bodhi full on.

Bodhi's usually placid expression was tense. The muscles in his face were tight and his eyes were clouded with thought.

"Actually, Sonny, I'd like to talk to you about some of my paperwork. If you have time, of course?"

Sonny nodded. "When you're done watching that pot boil, bring your tea into my office and we can pow wow."

"Thanks."

As Sonny turned to leave, Bodhi asked, "Would you like some? Tea, I mean? It's ginkgo leaf to promote mental clarity."

"Ginkgo, like those crap-smelling berries? No thanks," Sonny said with a shudder. "See you in a few."

~ ~ ~ ~ ~ ~ ~ ~ ~ ~

BODHI PAUSED outside his boss's half-open door to gather his thoughts before knocking lightly on the door frame.

"Come on in," Sonny said from behind the desk, his head bent over an Excel spreadsheet. "Working on the darn budget."

Bodhi lowered himself into a guest chair and folded his long legs beneath him. He sipped his tea in silence and waited until Sonny had reached a stopping point. He felt no impatience. And, having made up his mind to talk to Sonny, he also felt no lingering worry. His thoughts were calm. He imagined they were a lake on a day with no breeze.

"Alrighty, then," Sonny said, slapping the thick sheaf of paper down on his desk, "What's troubling you, son?"

Bodhi saw no reason to sugarcoat his words. He leaned forward slightly and held Sonny's gaze. "My files on the girls who died from myocarditis are gone."

Sonny sat back but otherwise showed no reaction. He was quiet for a moment, then he said, "When you say 'gone,' what exactly do you mean?"

Bodhi noted that Sonny's local boy accent had vanished.

"I mean, they're gone. It's as if my autopsy reports never existed. They're gone from the database. And my local copies are gone, too."

"That's not possible. It must just be … some kind of technological glitch." He waved his hands around in the air as if that would explain this unprecedented network malfunction.

"It's not a glitch, Sonny."

"Now, Bodhi, I'm no computer expert, but then neither are you. 'Course it's a glitch. The IT fellas musta screwed the pooch somehow. Who's the department liaison for technology? Stewart? I'll get him on it to have it all straightened out come Monday." Sonny ended with a too-hearty laugh and gave Bodhi an encouraging smile.

Bodhi chose each word with care and said, "I may not be a computer expert. But, I can't conceive of an error that would make the files— both the network and local copies—on the women with myocarditis disappear and only those files. Can you?"

Sonny gave him a blank look. "Can't say I know enough to answer the question."

"Ever hear of Occam's Razor?"

Bodhi was sure he had. If Sonny hadn't encountered the theory in medical school, he likely had in law school. Or while watching television. It was hardly obscure.

"The simplest explanation is generally the best—or something to that effect," Sonny mumbled.

Bodhi waited.

"So what are you sayin', son? Someone deliberately deleted your files? That's a pretty strong accusation." Sonny leveled him with a look.

"I know. And I hesitated to make it, sir, but there's one other factor to consider: I don't know if you're aware that it's my practice to keep personal journals, handwritten journals of my cases."

"News to me. Why? You thinkin' about writing a book?"

Bodhi smiled. The former Chief Medical Examiner had done just that. And then he'd leveraged his tell-all bestseller into a weekly program on Court TV.

"No. It's just a way for me to memorialize the lives that pass through my hands. They're private thoughts, of no medical or legal value."

Sonny shrugged. "Whatever gets you

through. Some guys drink. Saul golfs. I favor a long run, myself."

"My most recent notebook is missing. It contained my notes on the myocarditis cases. But, the rest of the books are undisturbed right where I keep them."

"And where's that?"

"In my office."

The room was perfectly still and silent for a moment. Then Sonny passed his palm over his eyes and muttered a low curse that Bodhi didn't quite catch. When he removed his hand, Sonny looked like he'd aged ten years. His skin was sallow and his eyes were bright with fear.

Before he could speak, the portable radio on his desk blared to life.

"10-55 incoming."

10-55 was the code for a confirmed coroner's case. It meant the police had arrived at a scene and determined there was no need for emergency medical services.

"I'll take it," Bodhi said, halfway out of his chair. There was no point in dragging in whoever was on call. He was already here.

Sonny raised a hand indicating he should wait. Then he picked up the radio and said, "Any details?"

The voice on the other end registered surprise that the boss himself was asking. "Uh, another young woman, sir. Neighbor called it in when she didn't show up for a breakfast date. She was dead in her bed. No evidence of trauma or foul play. Looks like the others."

"Roger that."

Sonny shook his head at Bodhi. "I'll take it myself."

Bodhi kept his expression neutral at this news. "Of course."

Sonny stood with uncharacteristic urgency. "I'll have Wally look into what happened to your computer files, Bodhi. Don't you worry." He patted Bodhi's arm and guided him toward the door.

Worry.

That unfamiliar undercurrent coursed through his body again, and Bodhi realized that he was, in fact, very worried.

Bodhi walked out of the building on autopilot, focused on his thoughts and not his surroundings. Once he realized he was acting mindlessly, he stopped at the edge of the parking lot to recenter himself before mounting his twelve-speed and pedaling off.

Do one thing at a time, do it slowly, and do it mindfully, he reminded himself.

Mindfulness usually wasn't difficult for him to achieve, but in his current mindset he found he had to force himself to watch a ladybug creep along the top rail of the bike rack until it reached the end and unfolded its wings. Only after it took flight, did he unlock his bicycle.

The white van with its tinted windows zipped into the parking lot and backed into the unloading bay. Bodhi paused and waited to see who emerged from the driver's seat. It was Jamal Parker, which was perfect.

Jamal was a relatively new employee and, despite the excellent benefits and stability that the job offered, Bodhi figured Jamal wouldn't last much longer. He hadn't managed to develop the shell that would allow him to chauffeur the dead without letting it haunt his dreams.

True to form, Jamal fumbled around in his shirt pocket for a cigarette and walked across the lot to smoke it, keeping his eyes averted from the heavy black body bag that his coworkers were unloading from the back of the van.

"Hey, Jamal," Bodhi said, as Jamal stopped to light his cigarette, cupping his hand around the flame to shield it from the late spring wind.

"Bodhi, my man." Jamal took a drag on his cigarette and exhaled, as he clasped Bodhi's hand in a friendly shake.

"You okay?"

"These young girls ... it ain't right." Jamal shook his head.

Bodhi nodded his agreement. "No, it's not. Same pattern as the others?"

"Yeah. Her downstairs neighbor told the cops she was out late partying but the neighbor heard her come home alone. They were supposed to get breakfast together this morning and the girl never showed. Her car was out front, and she didn't answer when the neighbor pounded on the door, so she called the landlord. He showed up with a key and ... they found her. Hispanic chick. She was pretty." Jamal's voice trailed off, soft and mournful.

Bodhi was glad for the information but sorry to see Jamal's pain.

"That's sad, man. You know that luxury car dealer on Baum Boulevard?"

"Yeah?" Jamal looked up at him quizzically.

"They're hiring drivers. The pay probably isn't as good, but it's full time, with benefits. And you'd get to drive Jaguars and Benzes instead of a hearse."

A smile spread like lightning across Jamal's face. "You for real?"

"I play volleyball with the assistant manager. Ask for Gary Flanders. Tell him I sent you."

"I will. Thanks, man."

Bodhi watched Jamal head back to his van, his step lighter now that his passenger had been removed. As he considered this latest death, the words that Bodhi had been avoiding came screaming into his brain: Pittsburgh was experiencing a cluster of sudden unexplained deaths.

A death cluster.

Protocol required Sonny to assemble an investigative team of pathologists to go out into the field and tease out any commonalities among the dead women—did they swim in the same pool, kiss the same person, eat at the same diner? The fact that there wasn't already a field investigation underway meant ... what *did* it mean?

Either Sonny had suddenly become incompetent or he had deliberately decided not to investigate a series of potentially related deaths. Bodhi thought of his missing files and stolen journal. Then he thought of Occam's Razor. He slipped his bike chain into his messenger bag and slowly pedaled away from the building.

As he bumped over the curb and eased out

into flow of light weekend traffic on Grant Street, a dark green Taurus started up and pulled out behind him. His mindfulness gave way to distraction as he tried to come up with a convincing argument against the existence of a death cluster. As a result, he didn't notice the car as it followed him at a crawl all the way through downtown, onto Bigelow Boulevard, and along his route through several residential neighborhoods.

When he stopped at the East End Food Co-op to pick up some rice noodles, it idled nearby in an alley.

He emerged with his package of food and continued through East Liberty, up the long hill that bisected the Pittsburgh Zoo & Aquarium, and on into his neighborhood.

He reached his house, hoisted his bike over one shoulder, and mounted the stairs to his front porch, thinking about a case that had been reported in a medical journal several years back —a sudden death cluster of six unrelated adults who all died from focal myocarditis. He couldn't recall having read an update.

He retrieved his mail from the box near the front door and secured his bicycle, eager to log onto his computer and research recent myocarditis clusters.

He didn't see the dark green car that crept past him and parked two houses down on the other side of the street.

Bodhi unlocked his door and went inside, letting the door bang shut behind him.

The driver of the Taurus killed the engine and settled in to wait.

9

Leo was surfing bridal websites, Java curled into a soft gray ball on his lap, when the harsh buzz of the front door intercom sounded. The cat jumped to the floor, legs going all directions.

"Yes?" Leo answered.

"Uh, Mr. Connelly? It's Kyle downstairs. You have a visitor. Says his name is Bodhi King."

From his tone, Kyle sounded like he very much doubted that.

"That's fine. Please send him up."

"Yes, sir."

Leo put the laptop into hibernation mode and straightened the piles of papers and journals that Sasha had stacked by the reading chairs. His stomach growled, a low, threatening grumble.

He'd been hungry for well over an hour now. Sasha'd called twice and told him not to wait on her for dinner, but, of course, he had. It was after eight, though, and she'd said she wouldn't stop working until she reached a spot in her document review where she could take most of the day Sunday to hang out. She even claimed to have a wedding-related surprise planned.

Maybe Bodhi would want to grab a bite. Just in case, he looked around for his shoes.

He was tying the laces when a quick, urgent rap sounded at the door.

Bodhi looked pale, tense, and out of breath. He smiled apologetically.

"Hi, Leo. I'm sorry for coming by without calling. But, actually, I don't seem to have your number. And I didn't want to put this in an email."

Leo considered this information. He didn't know Bodhi well. They played volleyball together on a team that one of the courthouse marshals at the federal court had organized. The team was good, made up mainly of former collegiate players, but beyond volleyball, they had little in common.

He knew Bodhi was a forensic pathologist with the county, a Buddhist, and a vegan. He could spike a mean volleyball. Leo was pretty sure he was single and straight. And he didn't own a car. That was the sum total of his knowledge.

"Come on in. Are you okay, man?"

Bodhi shook his head, setting his blond-streaked brown curls flying. "Thanks. Not really. I think I need your help."

He paced around Sasha's foyer. Java came running over to rub himself against the stranger's leg.

"Hello, cat." Bodhi said it in a conversational tone. Java mewled.

"I was just getting ready to go out and grab a bite. Have you had dinner?"

Bodhi looked stricken. "I'm sorry, I should have called first. Should I come back later?"

Leo took a quick mental inventory of the pantry.

"No, listen, you're here now. I'll make some soup, and you can tell me what's going on."

"You're sure?"

"I'm sure. Have a seat."

Bodhi sank gratefully into a stool at the kitchen island. Leo pawed through the cupboard and listed ingredients that would comport with

Bodhi's diet. "I have rice noodles, vegetable stock, ginger, and some veggies."

"Please don't cook on my account. I probably couldn't eat right now if I tried. My stomach's in knots."

He turned and searched the man's drawn face. "It's just soup. You know you need to eat. Fuel your body and your mind. Besides, I'm hungry."

Bodhi half-shrugged. "That'd be great. Thank you."

Leo grabbed a cutting board and started chopping carrots.

"Okay, you said you need help. Why? And, just out of curiosity, why me?"

"I don't know who else to ask. And, to be honest, I'm not even sure what you do-but, I have the sense that you still have connections with the federal agencies and can access their databases. Is that right?"

"Something like that. Are you in some kind of personal trouble?" he asked over the rhythmic slap of knife against wood.

He liked Bodhi. The man seemed like a low-drama, upstanding person. But he didn't *really* know him. He had no intention of putting himself on the line with his contacts at Homeland Security if this guy was trying to avoid a child support obligation or track down a former lover or something.

"No. Yes. Maybe?"

"Ah, well, thanks for clearing that up."

Bodhi gave a small laugh that seemed genuinely amused.

"I guess I should start at the beginning."

"Always a good place to start," Leo agreed. "Do you want a beer?"

Despite being half-Vietnamese, Leo wasn't entirely clear on the tenants of Buddhism regarding alcohol. He thought he recalled Bodhi cracking a few cold ones after summer volleyball matches, though.

"Love one."

Leo took two bottles from the refrigerator and twisted off the caps. He handed one to Bodhi and took a swig from the other.

"Great. You talk; I'll cook."

Bodhi took a small sip and placed the bottle on the island.

"You know I'm a forensic pathologist."

"Uh-huh."

He poured the stock into a copper-bottomed pot and lit the flame to heat it.

"Okay. I don't know how much attention you pay to the local news?"

"Exactly none. Unless it involves sports."

"Fair enough. Well, there's been a recent rash of deaths from myocarditis. The victims—"

Leo interrupted. "Three young women all in the past week, week and a half. Yeah, I did read something about this."

"Right. Well, three reported in the press. As of today, it's four. Four dead twenty-somethings in nine days." Bodhi's voice was grim.

Leo felt his eyebrows crawl up his forehead. "So, is this an epidemic?"

He hoped to God not. His nightmares about the winter's narrowly averted influenza pandemic had only recently stopped. Sasha's were still plaguing her.

Bodhi shook his head, his hands spread wide. "I have no idea," he admitted miserably.

Leo dumped the noodles, ginger root, and vegetables into the stockpot and gave Bodhi his full attention.

"Well, isn't it your job to investigate?"

"It is. But I think someone doesn't want me to. I caught the first three cases. And protocol would be for me to handle any suspected cases once the pattern emerged. But the office hasn't even actually acknowledged that there *is* a pattern. And then when the fourth body came in today, the ME himself handled it."

"Okay."

He shot Leo a meaningful look. "The boss doesn't usually get his hands dirty like that."

Leo had worked for enough governmental agencies to know that didn't mean there was a conspiracy.

"Couldn't that just be that this has the possibility of blowing up big? Unless the Chief Medical Examiner is different from every other elected official on the planet, he's going to want to cover himself in glory. Don't worry. If it goes south, I'm sure you'll get to take the fall."

Bodhi twisted his mouth into a small, wry smile. "I would have thought it was just politics as usual, if it weren't for my missing files."

"Your files are missing?"

"All of the records for the first two girls are gone. Like they never existed—they aren't on my hard drive, they aren't on the network. And my personal journal was stolen from my office."

"Well, crap, that sounds pretty shady," Leo admitted. "But, I don't know how I can help you. The county medical examiner isn't subject to federal jurisdiction. The people I used to work with can't retrieve your files for you."

At least not legally, Leo thought. He was fairly certain Hank Richardson could get his hands on pretty much any electronic files in the country, so long as he didn't mind violating innumerable privacy laws.

"I understand. Actually, I went to the Chief Medical Examiner this morning and he said he'll look into the missing files."

"That's good."

"I guess, but it doesn't feel right. Sonny seemed, I don't know, scared ... or worried. And he should have mobilized a team of field investigators days ago, and he still hasn't. There's been no concerted effort to draw a link between these deaths. This isn't being handled properly, and I don't know why."

Leo was about to share his view that one should never blame on malice what could be explained by incompetence but Bodhi leveled him with a long, impassive gaze and added, "Now there's another dead girl. I'm afraid she won't be the last."

They stared at each other in silence for a moment. Then Leo caved.

"What do you need?"

Bodhi acknowledged the offer with a slight bow of his head in thanks.

"I don't want to go mucking around in the county's files. Yet. I want to make sure there's really something here. I've spent the whole day trying to research clusters of SUD online, but I'm running into roadblocks."

"SUD?"

"Sudden unexplained deaths. They happen. Sometimes, you can trace a cluster to a common point of infection—like a guest who stayed in a hotel room where the next three guests fell ill and died—or a common origin—a group of hikers all ingested the same poisonous mush-room, things like that. SUD cases are rare but they generate a lot of interest, both academic and in the media. There's a wealth of literature on them. The methodology to uncovering the source of a SUD is part art, part science. So, I cast a wide net. I searched for myocarditis cases, of course, but also any other SUDs in the past year."

"And?"

Bodhi shook his head. "And I just keep finding dead pages. It's like someone's one step ahead of me, removing the information I need. Or, if they aren't a step ahead of me, they're right there with me—recording every key stroke, walking in my electronic footprints. I've tried to let those thoughts exist without obsessing over them, but I just can't find my peace with this. I sound crazy, don't I?"

Leo supposed Bodhi might come across as paranoid to a civilian. But if experience had taught Leo anything, it was that sometimes the truth of a situation is far-fetched—if not downright crazy. And if working for Homeland Security had taught him anything, it was that privacy of electronic data simply didn't exist. Properly motivated, and with sufficient resources or know-how, anyone could stalk another person's electronic presence virtually undetected.

He was about to share this hard-earned wisdom with Bodhi when he heard keys jangling in the hallway.

Sasha came through the door in a hurry, her arms full of files and a heavy paper-laden briefcase hanging from one shoulder.

"Sorry, I'm so late. I hope you went ahead and ate," she said, her head bent over the papers, as she kicked the door closed behind her. She looked up and noticed Bodhi. "Oh, I didn't realize you had company."

"Sasha, this is Bodhi King. We play volleyball together. Bodhi, Sasha McCandless, my fiancée, and hardworking, dinner-skipping attorney extraordinaire."

While he made the introductions, Leo pulled three deep bowls from the cabinet. "You're just in time to join Bodhi and me for some soup," he told Sasha.

"It's nice to meet you, Bodhi."

Sasha shook Bodhi's hand and gave him a warm smile. Then she walked around the island and pulled Leo close for a hug.

She wrapped her arms around his neck and stretched up onto her toes. He was enjoying the feel of her body pressed against his when she whispered, her breath hot against his throat, "Do we have a situation?"

He pulled his head back slightly and shot her a puzzled look. "A situation?"

She cut her eyes toward Bodhi and then reached past Connelly to roll open a drawer and remove three soup spoons. She spoke in a low, casual voice. "Maybe you're doing some freelance work for Hank?"

"What are you talking about?"

She met his gaze. "There's a car parked across the street, at the mouth to the residential lot. A dark-colored Taurus. The engine's killed and the lights are off, but there's a guy I've never seen before sitting inside staring up in the direction of the living room window. With binoculars."

It said something about his life with Sasha that she assumed her apartment was being watched and that he assumed she was right.

He shook his head and resisted the urge to go to the window.

"It's not me. I'm not doing anything exciting for Hank, it's just back office stuff."

It was a white lie. More of a fib, really. But the assignments he'd accepted for Hank so far had been sufficiently preliminary that he knew whoever was outside in the Taurus wasn't interested in him.

She arched a brow at that. He knew he'd need to talk with her about his work for Hank eventually. But not now, not in front of an outsider.

He nodded toward Bodhi. "Did you bring company, Bodhi?"

Bodhi, who had been lost in his own thoughts, snapped his head up. "Pardon?"

Sasha looked as confused as Bodhi did.

Leo ladled the steaming soup into the bowls. "Sasha says there's someone watching the apartment. Were you followed?"

Bodhi inhaled sharply at the news and then thought. Leo waited. Finally, Bodhi shook his head slowly. "I don't think so. I don't have a car. I biked over. I did cut through the park, and I think I'd have noticed a car then."

Maybe, Leo thought, *unless the driver was a pro.*

"Why would someone be following you?" Sasha asked, turning her bright green eyes on Bodhi.

Bodhi glanced at Leo, unsure.

"Sasha's whip-smart. And she knows her way around a crisis, unfortunately," Leo said with a wry smile. "Might as well fill her in. But, do it over dinner. Let's eat."

~ ~ ~ ~ ~ ~ ~ ~ ~ ~

BY THE TIME they'd finished dinner and cleared the plates, with Bodhi's cheerful assistance, the evening had given way to night. Connelly insisted they give Bodhi a lift home.

When they reached his narrow street, they found both sides parked up, the cars jammed in close to one another. Connelly left the engine running and idled in the middle of the road while Sasha hurried around to the back of the SUV and popped the hatch so Bodhi could retrieve his bicycle.

He balanced the bike against his left thigh and extended his right hand.

"Thanks again for the ride. It was very kind of you and Leo, but it really wasn't necessary."

She shook his outstretched hand and fixed him with a serious look.

"I know you think we're overreacting. But if you're right about the death cluster, you may be in danger. Whoever stole your files isn't going to stop there if they're trying to protect someone or keep a secret. You need to be careful. And alert."

He smiled gently at her.

"It's my practice to be mindful of my surroundings. I won't walk in fear, though, Sasha."

"Fair enough. Connelly will be in touch if he learns anything about who, if anyone, is monitoring your computer use. In the meantime, call us if you need anything. And, please, be careful."

She knew he didn't fully understand what he'd gotten himself into. But how could he? Most people had little experience with the sort of dangerous people she and Connelly seemed to attract. It was like she was wearing Eau de Psycho perfume.

He gave her another beatific smile. "Have a peaceful night."

Then he guided his bike up onto the sidewalk, waved to Connelly, and mounted the steps to his small brick duplex.

Sasha watched until he had unlocked his front door and disappeared inside. When a light appeared in the window, she turned and scanned the street behind her, looking for a Taurus idling down the block.

The street was quiet. Most of the houses were dark, except for a sprinkling of porch lights that dotted the rows of homes—probably homeowners tucked in bed, reading or watching the late night programs while awaiting the return of a teenaged child or a spouse who worked the evening shift.

She hopped back into the car, satisfied no one was sitting on Bodhi's house.

"See anything?" she asked Connelly, rubbing her arms to ward off the chill from the night air.

He shook his head. "No Taurus."

He turned his gaze from the rearview mirror to meet her eyes.

"So, you think he's right about the deaths?"

he asked, shifting out of park and easing the SUV out into the narrow street.

She shrugged. "His journal didn't get up and walk away, Connelly."

"Could be a competitive coworker. Or a jealous old girlfriend who thought it was a diary."

"Could be. But we both know that's not what's going on here."

He sighed heavily.

She knew what was bothering him. It weighed on her, too.

"Listen, we agreed not to go looking for trouble. Bodhi came to *you*. He clearly trusts you. If you can help him confirm whether someone's tracking his Internet usage, great. Maybe that's all this will be."

He twisted his mouth into a bow to let her know he was unconvinced.

"Given our track record? I doubt that."

"Okay, well, I doubt it, too. But we have to help him."

Connelly shot her a surprised look but just nodded his agreement.

The fierceness of her urge to help Bodhi surprised her, too. He seemed vulnerable. In need of protection. She hoped she was wrong. But she was probably right.

Connelly palmed the wheel and rounded the corner. As they passed the brick alley behind Bodhi's house, he inhaled sharply. She followed his gaze and squinted into the night. A dark car, shaped like a Taurus, hunkered between two tool sheds, away from the lone security light mounted in the alley. The interior dome light inside the car went dark. Someone was in there, watching.

Her mouth went dry. She swallowed hard.

"What do you want to do?"

He turned toward her. "Let's cruise down the alley. See if you can get a plate number. We'll call Bodhi and let him know, but other than that, nothing. What did you have in mind? Bang on the window and demand that the driver leave?"

Sort of, she realized, as adrenaline spiked through her body in a cold rush.

She laughed it off. "Yeah, right."

He gave her a knowing look then nosed the SUV into the alley and crept along. It was a tight squeeze. As they neared the car, he had to ease the vehicle up onto the narrow strip of grass that ran along the fences on the right side, narrowly missing a row of trash cans.

She turned to peer into the car. She was sure it was the same Taurus she'd seen earlier, she but couldn't make out a person inside. The occupant must have hit the floor when they entered the alley. Further evidence that the driver was up to no good.

She turned her attention to the license plate. It was completely obscured by an overgrown bush protruding from Bodhi's neighbor's yard.

"Can't see the plate," she whispered, kicking herself for not noting the license plate when she'd spotted the car outside her condo.

He nodded and drove on. He activated the Bluetooth calling feature and said "Call Bodhi."

While they listened to the phone ring, she said, "Maybe he needs to be scared, Connelly. I don't think he appreciates the situation."

"I'm sure he understands more than you think. He's just going to respond to it differently than you or I would. He's a Buddhist. And probably doesn't follow your steady diet of danger and intrigue."

She bit back her retort as Bodhi's voice crackled through the radio "Leo?"

"Hey, you're on speaker. The car is back. It's sitting outside your back door."

There was a pause, then a soft rustling sound, like he was pulling back curtains.

"I see it."

"Is your house locked up tight?" Connelly asked.

"Front and back."

"Check your windows. We didn't see anything out of place out front, but there's probably another car covering your front door. Or at least there is if these guys are any good. I think they're just watching, so go about your normal routine, but pay attention. Keep your guard up, okay?"

"I will. And thank you. I'm regretting dragging you into this ... whatever this is." His voice cracked.

"It's no problem. Really."

"Just please stay in touch," Sasha added. "Check in with Connelly tomorrow and don't go anywhere where you'll be isolated—just in case." She left the rest unsaid.

"I won't take any chances. Be well."

The call clicked off and quiet filled the car. Connelly turned off the Bluetooth connection and they drove through the sleepy residential streets, lost in their own thoughts.

Sasha broke the silence.

"I need to do a couple hours of work when we get home."

"It's after midnight."

"If I get it done, I thought we could scout some wedding locations tomorrow," she said in a casual tone.

"Really?"

"Really."

"Tomorrow's Sunday. Do you want to ask your mother to tag along?"

She stifled a groan. Sundays were reserved for lazing around her parents' house with the entire extended McCandless clan. If she invited Valentina to join them, she'd happily come along but would probably drag her daughters-in-law and their children, too. Sasha really didn't need an entourage.

"Let's do it in the morning while they're all at church. Who knows, maybe we'll make a decision and can report the big news at lunch."

"Yeah, right," he said leaving no doubt that he thought the prospect unlikely.

"We could," she insisted.

A slow smile spread across his lips. "We could. You could be a horse. I could be dreaming."

She tried not to laugh but couldn't help herself.

He coasted to a stop. As they waited for the

light to cycle, he turned toward her. "You need to get serious about your classes again."

It took her a moment, but she realized he meant her self-defense classes. She *had* been slacking off. Just last week, Daniel, her Krav Maga instructor, had called to hound her about the importance of everyone—even black belts— doing the necessary maintenance work to stay sharp.

They were right, of course, but she'd been so busy with work. And the wedding.

"Next week," she promised Connelly. She pretended not to see his frown.

10

S tone frowned down at the sheaf of papers on his gleaming desk and furrowed his brow in concentration. He was a businessman, not a scientist. The technical reports he'd pulled on Champion Fuel's herbal components might as well have been in Sanskrit. But he had to satisfy himself that his drink wasn't killing people. Even if his father and that figurehead of a mayor were willing to cloak themselves in ignorance, it just wasn't his way.

He stood and stretched, swinging an imaginary golf club, and felt his back loosen. He was missing his standing Sunday morning tee time at Oakmont. Or, as he liked to think of it, "worshipping in the great green outdoors." But his group had had no trouble finding a stand-in, and Deb had taken the kids to real church and then out for brunch. He had several hours of quiet time to puzzle through the blasted reports.

Might as well get to it, he told himself, turning his back on the golden sun that streamed through his floor-to-ceiling window and returning to his seat at the desk.

He pored over the report, a highlighter in hand. From what he could tell, the product was completely safe. Or should have been. He dragged the yellow highlighter through a line that read: "At the concentrations contained in Champion Fuel, a one-hundred-and-eighty-pound adult male would have to consume eight gallons of the beverage within a twenty-four-hour period to experience adverse effects."

He shook his head and re-read the line. There was no way anyone would drink eight gallons of *anything* in a day, was there?

But what about a much smaller woman? How much would she have to drink to experience adverse effects?

The report was silent. He assumed that meant there was no meaningful difference between the genders. So, the dead women couldn't have drunk enough Champion Fuel to have had an adverse effect. It didn't seem possible.

Stone dropped the marker and pinched the bridge of his nose. Then he moved his hand down his face and gripped his chin, giving it a rub.

Unless the concentration had changed. He grabbed the report and headed for the kitchen that served the executive floor. The stainless steel refrigerator drawer built into the cherry cabinets was packed with cans of Champion Fuel. He selected a sixteen-ounce can and checked the ingredients. Nope. No change. The amount matched that in the report.

Deflated, he rolled the drawer open to return the drink, then shrugged and popped the top. He could use a boost.

Back at his desk, he considered other options. Herbal Attitudes supplied the four constituent herbal ingredients that the company used in the energy drink. When they ramped up production and opened the South Side plant, they'd entered into a requirements contract with Herbal Attitudes. The smaller company had agreed to fulfill all of their ingredient needs. Sole sourcing, it was called.

He punched the home telephone number of

the company's contracts attorney into his desk phone and waited.

"Stone," Jude answered on the second ring. "What can I do for you?"

"Sorry to bother you on the weekend, Jude. I have a question about the Herbal Attitudes requirements contract."

"Shoot."

"Does the contract permit Herbal Attitudes to substitute a similar formulation of the three constituent herbals if demand exceeds their supply?"

"Nope," Jude answered immediately.

"You sure?"

"Positive. Herbal Attitudes' lawyers tried like hell to get that clause added, but your business people said no way."

Stone was silent for a moment.

"Stone? You still there?"

"Yeah, sorry. Okay, that's good."

"Do you need anything else?" Jude asked, obviously eager to get off the phone.

Stone could hear squealing kids in the background.

"No, that's it. Thanks, Jude."

"No problem. If you need a copy of the contract, I can email it to you."

"Sure. That'd be helpful."

"Will do, Stone."

"Enjoy the rest of your weekend," Stone said and ended the call.

He sat motionless at his desk and thought through his next steps. His pulse started to race, whether from the Champion Fuel that he'd mindlessly chugged while talking to Jude or anxiety over the dead girls, he couldn't tell.

He stood and paced around the office until his email chime sounded to let him know Jude's message had hit his inbox. He printed the PDF of the contract and scanned it looking for any nonstandard clauses. He and Jude had worked together to come up with the standard boiler-plate vendor agreement, and Jude tried hard to shove it down all their vendors' throats unchanged.

He flipped to the notice block. It looked as though Prescott & Talbott, the firm that repre-sented Herbal Attitudes, had choked it down more or less whole. There were some tweaks here and there to payment terms and an arbitra-tion clause that Jude always claimed was unen-forceable, but no major alterations.

Herbal Attitudes had no leeway on the product it was to deliver, and it was required to test each of the four herbal ingredients every ninety days as a matter of course or at Better Life Beverages' request in the interim.

Looks like it's time to request a test, Stone thought. He fired off an email to Jude asking him to do so first thing Monday morning and closed his browser.

He'd done what he could for the day; there was no sense in wasting the rest of the gorgeous spring weather. He checked his watch. He had plenty of time to drive over to the range and hit some balls before he collected Deb and the kids for the obligatory Sunday dinner with her parents.

11

Bodhi meditated for well over an hour on Sunday morning. He sat, cross-legged in a sunny patch on his living room floor and focused on nothing but his breathing. Only when his mind was completely clear did he turn from mindfulness of breathing meditation to loving kindness meditation.

He rarely took the time to do the loving kind-ness (or *metta bhavana)* meditation anymore. He usually felt such positive mental energy toward everyone that it seemed unnecessary to meditate on it. Now, however, he could tell he needed it. His nerves were jangling, he'd slept fitfully again, and he recognized feelings of anger and fear rising within him.

So, he rested his hands in his lap and turned

his attention to himself. He let the sentences run through his head: *May I be well and happy. May I be peaceful and calm. May I be protected from dangers. May my mind be free from hatred. May my heart be filled with love. May I be well and happy.*

When he felt safe, protected, and full of love he turned his thoughts toward his family. He considered Leo and Sasha, his new allies and friends, each in turn and wished them well. He then wished the families of the dead women well.

Next he considered his coworkers and neighbors—people he felt neutrally toward—and focused on them until he felt a loving kindness for each of them.

He turned his mind toward unpleasant acquaintances, like his co-worker Wally Stewart and the neighbor across the street who insisted on throwing her little plastic bags full of dog poop into his recycling bin. He held each of them in his mind until he felt warmly toward them.

Finally, he concentrated on the unknown people who were following him, taking his files, searching his computer, and trying to interfere with his job. Thinking of them filled him with a hot anger and a cold fear. He meditated for a long time on them until he was able to wish them well, too.

Only when he felt nothing but peace did he open his eyes and shift on his sit bones. He stood and walked to the kitchen and poured a glass of water. As he drank it, he enjoyed the feeling of contentment that had been absent for the past several days.

He slipped on his old gardening shoes and was halfway out the door, intent on tending to his small patch of herbs, when the telephone rang, breaking the silence.

He contemplated not answering, but at the last moment, he turned back. He'd later wish he hadn't.

"Hello. This is Bodhi."

"Bodhi, it's Saul." His fellow pathologist's voice boomed in his ear.

"Good morning, Saul."

"Morning. Listen, I need to talk to you."

"Okay." Bodhi waited for him to continue but the line went quiet. "Saul? Are you there?"

"Uh, yeah," his voice dropped to just above a whisper. "I need to talk to you in person. It's important."

"Is everything okay?"

"Not really. Can you meet me? How about at

the reservoir in twenty minutes? I'll meet you at the top of the steps behind the fountain."

Bodhi took a long, slow breath and noted the edge of fear in Saul's voice.

"Okay." Then he surprised himself by adding, "Make sure no one follows you."

Before Saul could press him on the statement, Bodhi ended the call.

~ ~ ~ ~ ~ ~ ~ ~ ~ ~

HE ARRIVED at the reservoir early. Taking his own advice, he biked a quick circuit through the lower loop that surrounded the reservoir, looking for a slow-moving car or anyone who seemed to be paying unusual attention to him, but he didn't see anything out of place. He passed the riotously blooming flower gardens and the spraying fountain and chained his bike to the rack at the bottom of the wide white stairs that led from Highland Park up to the reservoir.

'Reservoir' was a bit of a misnomer, since it had been drained of water for years. A covered water supply sat just down the road, but the reservoir remained an important hub of city life. Groups of women walked around the cement structure, some pushing strollers or herding small children, chatting and checking their pedometers and Fitbits. Serious runners stayed to the outside, pounding out a rhythm as their shoes slapped the hard ground. Elderly couples edged close to the rail and walked slowly, some no faster than a shuffle. A few held hands like teenagers.

On the far side of the reservoir, on a rare flat square of grass behind a cluster of benches, several ancient Italian men played a never-ending game of bocce. The men and their brightly colored balls and equally colorful bilingual shouted insults and laughter had been providing the backdrop for the walkers and runners and lovers for decades. They provided a welcome counterpoint to the new manicured gardens that had become the face of the reservoir.

He walked once around the perimeter, stopping to watch the bocce balls banging against one another amid the hoots of their throwers for several minutes before heading back to the main entrance to wait for Saul.

He looked up when Saul's shadow blocked the sun.

He started to stand, but Saul glanced around quickly and joined him on the bench.

"I don't think anybody followed me," he said in a furtive voice. "But why did you say that on the phone?"

Bodhi shook his head. "It doesn't matter."

"No, it does. It matters a lot. What do you know?"

"What do you know?"

They appraised one another for a long moment. Bodhi respected Saul as a pathologist and considered him to be a pleasant, likeable coworker. That was the extent of it. He imagined Saul's feelings toward him were similar. They shared very little in common in outside interests or lifestyles. They just happened to work in the same building. So, while there was no animosity between them, there wasn't exactly a deep well of trust, either.

Saul squinted at him and then, apparently having satisfied himself of something, spoke first. "I went into the office this morning to finish up some reports and heard someone banging around in your office. I figured you were in, too, so I walked over to say good morning. But it wasn't you."

"Did you see who it was?"

Saul shook his head. "No. All I saw was some clown's back as he climbed out the window, which is how I guess he got in. Looks like he smashed it in. There's glass all over the floor. He took your work laptop."

Bodhi exhaled, releasing his irritation.

Saul continued, the words tumbling out faster now. "I don't think he took anything else, but he messed up all your files and knocked over that box of rocks and sand. Your office is trashed."

"Thanks for telling me."

"But that's not all. I called security, obviously, and they came down to secure the scene, with Sonny trailing after them. I guess he was in working his new case."

Bodhi ignored the implicit jab at Sonny's sudden interest in performing autopsies. "I guess it's good that he was there."

"Yeah, right. I told him to call you so you could come in and confirm that nothing else was missing." Saul paused and let out an impressive snort. "He said we shouldn't bother you on the

Sabbath. Since when do Buddhists observe the freaking Sabbath?"

Bodhi found himself nodding. Saul had a point there.

"That's a little strange," he allowed. "But I'm sure Sonny was just preoccupied."

"Cut the crap, Bodhi. You've caught three of the four myocarditis deaths. And I know you were there yesterday when Martinez came in. I saw your name on the log. When's the last time Sonny made a cut? Everybody knows he'd rather not get his hands dirty. And then your office gets ransacked and you tell me to make sure I'm not followed. What's going on?"

Saul's face was mottled red with anger. Bodhi could tell he felt like he was being jerked around and it wasn't sitting well with him. He knew just how Saul felt.

"I honestly don't know. All I know is my files on those girls are missing. I went in and told Sonny yesterday and he seemed remarkably unconcerned. Now, this."

He saw no reason to mention his belief that someone was tracking his computer usage and Leo and Sasha's insistence that he was being shadowed.

Saul's eyes widened. "What do you think Sonny's up to?"

"I don't know that he's up to anything. In fact, I don't have the faintest idea what's going on at work at this point, but whatever it is, I think it's safer if you let me handle it."

Saul emitted another snort.

"No offense, but you're a little on the mild-mannered side to handle anything, don't you think?"

Bodhi smiled. "You'd be surprised."

Saul just shook his head, his disbelief palpable.

"What do you say we do a lap? It'd be a shame to let this weather go to waste," Bodhi suggested.

He unfolded his long legs and rose without giving Saul a chance to decline. The shorter man fell into step beside him. They walked the first quarter mile in companionable silence.

At the turn, Saul nodded to a harried mother carrying a girl of about four piggy-back style, while wearing a younger bald-headed baby of indeterminate gender in one of those front packs that seemed to be issued to new parents along with a squealing infant.

"Good morning," Bodhi said. "Looks like you have your hands full."

"And then some. She's the one who wanted to take a walk, and look at her!" The woman jerked a thumb backward at her daughter, who giggled and swung her legs.

She hoisted the girl higher onto her back. The movement jostled the baby, who let out a squeak of protest.

The sound of tires squealing on pavement caught her attention, and Bodhi followed her line of sight to see a dark green Taurus peeling out from a nearby spot. It drove by so fast the driver was a blur.

"Slow down, jagoff! There's kids playing in here!" the mother yelled, as the car disappeared from view.

She turned back to Bodhi and Saul, and they shared a disgusted head shake with her before continuing on their way.

After they'd walked several feet away from the woman, Bodhi said in a low voice, "I think that car's been tailing me, Saul. Whatever's going on could get messy. You have a family. You should stay out of it."

Saul blinked at the news that Bodhi had a

tail. "You think this is all about the myocarditis cases?"

Bodhi stopped to face him. "Don't you?"

"Could be. Thought you said there was no evidence of foul play."

"That was my finding."

"So, what then ..."

Bodhi didn't want to lead him to any conclusion. He watched Saul's face as the other man computed the information he had.

Saul frowned. "A SUD cluster?" he said at last.

"Possibly. But Sonny didn't want to hear it. There are four dead women, all with the same rare cause of death, in a short span of time, and the medical examiner hasn't mobilized an investigative field team."

"Yeah, he should have had guys beating the pavement days ago. It's the first thing you do."

"I know that, and you know that. And Sonny knows it better than anybody. So why hasn't he done it?"

They looked at each other for a long, silent moment.

Then Saul said, "Well, I'm not gonna let you twist in the wind. You need something, you let me know."

"I appreciate that."

Bodhi clasped him on the shoulder and turned to walk back in the direction they'd come from. By unspoken agreement, Saul continued around the loop in the opposite direction. There didn't seem to be any good reason to risk leaving together considering they didn't know who might be watching.

12

Still wired from skulking around late into the night, Sasha was unable to sleep soundly. She was up well before the sun rose in the hazy sky. With Java nestled in her lap for company and several oversized mugs of strong coffee for fortitude, she plowed through all the documents she'd brought home to review before Connelly woke up.

She deposited the purring cat on the couch and jammed a baseball cap onto her head, looping her ponytail through the back. Then she laced her running shoes and scribbled a note to let Connelly know she was dashing out to pick up bagels.

She considered the car keys hanging on the

peg beside the door for a second then shook her head. She needed to run, to clear her head, work her lungs, and shake off the unspecified dread that had settled in her chest.

She pushed through the lobby door and cut through the parking lot, swiveling her head to check for a green Taurus. All clear.

She ran down to Baum Boulevard, catching a wave of well-timed streetlights that enabled her to avoid that awkward jogging in place business runners did at red lights. When she reached the edge of the Einstein Brothers' Bagels lot, she slowed to a walk and dug her money out of the tiny zippered pocket sewn into the side of her exercise pants.

To her happy surprise, she'd managed to beat the Sunday morning after-church crowd. The deli was almost empty except for a couple working *The New York Times* crossword puzzle together at a table in the corner and a bleary-eyed father juggling what appeared to be two-year-old twins covered in yogurt.

She ordered her bagels, lox, and cream cheese and scanned the headlines on the stack of newspapers on the wire rack by the counter while she waited for the extremely cheerful teenager behind the counter to get the order together. The lead story was the death of the fourth young woman, Mia Martinez. The small color headshot accompanying the article revealed a vibrant, smiling beauty just this side of adulthood. A larger photograph in the center of the page showed the Chief Medical Examiner, somber-faced and grave, addressing reporters at an impromptu press conference in front of his offices. The mayor stood beside him with an identical serious expression. The pull-out quote under the picture assured Pittsburghers that this most recent tragic death was in no way connected to the others. *"People like to search for patterns, for reasons, but sometimes coincidences do happen. This is one of those times."*

Could he be right? Surely he wouldn't jeopardize the lives of an untold number of people in the city unless he truly believed what he said was true?

"Miss—?"

Sasha blinked and focused her attention on the voice. The girl at the counter holding out the paper sack and looking at her with some concern.

"Sorry," she said, flashing the girl a smile. "Got lost in thought. Have a good one."

During the short walk back to her condo, she continued to turn the medical examiner's position over in her head. Just months earlier, the city had been targeted as the release point for a highly contagious, deadly virus. She and Connelly had helped the authorities prevent the release, and, in the process, she'd gotten a crash course in pandemics.

She knew there was no danger of myocarditis sweeping the globe and killing millions of people, but the potential for a regional epidemic seemed like a real concern. And easily avoidable, to hear Bodhi tell it. So, why wouldn't the Medical Examiner assemble an investigative team to run the issue to ground, just in case there was a connection?

She took the stairs from the lobby to her floor and dug out her key. Inside, she was greeted by Java, who was mewing loudly and urgently.

She set the bag on the kitchen island and scanned the first floor for Connelly, who rarely slept past six. But there was no evidence that he was awake, so she shushed the cat and poured herself a fresh cup of coffee.

Java wound himself around her leg and continued to cry insistently.

"I fed you already," she told him but walked

over to the corner of the foyer where his food dish and water bowl sat. She checked to see if he had eaten his breakfast. The cat followed, darting between her legs.

"You have food, Java. What's gotten into you?"

He stared up at her and yowled.

The sound sent a small shiver up her spine. The last time he'd made that shrill cry was the night she'd found him and his badly beaten former owner in a parking lot.

Her heart sped up and she raced up the stairs to the loft bedroom to check on Connelly, not bothering to be quiet. Java tore up the stairs behind her.

Their bed was empty and had been made with Connelly's usual military precision. The door to the bathroom was open and ajar. Inside, the lights were off and the water wasn't running.

"Did he go out?" she asked the cat, wishing he could answer.

Java looked up, his blue eyes dilated and wide, but gave no hints as to Connelly's whereabouts.

She told herself he had probably just gone for a run or to pick up milk or something, but the fine hairs on her arms prickled. There'd been too much danger in their lives not to assume the worst.

She turned to go back downstairs to get her phone and call him.

As she passed her walk-in closet, strong arms grabbed her and pulled her inside. Her attacker covered her mouth with one hand and pulled the door shut with the other.

They were plunged into complete darkness. She couldn't see anything but she knew his eyes had already adjusted to the lack of light. A temporary advantage for him.

Her heart thumped like a drum in her ears. She forced herself to control her breathing.

The man dragged her roughly toward the back of the closet and her face brushed against a row of suit jackets.

She twisted her head, turning from one side to the other in an effort to free herself.

One hand was clamped firmly over her mouth. The other pinned her wrists together and wrenched them behind her back, forcing her to turn at an awkward angle.

She could hear his breathing, hard and fast. It was the only sound in the small space.

On the other side of the closet, the cat cried and scratched at the door.

Think.

She ran through her available options.

She could probably base her legs out and get enough leverage to bring a knee crushing into his groin. But she had good reasons not to use that maneuver.

She could head butt him. But that would leave her with a nasty headache and the bumps and bruises would require some explaining.

So she bared her teeth and sunk them into the soft, fleshy webbing between the thumb and ring finger of the hand over her mouth. She didn't stop until she tasted his blood, warm and coppery.

He yelped and jerked his hand away.

"Connelly," she said in the darkness, "let me go. I want to have breakfast."

She heard her fiancé's familiar rumbling laughter. Then he released her arms and pushed the door open.

She followed him out into the bedroom, where the cat rolled around at her feet purring in a spasm of apparent relief.

Connelly thrust his injured hand toward her. "Why the heck did you bite me if you knew it was me?" he demanded.

"You assumed the risk when you got the brilliant idea to ambush me," she said over her shoulder as she headed into the bathroom.

He trailed after her, grumbling.

She turned on the water and let it run into the sink until it was warm.

"How'd you know it was me, anyway?"

She took his hand and put it under the water, trying not to roll her eyes. She'd barely punctured the skin.

As she washed the bite mark with soap, she said, "We share a bed, Connelly. I recognize your smell and the way your body feels in the dark."

She rinsed his hand and patted it dry. Then she slathered it with antibacterial ointment and slapped a bandage on it.

"There," she said, admiring her handiwork. "Now can we eat?"

"After I've said good morning properly." He leaned over and kissed her.

"So, you acknowledge jumping me and forcing me into a closet isn't a proper greeting?"

"I told you. You've been slacking off on the Krav Maga. I just wanted to make sure your instincts are still solid."

"And ...?"

"And, I'd like to thank you for not kneeing me in the nuts."

"You're welcome," she deadpanned, "although, to be honest, I refrained mainly for my own sake. Let's eat already. We have reception venues to tour."

13

Sasha presented herself in Prescott & Talbott's gleaming main lobby at seven a.m. on Monday. Her best shot at an uninterrupted conversation with Will would be before his employees started to arrive in force. Her best shot at convincing him to reconsider his decision about Naya and the potential conflict was a face-to-face chat. So she had, yet again, skipped her Krav Maga class over Connelly's muttered objection.

Her heels echoed as they clacked against the bright marble. She crossed the silent lobby space and noted with mild surprise that the receptionist was someone she'd never seen before. A blonde woman, barely out of her teens, greeted Sasha with an impersonal smile.

"May I help you?"

"Where's Anne?" Sasha blurted.

Prescott & Talbott's morning receptionist had been a fixture for decades. She took one week's vacation a year to go to Myrtle Beach with her family. But that was always the first week of August, never in May.

The woman tilted her head. "Her daughter just had a baby, so Anne's helping her out. And you are?"

"Oh, sorry. Sasha McCandless."

The woman met her name with a perfectly blank expression.

"Who are you here to see, Ms. McCandless?"

"Will. Will Volmer."

A thin, shaped eyebrow crawled up the woman's face. "You aren't on Mr. Volmer's schedule. What are you here regarding?"

"Bread." Sasha raised the foil-covered sourdough above the level of the credenza that fronted the reception desk.

"Bread." The left eyebrow crept up to join its mate just under the receptionist's hairline. "I'll call Mrs. Masters, his secretary, and see if he can see you."

"Great. Tell Caroline I have a loaf for her, too."

The receptionist ignored that and punched a number into her phone. "You can wait over there," she stage-whispered, waving toward an arrangement of chairs.

Sasha smiled. She'd almost forgotten about Cinco's art chairs.

Charles Anderson Prescott, V, better known as "Cinco," had preceded Will as chair of the firm. An heir of the original Prescott, Cinco was a lousy lawyer, a so-so manager, and an art aficionado.

He had commissioned a sculptor and a fiber artist to collaborate to create iconic chairs for the reception area of the firm's lobby. The insanely expensive chairs were tall and angular. They were covered in snowy white slubbed silk—a fabric Sasha was able to identify thanks only to her recent forays into bridal boutiques. The chairs made a dramatic, not to mention unwelcoming, impression, just as they were intended to do.

Sasha had been a second-year associate when the chairs had arrived. Cinco's memorandum to the firm announcing the "chair installation" had included both a lengthy description of the aesthetic and artistic merits of his new acquisitions and explicit instructions that employees of the firm were not permitted to *sit* in the chairs. And as far as Sasha knew, no one—neither visitor nor employee—had ever dared to do so.

She gave the receptionist an innocent look and lowered herself into the nearest chair. Panic and disbelief flooded the woman's face, and she whispered furiously into the phone.

Sasha passed the next several minutes flipping through a marketing brochure that detailed Prescott & Talbott's dominance in multiple practice areas and pretending not to notice the receptionist glaring at her. The back leaf of the pamphlet described the firm's pro bono practice and community service programs. That was a new addition to the materials that could only have come from Will, who had been the firm's main champion of giving back to the community long before he took over as chairman.

Footsteps sounded along the corridor. Sasha glanced up, expecting to see Will's secretary, but it was Will's thin face that looked back at her. He suppressed a smile at the sight of her sullying Cinco's chair and crossed the space with his arms open.

"What's this I hear about bread? Is Leo baking again?" he asked, as she slid off the stupid chair and submitted to a quick hug.

"Nope. I made this batch all by myself."

Will seemed duly impressed.

"Have you met our new receptionist, Jayne? Jayne, Sasha was a rising star here until she struck out on her own for bigger things."

Jayne smoothed her scowl into a smile. "It's a pleasure." She offered the tips of her fingers in a lame lady-style handshake that drove Sasha bananas.

After shaking Jayne's fingers, Sasha followed Will to the stairwell.

"Stairs?" he confirmed.

"Always."

"So, are Cinco's chairs as uncomfortable as they look?" he asked over his shoulder, as they trudged up to the top floor.

"More."

"Next time, do me a favor and spill a cup of coffee on one. Then I can justify getting rid of them. Eighty thousand dollars on *chairs*." He shook his head.

They continued on in silence until they reached the hallway outside Caroline's office. As the managing partner of the firm, Will had a dedicated secretary who rated her own office outside his instead of a seat in a bullpen shared with three other secretaries.

He pushed open the door to Caroline's office.

"Caroline's not in yet; she had to take her car in for service. She'll be sorry she missed you."

"Oh, that's too bad. I brought her a loaf, too."

Sasha placed the second sourdough round on Caroline's immaculate desk and trailed Will to his personal office.

"Sorry to say, I haven't yet found a home for all of Cinco's trappings. But, at least I got the place repainted."

He pushed open the door to reveal a perfectly normal-looking office with tan walls in place of the vibrant orange that Cinco had favored.

Cinco's white leather furniture was pushed into one corner of the room behind Will's Amish-style coffee table and chairs.

"Have a seat."

Sasha deposited herself in the chair across from Will.

"So, aside from the freshly baked bread delivery, what brings you Downtown? You're not finally going to accept my job offer are you?" Will's tone was light, but he leaned forwarded with a look of anticipation.

She smiled. "Not today. Actually, I'm here to talk about Naya's job offer."

"We're very excited to have her as our first P&T Advancement Scholar."

"She's excited, too. I'll be sorry to lose her, but I think we all know she'll be a dynamite attorney. If she can manage to get through law school without alienating all of her professors."

Naya's disdain for authority was no secret around Prescott & Talbott's offices.

"True. So, what exactly's on your mind? I don't mean to rush you—it's an unexpected pleasure to see you here. But this managing partner business is one meeting after another. I barely have time to practice." Will seemed both surprised and saddened by the realities of running a major law firm.

"No, of course. Let me get to it. It's ludicrous to threaten Naya with the loss of her scholarship and job if I don't take her off my VitaMight case. She's with me for another four months, Will. I can't pay her to play Candy Crush all day. And, as you might imagine, she's been pivotal in helping me build my strategy. For Prescott & Talbott to drop that little bomb on me and then follow it up with a document dump ... well, I don't expect much from most lawyers, but I thought that sort of thing was beneath you. Not to mention, there's no ethical rule that supports your position." Sasha exhaled slowly.

She'd gotten more wound up during her speech than she'd intended.

Will cocked his head and wrinkled his brow. "What the devil are you talking about?"

Sasha mirrored his confusion. "You don't know?"

Naya had suspected as much, but it didn't make sense for English to make a threat he couldn't back up.

"Know what?"

She shook her head. "Friday afternoon, Garrett English called me to request that I wall Naya off from a case I'm handling for VitaMight."

"Why on earth would he do that? They remain a firm client. We still do some regulatory work for them; we wouldn't want to upset the apple cart."

"All I know is, he said if I don't pull her from the case, she won't be able to work on any Herbal Attitude matters when she joins you."

"He said that?"

"Yeah, and we both know you guys hire lateral attorneys all the time who are conflicted out from working for certain clients. But English hinted that she could be in danger of losing the scholarship and the job if I don't take her off the case. Then, right after we hung up, your mail-room delivered a small mountain of discovery. After five on a Friday. Classic bury the solo prac-titioner nonsense."

Will's eyes flashed. It happened so fast, she thought she'd imagined it. He was famous for never losing his temper. But he had one. She'd just seen the evidence.

When he spoke, though, his expression was placid and his voice was cool. "This must be a mix-up. Who did you say we represent—Herbal Attitudes?"

"Right. VitaMight spun off their herbal supplement division. Prescott's transactional group represented them in the sale to Herbal Attitudes. Apparently, the firm is now doing some litigation work for Herbal Attitudes, who, by the way, isn't a party in my case. I just sent a third-party document subpoena. So, why English responded scorched earth-style, I have no idea."

"Because Garrett English has the lawyering instincts of this loaf of bread," Will muttered, reaching for the phone on the side table and punching in a number.

"Kevin Marcus's office." Sasha's former secre-tary's voice sounded through the speaker.

"Good morning, Lettie. I'm here with your favorite trial-sized trial attorney," Will said, chuckling at his own joke.

Lettie processed that for a moment then squealed, "Sasha?!"

Sasha leaned toward the speaker. "Hi, Lettie. I'll stop by on my way out."

"You'd better. Have you and Leo set a date yet?"

"Not quite. I'll fill you in on all the wedding hubbub. Promise."

"Okay, then. What can I do for you? Mr. Marcus isn't in yet."

Will harrumphed at that even though it wasn't yet eight o'clock. "Ask him to come see me when he arrives."

"Yes, sir. Now, Sasha, don't you forget to come see me when you're done," Lettie demanded.

Will depressed the speaker phone button and turned toward Sasha.

"This must be a misunderstanding. I'll take care of it."

"Thanks, Will. I appreciate it."

She gave him a genuine smile and stood.

As he walked her to the door, he managed to sneak in another attempt at wooing her back. "You've said you aren't interested in coming back as a partner. You turned down the Director of Community Relations position. What would it take to get you back?"

She gave the question serious consideration.

What *would* it take to entice her to return of a life of endless billable hours, pointless position-jockeying, favor-currying, and petty unpleasantries?

"A miracle."

~ ~ ~ ~ ~ ~ ~ ~ ~ ~

SASHA CHECKED THE TIME, cursed under her breath, and took the stairs up to her office by two. She didn't even pop into Jake's for her late morning coffee.

She'd spent more time than she'd intended visiting with Lettie. Then a partner she knew only in passing had materialized and dragged her into his office to look at an endless supply of pictures of his kids.

She'd finally escaped and made the mistake of stopping by a boutique shop in the building lobby for a quick spin through the sale racks.

There, over a stack of discounted asymmetrical sweaters, she'd bumped into Kaitlyn Hart, a Prescott & Talbott junior associate who, not only remembered her, but—unlike the new receptionist—was impressed to the point of fawning with her notoriety.

Kaitlyn had insisted on dragging Sasha to a very early lunch with two other bargain-hunting Prescott associates. Watching them wolf down their sandwiches in great gulps while chugging their drinks in order to return to their desks and their mounds of work as quickly as possible both dampened Sasha's appetite and confirmed her belief that an act of God would be required for her to ever again toil in the employ of Prescott & Talbott.

Her frolic and detour had cost her an entire morning, and she hadn't even scored any accessories at the boutique.

When she reached her office door, it was both unlocked and ajar. She assumed Naya had gone in to drop off some papers, but when she walked through the doorway, she stopped short.

Connelly and Bodhi were camped out in her guest chairs, and Bodhi was holding an ice pack over his left eye. Dried blood stained the front of his shirt. Connelly raised his head at the sound of the door swinging open and met her gaze with concern in his eyes. He looked to be unharmed.

"What happened to you?" she asked Bodhi.

Connelly answered for him.

"He was attacked this morning behind his office building. He's okay. He's got some bumps and bruises and a nice shiner, but it could have been a lot worse."

"Did you get a good look at the person?"

Bodhi shook his head. "No. I was bent over, locking up my bike. He came up behind me and grabbed the strap of my laptop bag. The force wheeled me around and he popped me in the eye, then the nose. Took off running with my bag. It was all over in a few seconds. White guy. Taller than me. He was wearing jeans and a dark shirt. I'm sorry, but that's the best I can do for a description."

She wasn't surprised.

Connelly had told her about a Homeland Security training exercise where experienced law enforcement personnel had unknowingly witnessed a staged robbery. Afterward, they'd given conflicting, sometimes diametrically opposed, descriptions of the perpetrator. Their descriptions had differed on everything from race to the presence or absence of neck tattoos.

And she'd once attended a continuing legal education seminar in which a criminal law professor discussed a case in which a rape victim picked the wrong man out of a lineup and he was convicted. DNA evidence later established that the actual rapist had coincidentally also been in the lineup. The convicted man and the rapist bore no physical resemblance to one another aside from sharing a race.

The human brain reacted in strange ways to stress and the attendant flood of adrenaline. That was one reason she trained in Krav Maga: to take the need to think out of the equation in a crisis and to rely instead on instincts that had been honed through repetition.

"Did you report it?"

"Yes. To the police and to security at work." Bodhi's voice shook.

To Sasha's ear, the tremor sounded like anger, not fear.

Connelly interjected. "Over Bodhi's objections, he's been placed on unpaid leave while the Medical Examiner's Office investigates the attack and the thefts of his work and personal laptops."

Sasha blinked. "Work *and* personal laptops?"

"Yesterday, a colleague called me at home and asked me to meet him. He said he'd seen a guy in my office, who made off with my work-issued laptop. He'd broken the window to get in. I wasn't too worried because my personal laptop is a mirror image of my work laptop."

"And you didn't mention this to Connelly when you called last night because—?"

"You asked me to let you know that I was safe. I *was* safe. I didn't see the point in bothering you with the break in on a Sunday night, especially when work was going to be handling the investigation, anyway." He let out a shaky sigh. "I guess that was a mistake."

"It was, but it's done now, so let's move on."

As she was situating herself behind her desk and wondering how exactly to go about moving on and helping Connelly's friend, Naya appeared in the doorway, balancing a tray from Jake's.

"I thought I heard you running up the stairs," she said, handing Sasha a large latte. She passed an herbal tea to Bodhi and a cappuccino to Connelly, then took a sip from a bright blue bottle and screwed her face up in a grimace.

"What is that?" Connelly asked.

"Champion Fuel," Naya said with a shudder, "it's disgusting."

She placed the bottle on the table beside

Bodhi and caught Sasha's eye. "How'd it go at Prescott?"

"Will's going to take care of it," Sasha said distractedly. "But for now, we need to focus on something else."

"Him?" Naya asked, jerking a thumb toward Bodhi.

"Bingo. Connelly, have your contacts come up with anything yet?"

He shook his head. "No. And they're adamant that if there's any official action behind this, it's not federal. I trust my source on that."

Which meant his source was Hank, Sasha thought. She doubted he'd take anyone else at his word.

"Okay, well, clearly someone very badly wants some information that he or she thinks Bodhi has. Obviously, it's not in your reports on the dead women, it's not in your journal, and it's not in either of your laptops."

"Why do you say that?" Bodhi asked.

"Because they're still looking. If they had what they wanted, they'd stop."

"So what's left? What source of information remains?" Connelly asked Bodhi.

Bodhi was quiet for a moment. Then he said softly, "Nothing. They have everything."

"Wrong," Naya interjected.

Bodhi flashed her a confused look. "No, I don't have any other files or computers."

Naya leaned over and tapped him gently on the temple. "You have this."

He looked at Sasha for confirmation.

She nodded. "If you're right about it being a mirror image, they aren't going to find anything on your personal laptop either. That means they'll be back. And next time, they'll be looking for you."

14

Mackenzie slid into the chair across from Fred, waving him back into his seat as he halfheartedly rose to greet her. She snapped the folds out of the black linen napkin and placed it across her lap. It was a nice touch, the black napkin. It saved patrons who stopped in for a few midday drinks the trouble of picking tell-tale white napkin lint off their dark suit pants before returning to the office. If she'd shown up wearing a light-colored skirt, she'd have gotten a white napkin. She appreciated that level of attention to detail.

"Well? What was so important that you needed to drag me out of a meeting with the entire Economic Development team, Fred?"

Since Barry wasn't around, she didn't bother

to hide her irritation. Barry's unctuous style around his big donors had really begun to grate on her.

Fred sat back as though he'd been slapped.

He toyed with his half-empty rocks glass before meeting her eye and saying, "Now, Mackenzie, that's not very cordial."

She ignored the scolding. He opened his mouth to continue but cut himself off when she raised her hand to flag down a passing waitress.

"I'll get your server, ma'am—" the woman began.

"No, don't get my server. Get me a vodka tonic. Please."

The waitress bobbed her head and scurried away.

"You're a no-nonsense gal, aren't ya'?" Fred said with something approaching admiration in his voice.

"I'm a busy woman."

"Point taken. Okay, sweetheart, I won't waste your time. We have a problem." He tipped back his head and drained his glass.

"What kind of problem?" Mackenzie kept her voice low.

She'd scanned the busy restaurant when she'd come into the room. She hadn't recognized anyone, but that didn't mean that she hadn't been recognized. She'd gotten plenty of television exposure. It was her practice to stand right behind Barry's shoulder at press conferences, close enough to grab his elbow and whisper into his ear if he veered too far from his script, which happened with alarming frequency. And, as a result, she'd gained her own measure of fame among the local television audience.

Just thinking about her boss's idiocy kicked her stomach ulcer into activity. She hoped the waitress would hurry up with the drink.

"Someone's snooping around internally, trying to see if there's a connection between Champion Fuel and those dead girls."

"Internally? Inside your company, you mean?" she clarified.

There was no way Fred could have found out about the growing problem in the Medical Examiner's Office. All of her people knew better than to leak information. But even if he had somehow gotten wind of Bodhi King's meddling, Fred was getting plastered for no reason. Firing King would neutralize him. With no access to files or the investigation, he'd be unable to continue to try to connect the deaths.

A new, harried-looking waitress materialized

and placed a cocktail napkin and drink in front of Mackenzie.

"Thank you."

"Honey, let's have another one of these," Fred said, giving the woman his empty glass with an unsteady hand.

After she'd left, he nodded at Mackenzie.

"Yes, my company. What'd you think I meant?"

"Never mind. How do you know this?"

She sipped her drink and was pleased to discover that the bartender had used a generous hand with the vodka. She savored the slow, warm burn as it ran down her throat and coated the angry ulcer in her stomach. She'd pay for that in the morning, but, right now, she was just happy to dull the anxiety that rose in her throat like bile.

"He told me," Fred said.

"Who told you? The snoop?"

"Yeah."

"Why would he do that?"

She supposed some overeager company man might have thought he was doing his boss a favor by proactively clearing the company's name. But that seemed unlikely given that she'd been so successful in squelching any hint of concern about Champion Fuel in the media.

Fred turned his rheumy eyes on her and stared hard at her. Then he said miserably, "Because he's my son."

Not good, Mackenzie thought.

She gave a low whistle. "Stone Junior?"

"I don't have any other sons, honey."

"That is a problem."

"Yeah."

"Did he find anything?"

"No. Not yet. But, you know, he's tenacious. If there's anything to piece together, that boy'll do it. I told him to leave well enough alone, but that's just spurred him on." His voice contained the barest hint of admiration for his son, but he shook his head in dismay.

The waitress returned with his bourbon. Mackenzie let him take a long, greedy swallow before she posed the question.

"Are you going to take care of him or do you want me to do it?"

For a long moment, Fred didn't answer or give any indication he'd heard her. He stared into the bottom of his glass.

She waited, looking over his bowed head out the large window behind him, where the sun was setting over the city. The sky was streaked pink and orange, and she realized it had been months since she'd gotten home before dark. Her ulcer flared, and she turned her attention back to the miserable drunk across the table.

Just as she was about to repeat herself, he mumbled, "S.J.'s my boy. He's my problem."

15

Leo perched on the edge of the low couch and jiggled his right leg, antsy to get out of Bodhi's house before the sun set.

"Are you almost ready?" he called up the stairs.

After being thoroughly harangued by Sasha, with Naya providing back up, Bodhi had agreed to stay at the condo with them for at least the next few nights. Leo had offered to bring him by his place to pick up some essentials, but he hadn't envisioned it taking quite so long.

Apparently, Buddhists were even more unrushable than fiancées. Bodhi moved methodically from room to room, watering plants, unplugging appliances, *washing dishes*. Finally, he headed upstairs to pack. But that seemed to be slow going, too.

"I'll be right down," Bodhi said from the top of the stairs.

Leo stilled his leg and thumbed out a text to Sasha: *See anything out of place at the condo?*

His phone vibrated with her response almost as soon as he'd hit "Send."

Just Java eating your basil plant on the windowsill. ;-)

He smiled. He thought it unlikely that the Taurus would head back to Sasha's condo unless Bodhi and he led it there, but then again, he had no idea who their adversary was and what kind of manpower he, she, or they could wield. It could have been one lone guy who had done the tailing and all the thefts. Or it could have been a crew, fanning out across the city, scouring the streets in search of a reedy white guy with curly hair. There was no way to know.

He glanced through the front window at the fading sun. His leg began jittering again. He heard Bodhi's footsteps on the stairs, and he stood, exhaling in relief.

"All set?" he asked, managing to keep a casual tone.

"I think so." Bodhi zipped his gray and red

canvas backpack and slung it over his shoulders. He had a hardback book tucked under one arm.

Leo bent and picked up the reusable grocery bag that Bodhi had filled with unrelentingly healthy food from his kitchen.

"Okay, let's do this. Let me go first."

His heart thumped in his chest as he opened the front door and stepped out onto the porch.

"Do you want me to turn on the porch light? It's on a timer, but I can override it," Bodhi asked.

"No. It'll light us up like we're on display. Just stay close to me."

Leo swiveled his head from side to side, scanning the parked cars that were huddled up close to the curb on both sides of the narrow street. Nothing looked amiss.

He swallowed and waited for Bodhi to lock the door behind him, then he stepped off the porch and onto the stairs that led down to the street.

In a stroke of great luck, the spot directly in front of the house had been vacant when they'd arrived and it had been almost big enough for his Lexus. He'd managed to squeeze it in between two parked minivans with only the barest kiss to the bumper of the one behind him.

They had no more than twelve feet to travel

from the porch down the steps and into the car. But they were twelve feet of vulnerability and maximum exposure. The way to do it, if someone wanted to silence Bodhi for good, would be to crouch behind the cars on the right of the house and aim a rifle at the stairs. Clear shot, not a very long distance. And there wouldn't be a thing Leo could do to prevent it.

He looked to the right again, peering at the cars lined up behind his vehicle. The shadows were lengthening but there was plenty of light to get off a shot.

"Come on," he said over his shoulder. He angled his body so that his broad torso partially shielded the thinner man's and slowed so that they were walking side by side instead of single file.

Bodhi threw him a curious look but matched his pace.

Leo had the keyless entry remote out and ready when they hit the pavement. The Lexus's locks popped with a quiet *beep*, and Leo pulled open the door and shoved Bodhi into the passenger seat. He tossed the grocery bag onto the floor of the SUV and raced around to the driver's side.

They'd passed the first hurdle, and Bodhi was

safer than he'd been on the street, but Leo wouldn't relax until they were securely inside Sasha's condo unit.

He jammed the key into the ignition and locked the doors.

As the engine purred to life, he glanced at his passenger. Bodhi's face was pale and the muscles in his cheeks were taut.

"What was that about?" Bodhi asked.

Leo chewed on the inside of his cheek and tried to decide how to impress upon Bodhi the seriousness of his situation without terrifying him. He checked his mirrors and nosed the SUV out into the street, still debating with himself.

Finally, he said, "You're a logical guy, right? I mean, you're a doctor and a forensic scientist. You must like solving puzzles, finding answers."

It was a throwaway question, nothing more than a stalling tactic.

But Bodhi gave a serious response. "Of course. But I'm also a believer that there aren't answers to all questions. And sometimes it's better to accept that truth than to resist it."

Leo reached the stop sign and paused just long enough to pay homage to the notion of stopping and then rolled through it.

"Okay, but in this case, you believe that if you

look hard enough and long enough, you'll find a common connection between those dead women, right?"

"I do."

"And you could save some lives. If you identify the link and alert the public, it could prevent further deaths."

"True."

"So, it follows then, that whoever's trying to stop you is willing to let more people die. Right?"

Bodhi inhaled sharply. "You think someone deliberately killed them? They somehow caused those women to contract myocarditis intentionally?"

"Not necessarily. Their deaths could have been a fluke, an accident. But whoever's responsible hasn't come forward and doesn't want to be held accountable for whatever reason. And that person is willing to accept that the price of continued silence is more potential deaths."

Leo checked his rearview and side mirrors again, looking for a tail, but saw none.

"Okay. Yes."

They crossed over from the residential part of Highland Park and the mature leafy oaks and maples gave way to takeout restaurants and corner stores. He nudged the speedometer higher.

"And if this person is willing to let some unknown number of innocent citizens die, doesn't it stand to reason that he may also be willing to take it a step further and kill you to protect himself?" There was no gentle way to ask the question, but he tried to keep his voice calm and soft.

Bodhi's eyes widened then narrowed. Leo watched as he smoothed his face into a neutral mask.

At last he said, "That may be true."

They drove in silence through East Liberty and Shadyside. Leo scanned the road constantly for signs of an ambush. Bodhi leaned his head back on the headrest and closed his eyes. His chest rose and fell in a slow, rhythmic pattern. He seemed to be sleeping.

When he reached the condo building, Leo started to ease the SUV into the spot designated for Sasha's visitors. At the last moment, he backed out of the spot and continued past it, making a loop through the parking lot and around to the drop off circle in front of the building. He punched the speed dial for Sasha's phone.

"Hey, where are you guys?"

"In front of the building. Can you come down and help Bodhi carry up his stuff while I park?"

"Be right down."

He ended the call.

"I can manage," Bodhi said, finally opening his eyes.

"I'm sure you can manage the bags," Leo agreed, "but this is safer."

"You'll be with me."

"Look, the less time you're exposed, the better. There's no reason to walk you through the parking lot and past that tall hedgerow in front of the building. I know from personal experience that it makes an excellent spot for lying in wait."

Bodhi cocked his head quizzically but didn't have time to ask any questions because Sasha was already knocking on the passenger window.

Leo waited until Sasha and Bodhi had crossed the entryway into the lobby before driving around the circle and back into the parking lot. He locked the SUV, crossed the lot, and hurried past the bushes and into the vestibule.

Once he was inside the building, he exhaled a ragged breath of relief.

16

S tone sat in his study, poring over the documents he'd brought home from the deal team and the research and development team files. He vigorously highlighted nearly every line as he read, as if the bright yellow ink would somehow illuminate the secrets he was convinced the papers held.

The key to the deaths, he thought, was the carbonated drinks. The company had originally produced two versions of bottled Champion Fuel —carbonated, intended for sale to nightclubs as a mixer, and uncarbonated, which market research indicated home consumers preferred. It turned out that customers clamored for the carbonated version for home use, too, so they'd ended up offering both versions on the retail market.

The dense studies that the scientists had put together seemed to say that the proprietary blend reacted differently when mixed with carbonation, but what he couldn't quite puzzle out was how.

Frustrated, he bounced his highlighter off the mahogany desk and watched it fly to the floor.

He was tempted to wake his wife and ask her to read the study. She'd been a biology major. It had been ages ago and she'd never worked as a scientist. One summer interning at a marine habitat had been the extent of her career before she'd caught his eye at a Tri Delta/Sigma Chi mixer and set her sights on marriage, mother-hood, and tennis lessons.

But surely she could make heads or tails of the technical jargon.

He glanced through his office door, which stood ajar, and checked the time on the grandfa-ther clock that stood in the hallway. It was after eleven. Deb would kill him if he woke her at this hour.

He pinched the bridge of his nose and reread the passage he'd just highlighted:

Interaction and increased potency of withania somnifera, guarana, ginkgo biloba, and wild red ginseng when carbonated. Further study needed.

His shoulders were tight from hunching over the desk. He stood and turned to his left, then his right, cracking his back. It was time to hit the hay. He could watch "The Daily Show" and drift off to sleep to the sound of Deb's gentle snoring.

Stone stacked the papers neatly on his desk and shut out the green-shaded banker's light. He pulled the study door shut and headed for the main staircase.

He was halfway through the foyer when the doorbell chimed.

He froze and listened, convinced he was hearing things.

But through the frosted glass sidelights that edged the door, the New England-style lantern that hung over the door cast a man's shadow on the entry hall wall.

He hurried to the door before his late-night visitor could press the bell again. He pressed his eye against the peephole and reared his head back in surprise at what he saw.

"Dad?" He swung the door open and stepped out onto the wide porch, shutting the door softly behind him. "What are you doing out here at this hour? Is everything okay? Did something happen to Mom?" The words raced out of his mouth in a jumble, trying to keep pace with his brain.

"Calm down, S.J. I just had the girl out for a ride and thought I'd stop by and say hello." His father jerked a thumb toward the Ferrari that sat in the circular drive behind him, its engine still ticking as it cooled.

"Oh. Uh, okay."

Stone knew his father often took his sports car out for drives through suburban Pittsburgh late at night, when he could speed virtually alone on the windy back roads. He couldn't, however, recall his father ever just popping by unannounced at any time of day or night. That wasn't Fred's style.

"How 'bout a ride, son?"

Stone really just wanted to go to bed. But refusing any offer from Fred would guarantee the old man would hold a grudge for months, maybe years, over the perceived slight. The silent treatment he'd have to endure at work if he didn't just go for a ride would be worse than a few hours of lost sleep.

"Sure. Let me just get my shoes."

"Eh, you don't need your shoes. You'll have a better feel for the gas with your stocking feet, anyway," his father said.

"Better feel—? You're going to let me drive it?" He was sure he misheard.

Fred responded as if this were a perfectly ordinary occurrence, instead of the unprecedented event it actually was.

"Of course. Catch."

He tossed the key ring to Stone.

Stone snagged the keys and walked slowly toward the waiting car, more confused than he'd been when he was puzzling over the stack of scientific studies.

As he slid behind the wheel of the highly polished machine and inhaled the buttery leather smell of the interior, he realized he didn't have his wallet. For a brief moment, he contemplated telling his dad he needed to go back and get his driver's license, but he was half-convinced Fred would change his mind about letting him drive. So he belted the seatbelt, adjusted the mirrors, and turned the key in the ignition.

"Ready, dad?" He glanced over at his father in the passenger seat.

"Oh, I'm ready. Once you get down to the

main road, open her up and let her show you what she can do."

Stone pulled out, his heart racing faster than the revving engine, and the car shot out of the driveway onto the hill that led to the road below.

17

Sasha poured herself a cup of coffee as quietly as she could. As much as she loved her loft-style condo, she had to admit it wasn't exactly conducive to hosting house guests. Once she and Connelly were married, it would probably be time to think about getting a bigger place. Especially if they decided to have children. *Children?* She shook her head at her internal monologue and peeked over the island at Bodhi.

He appeared to be sleeping through her early morning routine undisturbed.

She'd offered to fold out the couch into what she could only imagine was an uncomfortable bed judging by the thin mattress and thick metal bar that ran across the middle of said mattress.

But he'd told her he'd brought his own bed along —which turned out to be a thin sleeping mat. He'd spread out on the floor, and Java had promptly kneaded himself a comfortable nest in one corner and curled himself into a ball.

She glanced over. Man and cat were both prone, unmoving on the mat. That was about to change, however. She pulled the tab back on a small can of strong-smelling salmon-flavored cat food.

A gray flash ran from the mat to the bowl at her feet and twisted itself around her bare ankle.

"Good morning. Did you keep Bodhi company?" she asked, bending to fill the dish and scratch Java behind his ears. He purred impatiently, then butted her hand out of the way so he could eat.

"He did," Bodhi said, unfolding himself and standing to stretch.

"Oh, no. Did I wake you?"

"Not at all. I'm an early riser."

"Do you want a cup of coffee?"

"No, thanks. I'll make some tea in a bit. Thanks again for letting me stay here. I know it's an inconvenience." He flashed a sheepish smile.

"It's really no problem. I just wish we had better accommodations to offer you."

He waved it aside. "I think Leo's overreacting, to be honest. I'd be fine at home. I'll talk to him."

She hid a small smile behind her coffee mug.

Connelly had been adamant that she not let Bodhi out of her sight while he went for a quick jog. The man didn't think that posting a live guard over a sleeping houseguest was overkill. She highly doubted Bodhi would be able to talk him into letting him go back to a house that was likely under surveillance by the same people who'd jumped him.

"How's the fat lip? Do you need anything for pain?"

"No thank you. Painful feelings are as valid as pleasant feelings. They can be welcomed."

She blinked and tried to form a response to that pronouncement.

Luckily, before she had to, the front door opened and Connelly returned from his run. He pulled his Department of Homeland Security-issued gray hooded sweatshirt over his head and hung it from the hook by the door. Then he tossed a newspaper onto the counter with a thud.

Something about the gesture seemed ominous to her. It must have struck the same chord with Bodhi, who looked up wide eyed.

"Not another dead twenty-something?" he asked.

"Not a twenty-something. A dead vice president of a local energy drink company." Connelly's voice was grim and tight.

"Myocarditis?" she asked, reaching over to unfold the newspaper.

Connelly shook his head. "No. Bullet to the back of the head."

"What?" Sasha asked.

Pittsburgh had its share of violence, but a mob-style execution was a rarity.

"His wife found him on the front porch of their Fox Chapel home late last night; well, technically early this morning."

Fox Chapel was not the type of neighborhood where the residents were murdered on their doorsteps. Maybe they were offed behind closed doors, by trophy wives or trust fund kids who had tired of waiting for the patriarch to go to the great beyond, but the denizens of the affluent suburb were not gunned down on their manicured lawns or in their circular driveways.

"That's strange," Sasha allowed.

It *was* strange, but it didn't explain the gloomy expression on Connelly's face. She scanned the article.

Stone Fredericks, Jr., was a devoted father of two, family man, member of the Oakmont Country Club, and second in command at a family-run business, which recently entered into a groundbreaking economic development partnership with the City of Pittsburgh to build a bottling facility for Champion Fuel, their flagship energy drink. He had been instrumental in creating the marketing plan that had enabled Champion Fuel to secure sponsorships as the official energy drink of all three of Pittsburgh's professional sports teams. According to the article, the Steelers, the Penguins, and the Pirates had all been swayed by Stone's vision and business acumen. He was one of the region's Forty under Forty rising stars in industry. The article was light on news about the murder, heavy on the dead man's business resume. Probably because they'd had to scramble to meet the deadline to even get the article to print; there wouldn't have been time to wait for law enforcement sources to get back to the reporter with information.

She looked up at Connelly. "Did you know this guy?"

He shook his head. "No, but his father's connected politically. The wife got up to use the bathroom around three and got worried because her husband hadn't come to bed. She went downstairs to see what he was doing and found him out on the porch. He was already cold. Her father-in-law showed up around four a.m. and started working the phones. Dad had the mayor on the horn before five. The mayor, in turn, called the governor. This game of phone tag went on all morning until it reached Hank, who, over his bowl of Wheaties, called to ask me to lend a hand to the authorities *unofficially* as a favor to the grieving family."

Politics. And money. That's how the world worked.

"Okay? So?"

"So ..." he trailed off meaningfully and jerked his head toward Bodhi, who had lost interest in the conversation once he'd established there wasn't another unexplained myocarditis death. He was working through a series of morning yoga asanas while Java swatted at his bare toes.

Sasha looked at him blankly.

He sighed and stepped closer to her. "We can't leave him alone, he can't come with me, and you have a lot of work to do. I'd planned to bring him with me to visit florists, but that's not in the cards now," he whispered.

She tried to suppress a giggle but failed.

Connelly glared at her.

"Come on, Connelly, he's an adult. I'm sure he can entertain himself for a few hours while you put on your secret agent suit and loom around a crime scene."

Connelly bent his head toward hers. "Buddhists won't harm any living thing, Sasha. Not even in self-defense. If they find him, he's as good as dead."

She tried to process this statement. "I don't understand. He'd just let them kill him?"

Connelly spread his hands wide. "It's involved, and he could probably explain it much better than I can. But I know a little bit, from reading up on Vietnamese culture when I was a teenager looking for my dad. A Buddhist simply doesn't value his own life more highly than any other life—whether that other life belongs to an insect, a stranger, or a criminal trying to harm him."

As if to prove Connelly's point, Bodhi stepped out of his Sun Salutation to gently scoop up a stinkbug that Java was torturing. He opened the living room window and set the bug free to Java's great disappointment and Sasha's barely concealed amazement.

Pacifist or not, she still thought a grown man could spend a morning alone in a secure apartment, but she knew better than to waste her time arguing with Connelly when he set his mouth in that thin, tight line.

"Okay, he can come to the office with me. I want to talk to him about filing a grievance against the medical examiner's office anyway."

It was Connelly's turn to fail to stifle a laugh. "Good luck with that."

~ ~ ~ ~ ~ ~ ~ ~ ~ ~

"ABSOLUTELY NOT."

Bodhi made the statement flatly, but kindly. His face was impassive. Despite the lack of outward indications of firmness, Sasha could tell he wasn't going to change his mind—no matter how forcefully she advocated.

"Okay." She threw up her hands, figuratively and literally. If he wasn't willing to file a grievance against the city for its unfair labor practices, there was very little she could do to help him get reinstated in his position in the short term.

But there was plenty he could do to help her.

"In that case," she said, grabbing a stack of papers from the nearest banker's box, "can you lend me a hand? This entire box is full of technical, scientific reports. I don't think any of them are actually responsive to my discovery request, but then again, how would I know?"

She doubted he'd be much actual help, but she couldn't very well set him up with a box of crayons, a pad of paper, and a tube of glitter glue like she did when she babysat her niece.

"I'm happy to pitch in. What exactly am I looking for?" Bodhi said. His eyes glinted with interest at the task.

She passed him a legal pad and a pen while she thought about how to explain the legal issues to a non-lawyer.

"Okay, my client is a company called Vita-Might. Ever hear of it?"

"Sure. They sell vitamins and natural supplements."

"Right. Sort of. They manufacture and distribute branded health products to retailers. In the 1990s and early 2000s, they owned and operated standalone VitaMight retail outlets, but about ten years ago, they stopped selling direct to consumers."

He nodded, following along.

"Since then, though, they've focused on wholesale sales. This case involves a breach of a requirements contract. VitaMight entered into a contract with Life Juice, Incorporated to sell as much ginkgo biloba and wild red ginseng as Life Juice needed to supply its company-owned smoothie stores nationwide. That turned out to be much more than VitaMight had anticipated, and management realized that to fulfill the contract terms and meet the retail demand for those products, they'd have to invest capital in upgrading and expanding their procurement and distribution facility."

He scratched out notes in that distinctive miniscule, indecipherable handwriting she assumed medical schools taught during the first year.

"That's a good problem to have, though," he commented.

"You'd think so. But VitaMight didn't look at it that way. They were in the middle of a five-year plan to pare down and right-size, not expand. So when they got an offer from a competitor called Herbal Attitudes, who was interested in their herbal division, they decided to spin it off."

Bodhi's pen stopped. "Spin it off?"

"They wanted to sell just that portion of the business. The way their lawyers structured the deal, VitaMight separately incorporated that business line into a wholly-owned subsidiary, which it then turned around and sold, along with the business's goodwill, assets, and liabilities, to Herbal Attitudes. The sale included the obligation to fulfill the requirements contract with Life Juice and all of VitaMight's other contracts. There was one carve out. VitaMight had been providing branded ginkgo biloba product to the Greenway Pharmacy chain. VitaMight and Herbal Attitudes agreed to leave that contract with VitaMight for complicated regulatory reasons until it came up for renewal, when Herbal Attitudes would take it over. Until then, VitaMight would purchase the supplement from Herbal Attitudes and continue to manufacture the store brand for the retailer."

"I hear a 'but.' Let me guess, Herbal Attitudes realized it couldn't supply both VitaMight and Life Juice with enough product."

She smiled. He was a quick study; maybe his assistance would turn out to be more than an adult version of an arts and crafts project.

"Exactly. For a while, that was okay. Vita-Might purchased the herbals from another company and got a credit from Herbal Attitudes. The problem arose after the Greenway contract was renewed and Herbal Attitudes took over filling the orders directly. First, they started shorting Greenway's order. Then, they just canceled the contract. So, the drugstore sued VitaMight for breaching the distribution agreement."

"But I thought you said Herbal Attitudes breached the agreement?"

"That's right. But, the renewal had a clause that allowed Greenway to look to either Herbal Attitudes or VitaMight for any damages. It was poorly drafted. VitaMight could have added Herbal Attitudes as a defendant, but the in-house counsel made a strategic decision not to."

And by strategic decision, I mean bone-headed mistake, she thought.

He looked unconvinced by her efforts to explain the interwoven rights and liabilities at issue in the case but changed the subject. "What's this stuff supposed to do anyway?"

Sasha rolled her neck to work out a knot while she tried to decide how to answer his question without revealing her personal belief that the supplement was a complete rip-off.

"Magic, apparently. It's been touted as aiding

in weight loss, muscle building, relaxation, increased energy, better sleep, and brighter, younger-looking skin."

As she spoke, Naya walked through the door carrying yet another bankers' box. From the way she held it, Sasha could tell it was heavy.

Yay, more paper.

"Don't forget increased brain function and sexual potency," Naya cracked, dropping the box on the nearest clear horizontal surface with a thud.

"Oh, right. What's that?" Sasha asked, although she suspected she knew.

"A present from your friends at Greenway Pharmacies. Supplemental document production —they just found these in a warehouse, allegedly." Naya's tone made clear what she thought of that explanation for the late documents.

"Just one box? That's not too bad," Sasha said, trying to convince herself.

Naya looked at her with a mixture of amusement and disbelief. "What have you been snorting? There's another eight boxes sitting in the hallway."

"I have a question. Shouldn't you be doing all this electronically?" Bodhi asked.

He was right. Typically, in the modern world,

discovery in civil litigation focused on ESI—electronically stored information. But Greenway hadn't yet entered the modern world. It maintained paper archives. The stores faxed their orders to the central warehouse. Who used faxes anymore? Greenway, that's who.

Sasha shook her head. "Usually, yes. But Greenway's a little bit behind the times."

That understatement drew a deep chuckle from Naya.

"A good bit behind the times, you mean. Those fools are still filling out forms in triplicate."

Naya plunked herself down in the free chair and looked over Bodhi's shoulder.

"What are you doing anyway? Did Sasha put you to work?"

"She was just filling me in on some background," Bodhi explained. "But, yes, I'm going to help out. It'll keep my mind busy and give me something to focus on other than the situation with my job."

Naya nodded at his explanation, but she threw Sasha a dark look.

"Hey, Mac, give me a hand with the rest of these boxes," Naya said.

Bodhi put down his pen and stood.

"I'll get them. I could use to stretch my legs. You said they're in the hall?"

"Yes. Thanks, that'd be great. Why don't you put them in the conference room across the hall for now. At this point, if I bump my desk, I'm afraid there might be an avalanche." Sasha smiled.

"Sure thing."

He strode out of the room with long, loping steps. The door shut behind him. Sasha counted silently, *one, two*—

"Come on, Mac. What are you thinking?"

Sasha exhaled. "Look, Will *said* he'd straighten things out with Garrett, but it hasn't happened yet. You can't work on VitaMight until we resolve this."

"Watch me," Naya snapped.

"Naya—"

"Don't Naya me. You can't let some Buddhist coroner mess up my system! I have a system, you know."

It wasn't clear to Sasha how Bodhi's occupation or religion would impact Naya's system, but she decided to leave that discussion for later.

"I know you have a system. I won't let him mess anything up. But, he's just sitting here. He needs something to do. And, frankly, even if Will does come through, we could use an extra set of hands."

Naya muttered under her breath.

"Why don't you walk him through the way you do a review. You can certainly train someone else, Chinese wall or no. Even Prescott & Talbott wouldn't complain about that," Sasha suggested, knowing full well that, given the chance, Prescott & Talbott would complain about the color of the sky. And probably file a motion to have it changed.

Naya continued to glower, but she nodded her assent.

"Great. I'm going to give Bodhi a hand with the boxes, then," Sasha said.

Naya followed her out into the hall and grabbed a box. Sasha could tell from the faraway look in her eye that her friend and paralegal was hatching a plan of some sort. She had no interest in finding out what it was.

18

L eo clasped his hands behind his back and leaned forward to study the wall of photographs that hung in the Fredericks family's great room, or family room, or whatever they called the large living space that sat adjacent to their kitchen and was anchored by a double-sided fireplace.

He deliberately ignored the heated discussion taking place in the marble foyer in the front of the house, where a Fox Chapel police officer and an agent from the FBI's Pittsburgh Field Office were circling each other like bears or MMA fighters.

Behind him, footsteps sounded. Someone was tromping down the back staircase, which originated in the kitchen and, Leo assumed, at one time led to the maid's quarters but now probably just served as a second set of stairs.

He turned and watched as a stocky, balding man hit the kitchen floor with heavy feet and headed straight for the butler's pantry, highball glass in hand.

The man drew up short when he noticed Leo standing in front of the photo gallery.

"May I help you?" He squinted at Leo suspiciously, and possibly slightly drunkenly.

Leo stepped forward and extended his hand.

"Leo Connelly, sir. My condolences on your son's death."

Fredericks looked at Leo's hand as if it were a dead animal but finally gave it a perfunctory shake.

"Do I know you?"

"No, sir. I recognized you from the pictures."

Leo nodded toward a series of glossy black-and-white shots of the junior and senior Stones deep sea fishing, shaking hands at what appeared to be Junior's wedding, holding an infant in a christening gown, and cutting a ceremonial ribbon at the site of their South Side bottling plant.

Stone Junior resembled JFK, Jr. He looked handsome, privileged, and earnest. Senior, even posing for pictures, looked like a hardened, unsentimental businessman, which squared with his reputation according to Hank.

Fredericks nodded, satisfied by the explanation and then turned away from the pictures.

"So, Mr. Connelly, which of the bumbling idiots out front do you belong to?" Fredericks asked, pulling the crystal stopper out of a heavy, round-bottomed decanter. He jerked his head toward the two law enforcement officers in the hallway, who were now staring at one another, thumbs through their belt loops, like outlaws squaring off for a duel at high noon.

Leo knew Hank had instructed the Bureau field agent to play the part of the overzealous fed with the hopes that the local police department would throw him out of the house. Hank didn't want there to be any official federal involvement in the investigation into Stone Junior's death. It was an admirable goal, but the agent in question wasn't ready for prime time. He probably wasn't ready for community theater—every word he uttered was stolen from the arrogant, self-righteous federal agent character in a movie.

Leo tried to block out the argument that raged in the foyer, mainly so that he wouldn't laugh.

"Actually, I'm retired—formerly with the Department of Homeland Security. Hank Richardson asked me to stop out on his behalf and convey his personal condolences on your loss."

The man's eyes glinted, and Leo knew he'd gotten the message: the politicians who owed Fredericks favors had delivered.

"You aren't here in an official capacity, then? Good. I'm tired of drinking alone."

He snatched a clean highball glass from the cabinet above and poured in several fingers of the same amber liquid that filled his glass.

"Twenty-one year old scotch," he said, handing the glass to Leo. "S.J. was saving it for a momentous occasion. Stupid thinking. Especially, now that he'll never drink it."

Leo tipped his glass toward the photographs. "In his memory, then," he said. He took a long swallow.

"Down the hatch," Fredericks replied, draining his glass. "Can you get rid of those two morons out front? S.J.'s wife, Deb, is upstairs trying to rest. The doctor gave her a sedative. I don't think a brawl in her entryway is really going to help keep her calm."

"I'll take care of it."

He found a marble coaster on the side table near the hearth and abandoned the scotch, which, while smooth, was not his preferred breakfast drink.

He walked through the hallway and, as he neared the front of the house, the indistinct angry voices grew less muffled and clearly heard the phrases 'pissing match,' 'jurisdiction,' and 'jagoff' echoing off the walls.

"Gentlemen," he said, keeping his voice low and his tone genial, "Mr. Fredericks' widow is upstairs resting under her doctor's orders. Let's show some respect."

The police officer had the decency to look abashed. Agent Central Casting rolled his eyes.

Leo cocked his head to the side and gave the field agent a meaningful look. "I'm pretty sure there's no federal issue here, Agent. Why don't you leave a card for Mrs. Fredericks and be on your way."

The guy opened his mouth, then thought the better of it, and shrugged. He plucked a business card from his wallet and tossed it on a carved marble entryway table that held a vase of lilies.

"Fine by me. I have better things to do."

He jutted his chin forward and stalked out

the door. Leo waited until he heard an engine start outside, then he turned to the cop.

"What a hard case, huh?"

The police officer eyed him, unsure if he should speak freely. Leo smiled in what he hoped was a trust-inspiring manner.

"Uh, yeah. You could say that. Aren't you FBI, too?"

"No. I was with Homeland Security, but I'm retired."

"You're kind of young to be retired," the officer commented. His eyes flitted over Leo's shoulder to the kitchen, where it sounded like Fredericks was fixing himself yet another drink.

Leo shrugged. "Got an offer in the private sector that I really couldn't pass up. Turns out, working for a big corporation wasn't my style."

The cop bobbed his head in understanding. "You should set up a PI shop. Guy I worked with did that. To hear him tell it, it's easy street. Serve some subpoenas, follow cheating husbands around, and take pictures of people out on workers' comp painting their houses and stuff."

And get your face blown off by a demented, quasi-military survivalist, Leo added silently. He decided to spare the fresh-faced patrolman in front of him the grizzly story of the late Deputy Russell's demise.

"Yeah, that sounds like an interesting gig. So, Officer—"

"Nederdorf. George Nederdorf. Friends call me 'Ned.'"

"Officer Nederdorf, it's been a long time, but I can remember what it's like to secure a scene. If you want to go grab a bite to eat somewhere, I'll sit on the house until you get back."

This was a blatant lie. He'd started his career as an air marshal and had spent the majority of his career doing internal affairs investigations, so he'd never gone through the stakeout/babysit a scene ritual. But, thanks to his fiancée, he'd been present at enough crime scenes to have a good sense of what it entailed.

Ned flashed him a look of appreciation then hesitated.

"I don't know. I do need to run over to Oakmont Bakery and pick up a cake my wife ordered for the kid's birthday party. But ..."

"Don't worry about it. Take your time. I'm retired, remember? I've got nowhere to be."

Leo smiled encouragingly.

Ned's eyes floated over Leo's shoulder to Fredericks drowning his grief in the great room.

Ned lowered his voice to a whisper. "Well, okay. But, listen; don't let the old guy leave." He leaned close to Leo and added, "My boss thinks he might be good for it."

"His son's murder?"

Ned nodded fast, like he didn't want Fredericks to catch him in the act. "He came out here late last night, close to midnight, and he and sonny boy took a drive. Says he dropped him off on the porch a little after one. He didn't mention any of this—until one of his grandkids said he heard a sports car engine revving and looked out his bedroom window and saw his Pap peeling rubber in the driveway."

Leo felt an eyebrow creep up his forehead. "Well, that's interesting. Stone, Jr.'s body was found on the porch, wasn't it?"

"Yup. And the medical examiner places the time of death at sometime between midnight and two a.m."

They looked at each other in silence for a moment, while Ned let this information sink in.

"Huh. Well, listen, he's in no shape to go anywhere. He'll be lucky to make it to the couch before he passes out. Go get your cake. How old's your kid?"

"Turning seven. It's a fun age, man. You have any?"

"Kids? No. I mean, not yet. I'm engaged."

"They'll change your life, but it's worth it. You know, if you're sure you're good with it, I am gonna go. I'll be back in forty-five minutes, maybe less. You want a donut or cookie or something? It's a great bakery."

Leo almost declined, but then he remembered something Sasha had told him once: People don't like to owe debts. If Ned went and picked up the cake, then he'd be indebted to Leo. Unless he brought Leo a pastry. Then Ned would consider them even.

"Sure. Pick something good—whatever they're known for."

Ned's face brightened and he touched the brim of his hat.

"Will do. See you in a bit."

As Ned hurried out the front door like he was afraid Leo was going to change his mind, Fredericks came clomping in from the back of the house.

"Good work. You got rid of both of them. Let's have a celebratory drink."

Fredericks' eyes were red and watery, but he wasn't slurring his words and seemed to be steady on his feet. Here was a man who drank a lot all the time.

"I'm good, thanks. I understand you were the last person to see Stone, Jr.?"

Leo watched the man's face for a reaction. He scowled at the question and snapped, "Aside from his killer, you mean."

"Of course."

"That's right. We had some business to discuss, so we went for a drive."

"At midnight?"

"I don't have a curfew. Do you?"

Fredericks' tone was more annoyed than defensive.

"No, sir, I don't. I didn't mean any disrespect."

That seemed to satisfy him. He turned on his heel and headed back to the comfort of his dead son's liquor cabinet.

Leo waited until he was out of sight, then he called out in a voice loud enough to give him plausible deniability but not loud enough for the man to hear him, "I'm just going to take a look at Stone's office, if you don't mind."

~ ~ ~ ~ ~ ~ ~ ~ ~ ~

STONE'S HOME office was large, masculine, and an utter mess. Leo eased the door shut silently behind him. He couldn't tell if the disarray was natural, part of the dead man's usual work habits, or the result of an overly enthusiastic search for evidence by Ned or other law enforcement officers—or Stone's killer.

He surveyed the chaotic office. Papers covered every horizontal surface and spilled out of folders and redwelds on the floor. Taking it all in, he was left with the distinct impression that someone had been looking for something in a hurry.

He stepped carefully over a stack of business journals and minced his way over to the desk, taking care not to disturb any of the papers where they lay.

The desk was stacked with discrete piles, at least. He examined each stack, working from left to right: invoices; human resources materials; a poster board mock-up of a marketing plan for Champion Fuel, with the smiling faces of a Steeler, a Penguin, and—half-hidden behind a person-sized can of the energy drink—he could make out the brim of the hat of a Pirate. Next, centered on the desk and positioned just in front of the leather desk chair, was a three-inch thick stack of reports stamped "Confidential R&D Materials—Do Not Distribute."

Leo checked his watch. He'd been in the office less than two minutes. This stack presumably was what Stone had last been working on. He could spare a few moments to thumb through it.

Twenty-five minutes later, Leo finished his frenzied review of the studies and sunk into Stone's chair, his heart thumping in his chest. He scrubbed his face with his hands and processed what he'd been able to understand of the scientific studies. Then he reminded himself that he didn't believe in coincidences.

He needed Bodhi to read these studies and tell him if he was right about what he thought they meant.

Leo sat motionless for a long moment. If he took them, he'd be stealing confidential, proprietary information from the Better Life Beverages. He'd be interfering with a homicide investigation. He'd be removing evidence. He'd be breaking too many laws to count.

His hand twitched toward the studies. Then he stopped.

Bodhi wouldn't read them. He would know what Leo had done and that, leaving aside legality and bureaucracy, it was wrong to take them. Plain, old, morally wrong.

Crap.

He didn't have time for an extended internal debate. Ned would be back soon, or Fredericks would come crashing through the office door in search of a drinking buddy.

What would Hank do?

Hank would shove the freaking documents down the front of his shirt and get the hell out of there.

Leo shook his head. He needed the information, not the documents. But there was no way he could copy down all the study results accurately, let alone quickly enough.

Okay, what would Sasha do?

He pinched the bridge of his nose, thinking. Then he laughed aloud.

Over the weekend, when they'd been scouting reception locations, Sasha had dragged him over to a display at the Carnegie Museum— some dinosaur exhibit that featured a creature her nephew had done a report on. She'd pulled out her cell phone and started taking pictures of the information placards so she could show them to Liam later.

He fumbled in his pocket for his iPhone and opened the camera application. He focused on keeping his hands steady and the phone square with the papers. He worked methodically and mechanically, flipping the pages and snapping picture after picture of the ten-point type, the bar graphs, the charts, and the tables.

He was straightening the stack to return it to its spot on the desk when he heard the front door open.

When Ned stuck his head into the office, Leo was standing, hands in his pockets, admiring the wall of diplomas, certificates, and awards that papered the wall behind Stone's desk.

"What're you doing in here?"

"Hiding from the old guy. I can't drink any more scotch on an empty stomach," Leo said, turning and shooting Ned a sheepish smile.

Ned's face relaxed.

"He's something else, isn't he? Good news. He's crashed out on the couch snoring to wake the dead. And I have crullers and coffee." He raised a white bakery bag as if to prove his point.

19

Mackenzie watched Barry pretend to react to the news of Stone Fredericks' death. His face reflected bewilderment and disbelief, a flash of sadness, and then, finally, an expression that she always thought of as pure statesmanship. She wondered how many years it had taken him to perfect his politician's mask.

"This is tragic," Barry intoned in a mayoral baritone.

"It is," she agreed primly, matching his somber tone.

She was impressed by the show he put on. She knew full well that Fred had called him before the sun was up and told him that Stone had been killed. She also knew Barry would deny receiving such a call—and deny the calls he subsequently made on Fred's behalf. His subterfuge was nothing personal. She'd have done the same thing. You can't very well announce that you've spent the morning pulling strings. Or the next time you need to, you just might find that your network's unraveled.

They let a respectful silence hang in the air for a full thirty seconds.

Then Barry said, "We'll have to convey our sympathies to Fred."

"My secretary's sending flowers. And, of course, you and I should attend whatever memorial services the family plans."

"Of course."

She waited a beat.

"The silver lining to this terrible loss is that Fred will be able to focus on moving our partnership forward without the distractions that Stone had been focusing on lately."

"Distractions?" Barry repeated stupidly.

She stared at him and willed him to figure it out.

"You mean—surely, you aren't calling a rash of deaths a *distraction*, Mackenzie."

He sounded genuinely offended. She arranged her face into a picture of mildly indignant piousness and backed away from the statement.

"Lord, no! How could you think such a thing? The deaths of those young women in our city keep me up nights. Getting to the bottom of their deaths isn't a distraction, Mr. Mayor, it's a *priority.*"

He nodded in relief and agreement.

She paused to marshal her thoughts before she continued.

"But, sir, Stone *was* adding to the confusion, with his insistence on following his wild theories that Champion Fuel was somehow responsible for the deaths. If he had continued down the path he was on, it could have clouded the issues and interfered with the Medical Examiner's investigation. There was a real danger he would have damaged the stellar reputation of the brand he and his father worked so hard to create. That's all I meant, sir."

Barry's cheeks flushed pink at the chastisement.

"Of course. I apologize if I suggested that you meant anything untoward." He hurried to change the subject. "Speaking of the Medical Examiner's investigation, has Sonny made any progress?"

"We have a briefing with him scheduled for right after lunch. He can fill us in then."

"Good," he said with a satisfied nod.

She briskly moved on to the mayor's daily agenda, walking him through his appearances, meetings, and engagements before he could realize she hadn't actually answered his question.

The benefit of having a boss with the attention span of a puppy was there was always another squirrel she could point him toward when the conversation got uncomfortable.

She made a mental note to check in with her own sources before they met with Sonny. Her ulcer couldn't handle any more surprises.

"If you don't need anything further, I'll leave you to your correspondence."

Barry loved answering letters and emails from his constituents on subjects ranging from pothole repair to the appropriate time for a city park's baseball field lights to go out for the night —the more mundane, the better.

Her hand was on the door when she heard him say, "I'm not as dumb as you'd like to think I am, Mackenzie."

Her heart skipped, and she turned back. "I beg your pardon?"

His head was bent over his pile of papers, and he didn't look up. "I didn't say anything."

She hesitated for a moment, sure of what she'd heard.

He continued to read his letters.

She tried to shrug it off, but as she stepped on into his reception area and pulled the door shut behind her, her pulse was fluttering in her throat.

20

Sasha returned to work feeling like an overcooked, beaten noodle from her lunchtime sparring session with Daniel. That was nothing new. But the exhausted bliss that usually followed a Krav Maga session was glaringly absent.

She was mad at herself. Door-slamming, foot-stomping mad. Daniel had gotten the jump on her not once, not twice, but three times in the thirty-minute workout.

His scolding echoed in her head as she stormed up the stairs and stalked down the hall to her office.

"Come on, Sasha. I've stabbed you, strangled you, and pinned you. Pull your head out of your butt

before you end up raped. Or dead. Or is your plan to let your fiancé protect you from now on?"

Hot, angry tears pricked behind her eyes as she remembered his disgusted lecture. As his star student, she'd never before been on the receiving end of one of his tirades. She wasn't sure what made her feel worse—his disappointment in her or her own.

She swept into her room, fuming, her cheeks still burning with humiliation.

Great.

Instead of the solitude she so badly craved, her office offered her an ensemble cast: Bodhi, Naya, and Connelly were all staring at her with varying degrees of concern. She took a deep, shaky breath and let it out slowly, releasing her self-flagellating angst with the air. It appeared she had other things to worry about at the moment.

"What now?" she tried to inject some levity into the question but failed.

All three of them started to talk at once. Their voices melded together in a frantic cacophony. She picked up enough to know that none of them was trying to communicate good news.

"Hold on." She raised a hand like a crossing guard.

The chorus of squawking ceased.

She pointed at Bodhi. "Guests first."

He graced her with a grateful smile that didn't quite reach his eyes.

"I've been served with a lawsuit," he said in a soft, disbelieving voice as he crossed the room and shoved a crumpled sheaf of papers at her.

He stood silently and watched her scan the complaint. The parents of Jasmine Courtland, the third woman to die of myocarditis, were suing him civilly in his personal capacity, alleging that he destroyed his files as part of an effort to cover up the connection among the deaths, resulting in intentional infliction of emotional distress.

She looked up and met his grave eyes. He was pale and drawn.

"Okay. First thing, an IIED claim is notoriously hard to win."

"IIED?" he repeated blankly.

"Intentional infliction of emotion distress. They'll have to prove that you deliberately caused their distress and that they've suffered actual, quantifiable damages. It's basically a junk cause of action that lawyers tack on to lawsuits. But, here, it's the only cause of action. That means these guys know they don't have a case. It's probably a money grab, I'm sorry to say."

She flipped back to the complaint to see who was representing the parents, but he put a hand on her arm to stop her.

"Wait. I'm sure they are genuinely grieving, Sasha." His voice shook.

"Of course they are. But, that doesn't mean they have a cognizable legal claim."

"You don't get it. Someone's manipulating them. Someone inside, I mean. How else do they know that my files are missing?"

And with that question, posed in Bodhi's calm, melodic voice, it clicked.

"You're being set up by your office."

He nodded mutely.

She chewed on the cap of her pen while she considered this.

"Where were you served?"

"Downstairs. Standing in line for a chai tea."

"Who from your office knows you're here?"

"Nobody."

She flicked her eyes away from Bodhi and shot Connelly a look that said *wanna help me out here?*

Connelly cleared his throat. "What about Saul?"

Bodhi shrugged. "I guess Saul might know. I told him you guys were helping me. But he's not in management. And it's not like he's got a tail on me ..."

He trailed off and grew even paler, if that was possible.

"So, it's safe to say that whoever has been shadowing you is (a) connected to city government somehow and (b) still following you," Sasha said.

He absorbed this news like a body blow. "Right."

"Okay. Let me read this more closely and think about our response. In the meantime, you go *nowhere* alone. Understood?"

His face clouded and, for a moment, she thought he was going to argue with her, but he didn't.

"Understood."

She shrugged out of her suit jacket and draped it across the back of her desk chair.

"Okay, who's next?"

She smiled at Naya and Connelly.

"Ladies first," Connelly said, sweeping his hand toward Naya and bowing with a flourish that made Sasha giggle despite the triage atmosphere of her office.

Connelly rewarded her with one of his lopsided little grins.

Naya huffed past him and braced her arms against Sasha's desk, the muscles in her forearms straining against her fitted blouse.

"Will called," Naya said in a flat, dangerous voice.

"And?" Sasha prompted, although she had a feeling she knew what was coming next.

"*And* he's really sorry but the business and finance lawyers and the litigators have put aside their constant internal sniping to join forces and demand that I stay off the case. He said Marcus threatened to force him out of the chairmanship if he doesn't roll over."

Sasha felt her eyes widen.

"He told you that?"

"He's almost as disgusted as I am, Mac."

Sasha could see that. Will wasn't one for playing games.

"Well, our hands are tied. It sucks, and it still makes zero sense, but it is what it is, Naya."

"Screw that noise. I told him to stick his scholarship where the sun don't shine."

Naya's body actually vibrated with tension.

Sasha narrowed her eyes and stared at her legal assistant.

"Tell me you didn't?"

Naya fixed her with a dark look.

"Naya—"

"Don't even bother. Just tell me which box to start with."

Sasha tried to beat back the guilt that rose in her chest. She reminded herself that Naya was an adult who could make her own choices. It didn't work.

"We're going to talk about this later, okay?"

"Whatever Mac. Which box?"

Sasha shook her head and pointed at the mountain.

"The top one, I guess."

Naya grabbed it and heaved it off the pile.

"Come on, Buddha. You can help," she said in Bodhi's general direction.

He trailed her out of the office.

Sasha turned to Connelly.

"Well, what's your drama?" she asked.

"Mine can wait until you tell me what happened."

He crossed the room and tilted her chin up with one hand, staring at her with his light gray eyes that reminded her of her softest cashmere sweater.

"Nothing happened."

"Liar."

He searched her face, and she felt her cheeks grow pink again as she remembered Daniel's parting words to her.

"It's nothing, I mean it's stupid. I had a bad workout."

"Workout? Or sparring session?"

His tone was innocent, but she stiffened.

"Did Daniel go behind my back and *call* you?"

"He's worried about you, Sasha."

She sputtered, trying to formulate a response that didn't sound like a petulant teenager and failing. "I can take care of myself, Connelly. I don't need two big strong men to put their heads together to keep the little lady safe. How dare—"

He covered her mouth with a finger.

"Take it easy, tiger. Nobody's doubting your capabilities—least of all me. Come on, I know you're a badass."

She huffed out a breath and let the tension out of her shoulders. "But?"

"But, we seem to have landed in the middle of another ugly situation. And, so far we've been lucky getting out of jams. One of these days our luck is going to run out, and when it does, it'll be important that you haven't lost your edge. I might need you to save me. So, Daniel thinks you should go back to the morning class and brush up, okay?"

She had the distinct impression she was being handled, and she didn't like it. But everything he said made sense and rang true. So she nodded.

"Okay."

"Good. Also, just so you know, he didn't call to give me a report on you. He was returning my call and just mentioned that Hurricane Sasha was headed my way."

She couldn't help laughing at that. She had left Daniel's studio in a foul mood; the warning had probably been warranted.

"Why did you call him? Are you setting up a time to meet with Chris about the music?"

Daniel's boyfriend was a gifted pianist and had offered to play at their wedding, if they ever got around to having it.

"I wish. I wanted to see if he had any ideas for nonviolent self-defense tactics we could teach Bodhi."

"And?"

"Nope. I mean, it's no surprise. You can't protect yourself if you aren't willing to cause harm to someone else if necessary."

She contemplated the implications of that basic fact. Bodhi was, in the truest sense, defenseless.

"Do you really think it's going to come to that?"

He worked the muscle in his cheek while he considered his answer. Finally he said, "I do. I think Stone Fredericks' murder is connected to Bodhi's death cluster." He reached into his pocket and pulled out his phone. "Let me show you some pictures I took at Fredericks' house."

~ ~ ~ ~ ~ ~ ~ ~ ~ ~

BODHI SQUINTED at the printouts that Naya had made from Leo's cell phone photographs. The quality was better than he had any right to hope for, but they were still hard to decipher. His eyes were tired and a dull headache was forming in his skull.

He acknowledged his physical discomfort and sat perfectly still for a moment, then encouraged his awareness of his pain to leave his consciousness. While he waited, he sipped the lemon water that Naya had been kind enough to bring him and reviewed his notes.

Leo's instincts had been solid. Better Life Beverages had been worried about the effects of their herbal concoction. But judging by the results of the studies Leo had photographed, Bodhi thought their concerns were misplaced.

The door opened and Naya and Leo appeared in the doorway.

"Are you at a stopping point?" Leo asked.

"I can be."

They came in and sat across the conference table from him.

"How's it going?" Naya asked, toying with her energy drink.

"Well, as far as I can tell, the studies establish that *withania somnifera* is perfectly safe in the quantities they use, even in the carbonated formulation. Lucky for you," he added pointedly, gesturing toward Naya's Champion Fuel. "You drink that stuff by the gallon."

She twisted her mouth into an irritated little bow and cleared her throat, reading from the back of her can in a commercial announcer's voice, "*Withania somnifera*, guarana, gingko biloba, and wild red ginseng combine in Champion Fuel to provide a safe yet effective boost of mental focus and clarity, physical stamina and alertness, and vitality."

"Could the combination of those herbs cause myocarditis?" Leo asked.

Bodhi shook his head slowly. "I don't think so. The only one that's there in any appreciable amount is the *withania somnifera*. That and caffeine are the main ingredients. The rest are there in trace amounts only. Like, when you order crab soup at a restaurant, and it seems like the crab must have walked through it? It's like that. Naya's paying mainly for her shiny can and the imprimatur of her favorite professional athletes." He smiled at Naya to lessen the blow.

She rolled her eyes.

"Whatever. It tastes like dirt, but I can almost keep up with Mac when I'm drinking this stuff."

Bodhi leaned forward. "Does it really?"

"Really what?"

"Really taste like dirt?" He could feel the excitement of discovery rising in his chest.

"Well, yeah, it kinda does. I mean, it's not totally nasty. It just tastes ... earthy. Here, try it." Naya pushed the can across the table toward him.

He picked it up and gave it a cautious sniff. It had a generally pleasant aroma. He took a small sip and held it in his mouth as if he were tasting wine. As the liquid washed over his taste buds he had to agree with Naya. It did have an earthy taste, like soil. Or mushrooms.

"What?" Leo asked, startling him.

"Nothing," he said.

"No, you're thinking. It's showing in your face."

Bodhi chose his words carefully. "It's just the beginning of an idea."

"We'll take what we can get," Leo told him. "Spill it."

He turned the can in his hand for a moment then passed it back to Naya. "Well, do you remember the electronic studies that I was trying to track down, the ones that were all dead pages or 404 errors?"

"Sure," Leo said.

"Well, based on what I could tell from the truncated abstracts, they involved instances of viral myocarditis death clusters that were caused by naturally occurring toxins. In one case, it turned out to be a rare mushroom that grew only outside some small Asian village. Another one was a case where several vacationers in an Austrian town died after drinking a tea made from a local wildflower. I wonder ..."

he trailed off, hesitant to voice his untested hypothesis.

"You wonder what?" Naya urged with a hint of impatience.

"I wonder if the wild red ginseng could be contaminated in certain batches. If it's toxic, the fact that it's a trace amount might not matter."

"Why are you focusing on the ginseng, and not one of the other ingredients?" Leo wanted to know.

"Wild red ginseng is rare. It's being harvested faster than it grows. So, if it's hard to come by and in short supply, it's possible that some resourceful, entrepreneurial villagers some-where might be cutting it with a local fungus or something."

Naya laughed. "Like drug dealers cutting their marijuana with oregano?"

Bodhi didn't laugh. "No, more like dealers cutting their cocaine with levamisole."

Naya and Leo looked at him questioningly.

"A few years ago we had an epidemic of deaths from cocaine. The users weren't overdos-ing, but they all had cocaine and levamisole in their bloodstreams. It turns out some cost-conscious South American drug lord who also raced horses got his hands on levamisole, which is a veterinary de-worming agent. He decided to cut his stash with it."

Leo and Naya's faces were identical masks of disgust.

"Yeah," Bodhi continued, "I'll spare you the description of the effect that levamisole has on humans. Anyway, it could be that there's something in Champion Fuel that's not supposed to be there."

Naya lowered her can to the table and pushed it away.

Leo leaned forward. His eyes were bright and interested. "Can we test for that?"

"It can be tested for, but I can't do it. You'd need to hire a commercial lab. It'd be easy enough to analyze the contents of a can of Champion Fuel and see if the ingredients match up with the printed information."

Naya raised a hand. "Hold up. I don't want to be a buzz kill here, but if all the dead women drank Champion Fuel that contained something toxic in it, wouldn't you have seen that in your autopsies?"

"Not necessarily." Bodhi didn't like to equivocate, but sometimes the answer wasn't clear cut. "I did analyze the contents of the dead women's stomachs and had their blood tested, but that wouldn't provide a granular analysis of the makeup of any one item they'd ingested. And, at the risk of further disheartening you, I can't even say for sure that they all drank Champion Fuel before they died."

"But, I thought you said—" Leo began.

"I said they had all consumed *withania somnifera*. I didn't think anything of it at the time. It's not usually toxic in the amounts consumed by humans. I can't consult my notes, obviously, but I don't recall any of the other ingredients registering on the tests we ran. Then, too, that could simply be that they were present in such small amounts that they weren't detectable."

"But how could you dismiss it as nothing? I mean, it was a common thread," Naya insisted.

"It was a common thread, but it's also a common herbal supplement. Other names for it include Indian ginseng and winter cherry. It's used in several brands of energy bars and drinks. The dead women all shared a profile. They were young, fit, and relatively health conscious. It wasn't surprising to see that they all had consumed a fairly common herb. They all also had eaten Greek yogurt, albeit different flavors, and some variety of leafy greens before they died, too. It just didn't seem remarkable."

"But it must be. Because someone's willing to kill over it. Well, over the fact that they drank Champion Fuel, at least. I'm sure of it," Leo said.

Bodhi shook his head, unconvinced. "How can you be so sure?"

"Even if these studies aren't conclusive, the fact that Stone Junior was poking around in research and development reports that raised a concern about the interaction among the various herbals is material. It wasn't something that would have fallen under his area of responsibility. He was worried. And now, he's dead. I find it hard to believe that's a coincidence."

"There's no such thing as coincidence, as far as I'm concerned," Naya opined.

Leo nodded his agreement. "What about the fact that all the deaths have been women? Plenty of men drink Champion Fuel. At least half our volleyball team drinks it in the hopes of achieving the athletic prowess of the Steelers' offensive line. Why haven't any men died?"

"I'm just theorizing, but the fact that deaths all occurred in women, more specifically, thin women, with low body mass and low body fat percentages, *could* lend further credence to the fact that the ginseng is tainted. A small amount of poison will be absorbed much more readily and will have a greater effect on a smaller person."

"See? So, the theory hangs together," Naya said.

He opened his mouth to caution them again about jumping to conclusions. He was a scientist at heart. These leaps of logic unsupported by anything but gut feelings made him supremely uncomfortable.

Sasha burst into the room noisily before he could get out the appropriate caveats.

Everyone turned to look at her.

Her face was flushed and long tendrils of hair had worked their way out of the smooth knot she'd secured at the nape of her neck with an old-fashioned hairpin. Bodhi wondered idly if the jeweled hairpin was purely decorative or if she could also wield it as a weapon.

"What's going on?" Leo asked.

From the spark in her eye and her breathlessness, it was clear something noteworthy had happened.

"You're never going to believe this. Greenway dismissed the case." she said, the words rushing out of her mouth in a jumble. "You'll never believe who just made a settlement demand."

"With prejudice?" Naya asked.

"Yep."

"You didn't tell me you were talking settlement."

"We weren't."

"Then, why—?"

"I have no idea. I mean, they were going to lose, probably on summary judgment. Definitely if we went to verdict. But, who just gives up and goes home in the middle?"

Naya stared at Sasha. Leo caught Bodhi's eye and shrugged. It sounded strange to Bodhi, but the world of civil litigation was foreign to him.

"They must be afraid of you," Naya said with a smirk.

"It's crazy. Totally crazy. But who cares. Vita-Might is thrilled. A happy client is a happy client. And if there's no case, there's no conflict. So you should smooth everything over with Prescott & Talbott."

Naya glared at that statement but held her tongue.

Leo's eyes fell on the rows of banker boxes. "Do you have to return the documents if the case settles?"

"Ordinarily. I have to shred Greenway's production and certify that I haven't kept any copies. That's fairly standard, and it's required by the confidentiality agreement."

"But not Herbal Attitudes?" Naya asked.

"Our good friend Garrett didn't produce them subject to a provision to return or destroy them. Sloppy, if you ask me." She shrugged.

"So we can keep looking at them?" Bodhi wanted to know.

Sasha scanned their faces and wrinkled her forehead at their sudden heightened interest in the mountain of documents.

"Why would you want to?"

"Wrong question. Why don't they want us to?" Naya said. "There's something in those boxes, Mac. I know it."

Bodhi felt in his bones that she was right.

"Knock yourselves out."

21

Mackenzie had spent two college summers hawking an overpriced, unproven early learning curriculum door to door to suburban parents staring down the barrel of a long, hot season of sticky children whining 'I'm booooored.' Both years, she was the top salesperson in her region.

Although the company trained the sales force to use high-pressure tactics to get a foot in the door and then refuse to leave until the sale had been closed, Mackenzie's success came from her innate ability to find the secret fear hidden in the heart of a given mother and bear down on it until the checkbook came out.

Dusty piano sitting in the family room while a gaggle of boys rappels down the side of the staircase (or, even better, climbs out a bedroom window to the roof)? The curriculum would build concentration and enable the kids to sit quietly and focus.

Sunday *New York Times* on the front porch and a Subaru in the driveway? Time to trot out the terrifying statistics about the 'summer slide' and the prospect of mom's well-groomed children losing two grade levels of learning during the three-month break.

If there was a Darwin fish on the bumper of the Subaru and/or an infant wrapped in a cloth sling hanging from the front of the mother, she'd go one further and throw in a spiel about how European countries handle the break, appealing to the former global citizen she figured was trapped inside the harried-looking woman.

Her finely-tuned instincts had paid for her junior and senior years of college and had served her well ever since.

So she took a full minute to size up Sonny Jackson and determine his biggest professional fear. While she eyed him, he shuffled his feet, cleared his throat, coughed awkwardly into his hand, and looked around his own office with darting, frightened eyes, as if he'd never seen it before.

Perfect. The Chief Medical Examiner was afraid of scrutiny. *This should be easy.*

She allowed a slow, warm smile to spread across her face and stretched out her hand.

"Dr. Jackson, thanks for seeing me. The Mayor is so sorry he had to cancel, but please know this issue is of the utmost importance to him."

Sonny accepted her hand with some reluctance and gave it an unenthusiastic pump. She didn't hold it against him; it was pretty disappointing to learn that your meeting with the mayor had turned into a meeting with his top lackey. She never took that response personally.

"Mizz Lane," he drawled, belatedly pouring on the charm, "you tell the mayor he can cancel on me any time if he's gonna send a looker like you as his stand in."

Classy.

She smiled wider and let her dark lashes flutter over her eyes and land on her cheekbones.

"I'll be sure to deliver that message, Dr. Jackson."

He raised a hand to wave off the honorific and then rolled it in a flourish toward the empty visitor's chair in front of his desk.

"Please, call me Sonny. And make yourself comfortable."

She lowered herself into the seat and crossed her legs. He remained standing until she was settled, then he smoothed his tie over his chest and deposited himself into his tall-backed leather desk chair.

"Well, I know you're a busy man, Sonny, so I don't intend to take up much of your time. The Mayor is looking for an update on this myocarditis problem, as I'm sure you can imagine."

Sonny dragged his eyes away from her left foot, where her red pump dangled from her toes as she swung her leg in a steady rhythm.

"Of course, of course." He pawed through a stack of papers and retrieved a slim manila folder.

She folded her hands in her lap and kept her eyes pinned on his.

He scanned a sheet of paper and then looked up.

"Well," he began, "I know this is gonna be cold comfort for his honor, but the plain truth is those dead girls are nothing but a coincidence. Nobody wants to hear that, but look, aside from the fact that the cause of death is the same in all four cases and they're temporally close to one another, there is simply nothing to connect them. Nothing."

She hitched her lower lip up slightly to convey mild disbelief. She was thrilled that he seemed committed to covering up the missing files and stolen computers. If he didn't tell her about them, then Barry would have something even better than plausible deniability. His office would have an actual lack of knowledge.

He blinked at her.

Better yet, if the chief medical examiner was that desperate to keep his office's secrets, it would definitely play to her advantage.

"What's wrong? You look like you aren't convinced."

She took her time answering, letting his anxiety build.

"Well, you're the medical expert, Sonny. But, it seems you've forgotten another thing that connects those dead girls."

He blinked faster.

"I ... what's that?"

"At least the first three all shared the same coroner, isn't that right? Dr. King?"

Sonny exhaled. His relief that she didn't seem to know about his missing files was splashed across his face. "Uh, I believe that's right."

"And Dr. King is currently on unpaid leave, isn't he?"

Now Sonny was boxed in. He couldn't tell her why King was on leave without raising serious issues about the security of his office's data, in particular, the evidence related to the myocarditis deaths.

She waited and watched his face.

Finally, he mumbled, "That's correct. It's an internal personnel issue. Got nothin' to do with the dead girls."

"Well, that's a relief. Of course, the Mayor's Office will have to launch an investigation into Dr. King's role in those three autopsies, anyway. I'm sure you understand," she said brightly,

"What? Why?"

"Sonny, surely you've heard that Jasmine Cortland's family has sued Dr. King."

His eyes widened. She wasn't sure whether he actually hadn't heard or whether he was just stunned that she had.

"Uh—"

"I understand that Dr. King was served earlier today and that the complaint alleges he destroyed official files related to the Cortland woman's autopsy. I'm sure there's no truth to that allegation, but in light of the civil lawsuit against an employee of your office, the Mayor can't risk being seen as complacent. He'll have to announce that your office is under investigation. I believe his press secretary has already scheduled the press conference for this afternoon. Of course, you'll stand next to him and vow to cooperate." She kept her voice gentle but firm, as if to signal there was no room for negotiation.

Sonny blanched. He pushed both palms down flat on his desk in what Mackenzie suspected was an effort to steady his shaking hands.

"An investigation? Press conference? Come on, now, honey, you gotta know that's not necessary. And, in fact, it's gonna be a big distraction for my people."

Just like an overtired housewife who only wants every educational advantage for her kids, Sonny was doing her work for her. She moved in for the kill.

"An investigation *would* be unfortunate, wouldn't it? What with you on the short list to head up the Forensic Science and Law Program at Duquesne when Jim Clark retires."

He blinked. A rapid fluttering of his eyelids. He looked just like a startled rabbit.

"Uh—"

"Oh, don't worry, we know the appointment is very hush hush right now. But you're a strong contender. The school has already called and asked the mayor about you. He's thrilled. For you and for us—it'll be quite a feather in his cap if his Chief Medical Examiner gets such a prestigious position. In fact, he mentioned something about a raise if the directorship comes through. Since you'll be so busy with two high-profile jobs."

The blinking slowed and he puffed up just a touch.

"Well, three, actually. The director also heads the Wecht Institute, you know, for continuing education and the masters programs."

She smiled like she was impressed and said, "But, of course, the mayor can't very well give you a glowing recommendation if your department's under investigation. It wouldn't look right. You understand."

His short-lived relief vanished, and horror painted his face.

"Surely we don't need to investigate this formally. Can't his honor do ... something else?" A plaintive whine snuck into his voice.

"What do you suggest?"

"I don't know. Something. Anything!"

She waited a beat then said in a doubtful tone, as if she were speaking more to herself than to the desperate man sitting across from her, "I wonder if we could..."

He leaned forward. "What?"

"I'm just thinking aloud here. I wonder if you terminated Dr. King, if that might not satisfy the Mayor and obviate the need for a public inquiry. Because you're right, the media and governmental attention will put your people under a microscope. That'll make it hard to do their jobs. That's no good for the department ... or for you."

He huffed out a breath. "Fire Bodhi? He's one of my best coroners. I mean, I haven't seen this complaint, but I'll tell you right now, he never cuts corners, never plays politics. He won't advance into management, of course. He's got no stomach for it. But he's a damned fine forensic pathologist. I can't just fire the guy."

She edged her tone with steel. "Actually, you *can*. You need to decide if you *will*. It's your choice, you can sacrifice one easily replaceable worker or you can sacrifice the reputation of the Medical Examiner's Office and your own academic career. Just know that if you choose the latter, the Mayor's Office has no intention of going down with you."

Sonny swallowed hard. "But what about Bodhi?"

She waved a hand. "What about him? Work out a package so he'll get his pension and give him a soft landing. Bring him over to Duquesne as an adjunct professor after they name you director. He's the least of your worries."

She leaned back against her chair to wait him out. Her summer sales job had also taught her that once she'd fully exploited a person's fear, she didn't need to pressure him to close the deal. Sitting in silence for a few moments and letting him talk himself into it was all that was required. She calculated that it would take Sonny three minutes, tops, of hemming and hawing before his loyalty to Bodhi King was nothing but a distant memory.

22

The silent concentration that Sasha and Naya brought to their work was comfortingly familiar despite the differences in their tasks, Bodhi thought. The rhythm of their softly turning pages was similar to the quiet scratches of instruments in his autopsy room; the aura of intense thought and careful consideration was the same. It soothed him, but he could tell that it was agitating Leo.

His friend was squirming in his seat as he flipped through the documents. Leo's left leg pounded out a constant jiggle under the table.

Bodhi paused and considered the task from Leo's point of view: Leo was a man of action. A doer. And, Bodhi suspected, to him, scanning page after page of irrelevant paper hardly seemed like doing anything.

Bodhi checked the time. It was nearly seven p.m.

"Do lawyers take a break to eat?" Bodhi asked.

Although he kept his voice soft, it seemed to break the hush sharply. Both Sasha and Naya looked up immediately and in unison.

Hope flared in Leo's eyes.

"When absolutely necessary," Sasha admitted. A small frown creased her face. "Are you guys starving? Because if we could just push through another couple hours, we could order in—"

"Why don't Leo and I run out and pick up something, better than takeout. We can go to Whole Foods and then Leo can cook for all of us back at your place?" Bodhi suggested before she could force them all to continue to work without a break until midnight. For all her initial skepticism about the value of continuing to look through the documents, she'd jumped right in and was enthusiastically plowing through the stacks of paper.

Leo was already on his feet.

"That's a great plan. I need to feed Java

anyway. We'll meet you at the condo. Naya, you in?"

Naya scrunched up her face and considered. "You making something with tofu or with bacon, Flyboy?"

Leo smiled, pointing at Bodhi. "Dr. King here is a vegan, but I promise not to sneak any soy products onto your plate."

Naya shrugged. "Okay, then. Thanks."

Sasha wore the look of a woman who knew she'd been beaten. She had the good sense to capitulate with grace. "Do you want to ask Carl to join us?"

"Nah, he's got tickets to the game."

"The hockey game?" Sasha asked, with a guilty expression.

"Don't sweat it, Mac. He was taking his brother all along. I'm not missing anything."

Sasha narrowed her eyes but accepted the explanation, which had the ring of a lie to Bodhi's ear.

"Great. Come on, then," Leo said to Bodhi, eager to escape the room.

The women had already returned their attention to their documents, their heads bent like monks over sacred writings, their focus solely on the words in front of them.

~ ~ ~ ~ ~ ~ ~ ~ ~ ~

THEY WERE CROSSING South Highland Avenue when a glossy Mercedes S Class slid to a halt next to them and the driver's window buzzed down.

"Yo, Bodhi!" called an excited voice.

Bodhi turned and squinted in the fading light. Beside him, Leo tensed and shifted his broad shoulders in an effort to create a shield.

"It's okay," Bodhi said in a low tone, as he recognized the driver.

"How's it going, Jamal?" he asked, skirting around Leo and approaching the highly polished car.

"It's freaking great, man. This job is awesome."

Jamal reached an arm through the open window and patted the side of the car gently, as if he were petting the flank of a horse. He smiled broadly.

Leo stepped forward and whistled at the car.

"Nice ride."

Jamal laughed. "Sure is. Wish it was mine."

Leo cocked his head.

"Jamal used to work with me at the Medical Examiner's Office," Bodhi explained. "He drove the hearse. I suggested he talk to Gary about getting a job as a driver at the dealership. Looks like he took my advice."

Jamal nodded. "Jamal Parker. Nice to meet you."

"Leo Connelly. I play volleyball with Bodhi and Gary. Congratulations on the new gig."

"Thanks. How's it going at the morgue?" Jamal asked.

"I wouldn't know. I'm out on unpaid leave," Bodhi replied with no trace of emotion.

Jamal's eyes widened. "No freaking way."

"Way."

"You're like ... the perfect creepy coroner, man. I mean, no offense. Sonny loved your skinny arse." Jamal was shaking his head in disbelief. "What'd you *do*?"

"Nothing. It's a long story. It'll all work out."

Jamal shot him a skeptical look. "Hope so. But, that place ... the politics are hyper, man."

"Hyper?" Leo asked.

"Yeah, it's in overdrive. People stabbing each other in the back. I mean everyone from the janitors on up to the MEs. Like, stealing each other's cases? Man, that's sick. They're fighting over dead people."

"There's certainly some ambition and healthy competition at play," Bodhi agreed.

Jamal laughed knowingly. "Come on, now, it's way more than that. Look at Saul."

"Saul?"

Bodhi had never heard anyone complain about Saul's ethics.

Jamal's right eyebrow shot up his forehead. "Yeah, Saul. He's got a blonde honey on the side. Brings her into the freaking morgue for sexy time." He shuddered at the thought.

"That's not—that can't be true. Saul has a wife and four young kids. No way." Bodhi shook his head, rejecting the possibility.

"I'm telling you, Bodhi. It's true *and* What's His Name—the coroner with the red hair? He walked in on them in cold storage one night. He's been lording it over Saul ever since."

"Lording it over him how?" Leo asked, suddenly interested in the office gossip.

Jamal shifted his gaze to Leo. "He's got Saul writing up his reports for him. When that model came in, you know, Bodhi, the overdose—"

"She was dating some ballplayer?"

"Yeah, her. Sonny caught that case and redhead dude told him to hand it over. Figured it would get some prime time play."

"The redhead? Do you mean Wally?"

"I don't know, dude. He's got the office on the other side of Saul's."

Leo looked sharply at Bodhi.

"That's Wally," Bodhi confirmed. "Wally Stewart."

"Anyway, that joint is a snake pit. You should get out while the gettin's good. Listen, I gotta get this baby back to the dealership. Thanks again for the hook up."

Jamal extended his arm straight out and Bodhi gave him a quick fist bump. He eased the car out into the flow of traffic and Bodhi and Leo watched him glide away, the steady purr of the engine growing fainter.

After a moment, Leo started walking toward the grocery store. "Do you think Saul could be involved?"

Bodhi considered the question dispassionately as they walked, matching Leo's long stride and turning the possibility over in his mind.

Finally, he said, "I don't know. My heart says no. But my heart would have said he wouldn't have an affair, either..."

He trailed off and they walked on in silence.

As they clattered down the metal stairs that led to the Whole Foods Market parking lot, Leo said. "What about this Stewart guy?"

Bodhi had known the question was coming. He tried to answer it fairly.

"Wally Stewart is a smart man, but he's suffering terribly."

"Suffering? From what?"

Bodhi smiled.

"Some people believe that when another person makes us suffer, it's not personal; it's his own suffering spilling over."

"And Wally makes you suffer?"

Bodhi exhaled. "Wally makes everyone suffer."

23

"Why don't Connelly and I just set a date and then we'll book whatever venue is available?" Sasha proposed, both because she thought it was a reasonable solution and because she was eager to stop having this very same weekly conversation with her mother.

Valentina McCandless wasn't wearing pearls, but if she had been, she would have clutched them.

"Absolutely not," she sniffed without even bothering to look up from the soft bare bottom she was expertly diapering.

"Why not?"

Sasha's mother gently pressed the Velcro tabs together on the cloth diaper and picked up her grandson's feet, pumping them in a bicycle motion.

"That's better, isn't it, my little bean? Yes, it is, nice and clean," she cooed to Julian. He rewarded her with a lopsided smile.

"Look, he's smiling!" Sasha said, amazed despite herself.

"Probably gas," her mother replied in her normal voice.

She handed the baby to Sasha. "Here, hold him while I wash my hands."

Sasha took the flailing lump and jostled it awkwardly, one hand supporting his floppy neck. She didn't know a ton about babies, but that much she knew—they couldn't hold up their own heads.

As Valentina scrubbed her hands at the kitchen sink, she spoke over her shoulder.

"To answer your question, your notion that you'll just pick a date you like and miraculously find, not only a church and a reception site that you like, but also vendors that are available is just naive. Where were you when your sisters-in-law were planning their weddings?"

Working, probably.

"Mom, it really doesn't matter to me *where* Connelly and I get married, just *that* we do."

Sasha took one last stab at getting her mother to understand her viewpoint, knowing full well that it was futile. She jiggled Julian against her shoulder.

Her mother turned and arched an elegant brow.

"Careful he doesn't spit up on your suit jacket."

Sasha grabbed a burp cloth off the freshly laundered stack and shoved it between her nephew's tiny milky smelling head and her five hundred dollar jacket.

"Mom, did you hear me?"

Valentina locked eyes with her daughter and her expression softened.

"I heard you, Sasha. But, I think that's just your frustration talking. I know it's a lot of work, but when you look back on your wedding day, you'll be glad that you took the time to make everything perfect."

Perfect for whom?

"If Connelly and I are husband and wife at the end of the wedding day, I'll consider it a roaring success."

Her mother cocked her head and considered her like she was an alien life form.

Sasha knew the feeling

When she was ten, after yet another go around with her mother about appropriate behavior for a lady, she'd cross-examined her older brothers about whether they were *sure* their mother had been pregnant before a baby girl arrived. Despite their insistence that Valentina had definitely been pregnant and had returned home with a squealing green-eyed baby, Sasha clung to her suspicion that someone had left her on the McCandless family's doorstep —or that there'd been a mix-up at the hospital. Only after her father had pointed out that she was a younger carbon copy of her maternal grandmother had she reluctantly conceded that she must be related to Valentina.

But, sometimes ...

"And does Leo share that unsentimental view?"

Sasha gritted her teeth to stop from shouting 'No, but that's because you've been working him over every time you see him.'

Say what she would about her mother, Valentina was shrewd and very smart. She knew her future son-in-law craved family and connection and had spent the past several months drilling into him the idea that a big, fancy wedding was what family was about.

"Well? Does he?"

Sasha wished she'd visited her mother before her Krav Maga class instead of the other way around. She was going to leave her parents' home with pounds and pounds of pent-up aggression.

"No, Mom. I guess he doesn't."

"It's his special day, too, honey," her mother said gently.

As if to express his agreement with this point, Julian shot a thin stream of partially-digested breastmilk at Sasha's lapel, just to the right of the protective cloth. He looked right into her eyes with his own enormous blue eyes and smiled.

"Now *that's* a real smile," her mother observed.

Sasha wondered how much worse her day could get.

24

Leo couldn't spend another day cooped up in Sasha's office staring at contracts and purchase orders until his vision blurred. He'd tried to talk Bodhi into playing hooky with him, but the forensic scientist seemed to enjoy the document review and had headed into the office with Sasha.

Leo decided to spend some time digging into Saul and Wally's personnel records. He could have invoked Hank's name and called in some favors at the National Security Agency to get pretty much everything he wanted, but he decided to try it the old-fashioned way first. He trusted Hank completely, but he had no illusions that every civil servant working for the federal government was squeaky clean. The fewer people who knew what and who he was investigating, the better.

He picked out a suit that didn't scream 'G Man' and paired it with a sloppily knotted tie. He refrained from his usual precision when styling his hair and left it slightly mussed, even though doing so made him feel off-balance and unfinished. He was fairly confident he could pass himself off as a freelance writer. And, if he couldn't, he'd try the old Connelly charm.

The cat appraised him from his perch on the counter and gave him an approving *meow*.

"Thanks, Java."

Leo grabbed his keys from the valet tray. In the process, he knocked a glossy tri-fold flyer off a small stack of junk mail destined for the recycling bin. He bent to retrieve it. *Your Destination Wedding Starts Here!* promised the brochure. A sapphire blue sky met impossibly bluer water and the silhouettes of a barefoot bride and groom walked through the snowy white sand.

He turned the paper over in his hand, noted Sasha's name in the recipient field, and then folded the pamphlet in half. Instead of returning it to its place on the entryway table, he stuffed it into his pants pocket.

~ ~ ~ ~ ~ ~ ~ ~ ~ ~ ~

GETTING into the office of the Medical Examiner's Press Officer proved harder than he'd antici- pated. He spent twenty minutes loitering in the hallway outside the door that he'd been directed to by the security guard manning the entrance to the building. He was just about to try another fruitless round of knocking on the windowless wooden door when he heard the clatter of high heels drawing closer.

A hugely pregnant woman, with a complexion like peaches, came hurrying along the corridor. Her belly preceded the rest of her by a good six inches.

"Oh." She drew up short when she saw him and blew a stray curl of hair out of her eyes. "Are you waiting for me?"

"I don't know. Are you the press officer?" He smiled disarmingly.

She smiled back right away but a cloud passed over her face when she answered. "That's my title, all right. Are you a stringer?" She eyed his rumpled attire.

"Freelancer. I'm doing a piece on the myocarditis deaths."

"Well, if you're looking for a comment for that story, you're going to have to go through the Mayor's Economic Development Deputy Director."

"Why would I have to do that?"

For a moment, the woman looked as if she were going to launch into a rant, but instead she clamped her top teeth down over her lower lip hard. Then she said, "Good question. You should feel free to ask Ms. Lane."

"Lane?"

She nodded and dug a small notepad out of her overloaded leather handbag. She rested the pad on her stomach as a ledge and scribbled a name and telephone number.

"Mackenzie Lane." She tore the sheet from the pad and handed it to him. "Call first or she'll have you cooling your heels forever."

"Got it. Thanks."

"You bet." She turned and jammed her key into the door.

"Wait. Can I a least get some background from you?"

She turned, halfway through the door.

"What kind of background?"

"Stuff like how many coroners—I mean, forensic pathologists—work for the office. Who's senior? Who's not? What the atmosphere's like. Whether there are any feuds. You know, background." He smiled.

She stuttered for a moment, and he thought he had her. Then she shook her head and spoke in a low whisper. "I'm sorry. Things are ... tense ... around here. I can't risk losing my job, not with the baby coming. You have to talk to Ms. Lane. But, just between you and me? It's like any other workplace with the usual in-fighting and back-stabbing. Just add dead bodies."

She turned back to her office.

"Got it. Thanks. Oh, and congratulations on the, um, baby," he said.

She tossed him a smile over her shoulder before disappearing behind the door.

He stared down at the name and phone number and then shoved the paper into his pocket along with the resort wedding brochure. Try as he might, he couldn't come up with a good reason why the mayor's deputy director of economic development, rather than the county's chief medical examiner, would be fielding questions about a rash of deaths.

Out of Sasha-enforced habit, he took the

stairs and emerged in the main hallway, which was filling with city worker bees swarming on their ten o'clock breaks.

As he passed the line at a coffee kiosk, a shock of ginger hair caught his eye. A gangly red-headed man and a morose-looking colleague, both wearing white lab coats, stood together, waiting to order their mid-morning jolt of caffeine.

A hunch told him the pair was Wally and Saul. Connelly didn't believe in luck, and he knew he was unlikely to hear anything relevant, but it seemed imprudent to pass up a perfect eavesdropping opportunity if the universe was inclined to hand him one.

He hesitated in the middle of the concourse for a moment, then stepped into line behind them and pulled out the brochure, pretending to examine it while he tuned into their conversation.

"—not going to happen, Wally," the man he assumed was Saul insisted.

"It did happen, you moron. Sonny told me himself. Bodhi's not coming back. And I'm getting his lab."

"Who cares who gets his lab? What difference

does it make? No way would they fire Bodhi. He's out on admin leave, is all."

Wally flicked an impatient hand at his co-worker. "He was, but Sonny's drawing up the termination papers now. And you say you don't want his lab, but the next time you're bending your honey over your piece of crap desk, you'll be wishing you had it. It's private. He has that sweet stainless steel desk. Hey, maybe, I'll invite your girl over to check it out."

Saul balled his hands into tight fists at his sides.

Leo waited to see what he did next. But the shorter man just took three deep breaths and muttered, "Don't talk like that."

Wally responded with a nasty laugh.

Saul looked nervously over his shoulder, and Leo stared down at the pamphlet.

They shuffled forward as the line moved up closer to the counter.

Leo shoved the paper back into his pocket and made a production of looking at his watch. With a loud sigh, he stepped out of the line and hurried toward the door as if he were late for an appointment.

25

Connelly came banging through the office door like he was being chased. Given their history, Sasha craned her neck to peek through the swinging door and confirm that there wasn't a pursuer running down the hallway.

"Listen, this is important. I was lurking around the Medical Examiner's Office this morning. I learned three things. Saul is absolutely having an affair; Wally is definitely suffering; and Bodhi—"

"—Is about to be fired," Naya finished.

Connelly blinked. "That's right. How—?"

"Saul just called my cell phone to give me the head's up," Bodhi said in an oddly flat voice.

Sasha recognized that lack of intonation as

the voice of someone who hadn't yet accepted the reality of his situation.

"Did Saul also mention that all comments from the Medical Examiner's Office must now go through the Mayor's Deputy Director of Economic Development?" Leo asked.

"I don't—that doesn't sound right. I don't know what's going on over there," Bodhi managed.

Sasha stared hard at him. "How exactly did you learn all this, Connelly? Who did you talk to?"

"No one. I hoped to get something from the press secretary, so I posed as a freelance writer—"

"That explains that tie," Naya observed.

Sasha bit her lip to suppress a laugh.

Connelly ignored the jab and pressed on. "But the press secretary told me comments on the myocarditis deaths had to come from this Mackenzie Lane woman in the mayor's office. As I was headed out of the building, I noticed two men in white lab coats in line for the coffee kiosk. One of them had red hair, so, on a hunch, I got in line behind them and overheard their conversation. The redhead, Wally, was needling Saul about his mistress. They were also talking about Bodhi's, um, termination. I'm sorry, man."

"Thanks," Bodhi muttered.

Connelly turned his attention from the newly unemployed man and sought Sasha's eyes, giving her a meaningful look that said *what the devil is going on?*

She shook her head, slowly. She had no idea.

Meanwhile, Naya was typing furiously on Sasha's laptop.

"This Mackenzie Lane woman is all over the Champion Fuel deal," Naya said, scanning a page of search results. "I mean *all* over it."

Sasha watched the others' faces. Naya and Connelly were scowling, making the same unpleasant connections between Bodhi's situation, the VitaMight settlement, the dead young women, and the murder of Stone, Junior, that she was trying to ignore.

"It's too neat, you guys," she said. "There's no way I just happen to have a case that's somehow related to this death cluster scandal."

"Well, Prescott & Talbott's tied up in it. So, it's not really all that surprising," Naya muttered darkly.

Connelly added, "And you *are* a trouble magnet, don't forget."

She bristled. "Hey, Bodhi's your friend, so this one's on you."

Connelly just laughed, but her face flushed as she realized what she'd just said.

She turned to Bodhi. "I'm so sorry. I didn't mean that the way it sounded."

Bodhi tossed his curly hair like a dog shaking off water.

"It's okay. It's true, I've brought trouble into your lives."

He said it in a matter-of-fact tone that only made her feel worse.

She crossed the room and searched his face. His eyes were sad.

"Bodhi, listen. Honestly, I was just needling Connelly. You wouldn't know this, but the past two years or so have been one dangerous crisis after another. I mean *dangerous*, like people trying to kill us with alarming regularity kind of dangerous. This—whatever it is—is a kerfuffle, a little blip in comparison. The only one who's truly in danger here seems to be you. And, we're going to do whatever we can to protect you and force the City's hand to investigate the connection between the myocarditis deaths and Champion Fuel."

"I can't ask you to do that."

"You didn't. We offered. And it's settled. So, let's move on." She looked around the room to include Connelly and Naya in the conversation. "Anybody have any brilliant ideas about our next steps?"

The early afternoon sun slanted through the window, throwing a beam of light across the middle of Naya's face. She met Sasha's gaze and shook her head slowly. Connelly looked equally defeated.

She felt her own shoulders sag. They were in the middle of a sticky, interconnected web, and she knew without a doubt they were the fly, not the spider. Beyond that, she knew little else.

Bodhi coughed.

"Let me talk to Sonny."

"He's not going to tell you anything. He just fired you to avoid your finding out more than you already know," Naya protested.

"Maybe so. But I've worked for him for a long time. He can't expect that I won't have questions. And maybe he'll say something that he doesn't realize is significant. Sonny can be ... loquacious. If I can get him started talking, he'll have plenty to say."

Connelly's clenched jaw told her what he thought of this plan, but Sasha shrugged.

"It's not like anyone else has a better idea. If you feel comfortable talking to him, then I say go for it."

A smile flitted across Bodhi's face. "I'll try to catch him outside the office. He likes to take an afternoon constitutional when the weather's nice."

"I'm coming, too," Connelly said. "I'll stay a half block behind, but you aren't going to wander around without protection."

Sasha was glad to see that Bodhi acquiesced with more grace than she would have in his shoes.

As the men walked out of the room chatting about volleyball, Naya turned to Sasha.

"What about us."

Sasha smiled at her. "VitaMight signed the settlement agreement this morning. The case is over."

"So?"

"So, there's no case for you to be conflicted out of. You can paw through those boxes to your heart's content and find whatever it is that Prescott doesn't want us to find."

Naya smiled back, a wide, eager grin that lit her eyes.

"I thought you'd like that."

They both knew Naya wouldn't rest until she found the document that prompted Herbal Attitudes to foot the settlement bill.

"What are you going to do?"

"Pay a visit to an old enemy."

~ ~ ~ ~ ~ ~ ~ ~ ~ ~

DISTRICT ATTORNEY DIANA JEFFRIES wasn't exactly an enemy, but the woman was certainly not a friend.

She'd managed to win her last election despite her office's well-publicized mishandling of two murder cases. Sasha's role in defending the accused hadn't endeared her to the district attorney. But, Sasha told herself as she checked her reflection in the mirror that inexplicably hung on the wall over the desk of the district attorney's secretary, she *had* made up for that later. Two killers were behind bars, and while Diana had taken the credit, Sasha had done all the work.

Her green eyes looked back at her, skeptical and unconvinced.

The secretary started as Diana's office door swung open.

Diana strode out into the reception area and offered Sasha a limp hand.

"Attorney McCandless, to what do I owe the pleasure of this little surprise visit?"

Her dark lips parted into an approximation of a smile, but she was looking over Sasha's shoulder at herself in the mirror. She dropped Sasha's hand and straightened the patterned scarf draped artfully around her neck.

"Thanks for seeing me without an appointment."

"My secretary says you told her it was urgent," Diana said flatly, finally turning her attention from her reflection to Sasha.

"It is. Can we talk privately?"

Diana bobbed her head and then snapped at her secretary. "Hold my calls."

She swept back into her office, and Sasha followed, after giving the harried-looking secretary an encouraging smile.

Diana had put her stamp on her office. The standard-issue dark wood furniture, so masculine and serious, was covered with vases of colorful fresh-cut flowers and pastel ceramic pottery. A sheer window dressing fluttered across the top of the large window behind her desk, softening the cold, institutional window frame.

She didn't take her seat or direct Sasha to a chair. Instead she stood in the middle of her office and dropped all pretense of friendliness.

"So, what's your problem?"

Sasha stood across from the taller woman. She was forced to crane her neck back to meet Diana's eyes.

"Oh, I don't have a problem, you have the problem."

Diana stiffened. "Is that so?"

"Well, I'd consider it a problem if I were the District Attorney and someone within city government was violating Section 4702."

Sasha watched Diana's eyes widen in shock and then narrow with distrust.

"4702—threats and other improper influence? Are you suggesting a government official is being blackmailed or threatened?"

"Oh, no, I *know* a government employee has been physically attacked and retaliated against in an effort to prevent him from carrying out the duties of his office. What I'm *suggesting* is that the attacker is also a member of city government."

She stared impassively at Diana.

The older woman swore under her breath and then sighed, a long, slow sigh.

"I guess you should have a seat," she said with palpable reluctance, waving vaguely in the direction of two Queen Anne chairs.

Sasha took the closer of the two, and Diana sat across from her and leaned forward, close enough that Sasha could smell her heady, floral perfume.

Sasha gathered her thoughts. She needed to deliver a story that impelled Diana to take action without providing any details.

Diana watched her face in silence, with her legs crossed and one high-heeled foot swinging like a metronome.

"You're aware that four young women have recently died from myocarditis?"

"Of course."

"The coroner, er—forensic pathologist—who did the first three autopsies has been followed, mugged, and robbed in the past several days."

"And you think his troubles are related to his autopsies?"

"I do."

"Has he been threatened? Has anyone told him to make a specific finding or else?"

"Not in so many words—"

Diana cut her off. "Then how can you establish someone, let alone someone within city government, is trying to influence him?"

"Well, his files on those three cases disappeared. Then he was placed on administrative leave. Now he's been fired. It seems fairly clear that someone—either someone in the Medical Examiner's Office or even higher up in the food chain—wants to keep him quiet."

"Quiet about what? The Chief Medical Examiner's official position is that those deaths are unrelated."

"This employee disagrees."

"You mean, this *former* employee disagrees." Diana leaned back, and her features relaxed. She smiled broadly. "As you undoubtedly know, the statute prohibits threatening or otherwise attempting to influence a public servant, Sasha. If your friend is no longer employed as a medical examiner, he can't be taking any official government actions or making any decisions to influence, now can he?"

Diana's satisfaction radiated like a light as she beamed at Sasha.

Sasha spoke slowly, as if Diana were a not-overly-bright child. "But, his termination was just part of the pattern of intimidation and improper influence. It's part of the effort to keep him from acting as he's obligated to do. See?"

Diana shrugged. "I would have to have someone research the legislative intent behind the statute to see if that circumstance is covered."

"Will you?"

Diana laughed humorously. "You can't be serious. My assistant district attorneys are carrying full caseloads, prosecuting actual crimes. I'm not about to assign any of them this academic exercise."

"What about an intern? Don't you care that someone in the government machinery is trying to cover up a connection among these deaths?"

"I am certain that the Chief Medical Examiner stands behind the findings of his office. It's not my place to second-guess his decisions. Nor is it yours," she scolded Sasha in a cold tone.

"What about the public's right to know?"

"Aren't you cute when you're earnest."

Appealing to Diana's apparently underdeveloped sense of morality was clearly futile, so Sasha tried a different tack.

"Respectfully, I think this goes higher than the Chief Medical Examiner. It might implicate the May—the highest levels of city government. You're the District Attorney, Diana."

"I know my title, and I'd like to keep it, thank you very much. I'm not going to be drummed out of office to help some schmuck who couldn't hack it at the M.E.'s office."

"This isn't just about the Medical Examiner's Office—the Mayor's Office may be involved. You could break this wide open. Don't you have any ambition?"

"Honey, I'm ambitious, not suicidal. If you think I'm taking on that viper's pit, you've taken leave of your senses," Diana said in a frank voice.

Sasha blinked. "So, that's it?"

Diana's politician's smile slipped back into place and she stood, arranging the fringe on her scarf.

"I assure you, Attorney McCandless, that this office takes seriously any charges of improper influence. And when or if someone brings me a colorable charge, it will be treated as such. Thank you so much for stopping by, but I'm afraid I'm late for a meeting."

26

Bodhi timed his arrival to the parking lot behind the Medical Examiner's Office almost exactly with Sonny's mid-afternoon walk. He situated himself under the same tree where he'd provided Jamal his unsolicited career advice just days earlier. Before he could settle in to wait, the windowless metal fire door in the back of the building swung open, and he stepped forward.

Behind him, he sensed Leo moving closer on the sidewalk outside the lot. He wanted to turn his head to confirm that Leo was far enough back to remain undetected but stopped himself. Leo was a professional, after all.

Sonny's head was bent, and he didn't hear Bodhi approaching.

"Sonny, sir," he said, falling into step beside him.

Sonny started when he saw Bodhi but covered it immediately.

"Aw, son, I'm so sorry." He patted Bodhi's forearm in a clumsy attempt at sympathy.

"So it's true? You're firing me?"

"It's done. As of this morning. You'll have to sign for the papers when they're delivered. You gotta know, I didn't want to. I ... I had to."

"Why is that?"

He held his former boss's gaze until the older man looked away and mumbled an inaudible response.

"I beg your pardon?"

Sonny cleared his throat and quickened his stride. He swiveled his head around the deserted parking lot and then his eyes returned to Bodhi's.

"Let me buy you a drink. I owe you that much."

"Respectfully, I'd say you owe me more than that, sir. But, I'd like that."

He would like that. It would make his task that much easier. Nothing loosened Sonny's tongue like a highball.

He risked a glance at Leo over his shoulder as they jaywalked across the side street, dodging a van. Without having to ask, he knew their destination was the bar at The Carlton.

They walked in silence. He could feel nervous energy radiating from his former boss. Twice Sonny threw furtive looks behind them, as if he knew Leo was following them. Or he was worried that someone else might see them together.

They ducked under the awning of the office building that housed The Carlton and hurried across the hushed lobby to the restaurant. It was equally quiet, the staff enjoying the mid-afternoon lull between lunch and happy hour.

The dark-haired hostess looked up from flirting with the sommelier and feinted toward her post, but Sonny waved her off. "Don't mind us, honey. We're heading to the bar."

Bodhi trailed him across the room to a gleaming brass rail that set off the bar from the rest of the room. Sonny headed for a small table and two leather club chairs at the far end. The few drinkers who sat on the stools lining the bar would be unlikely to notice the two of them, let alone to overhear their conversation. Bodhi doubted the table selection had been an accident. He hoped it meant Sonny planned to talk frankly.

As Sonny was giving his highball order to the waiter, Leo strolled into the room and made his way to the bar without so much as a glance toward their table.

"Sir?" the smiling waiter repeated.

"Sorry?" Bodhi said, jerking his attention away from Leo.

"Your drink order?"

"Oh. Any organic red that you have by the glass would be great."

Bodhi rarely drank wine, but the Carlton was known for its list. He assumed the waiter wouldn't steer him wrong.

"Very good sir."

As the waiter walked away, Bodhi leaned toward Sonny.

"Why'd you fire me?"

Sonny gave him a wry smile.

"Just like that, huh? No chit chat first? Fair enough. I had to."

"Why?"

Sonny's clear eyes pierced him and he said, "I'll be blunt. It was politics. Nothing to do with you or your job performance. For crying out loud, you're my best pathologist without a doubt. But those missing files—"

He trailed off as the waiter returned with

their drinks. They watched in silence as he removed them from his small silver tray with a studied flourish and placed them on the table in front of them. A small bowl of cashews followed. Then he stood ramrod straight and waited for them to each take a sip and proclaim their drinks acceptable, before giving them a small nod and backing away.

Sonny turned his attention to his highball, but Bodhi pressed on. "What about the files? I came to you and told you about them. I didn't delete them, you know that."

"I do, son, but they're a complicating factor. The press would love to claim that the myocarditis deaths are related and maybe some of them could've been prevented if we'd made the connection. That's a load of crap, of course, but you know how they'd spin it if word got out that we didn't even have the records ...." He winced at the thought.

Bodhi swirled his wine and watched the sugary trail as it ran down the side of his glass.

Finally he looked up at Sonny again, "You know there *is* a connection, right? Among the deaths? I've been doing some research and I think the women all reacted to an herbal supplement in—"

Sonny slammed his glass down on the table. The white linen tablecloth muffled the sounds, but it was loud enough that Leo swiveled on his barstool to see what was happening.

"Don't!" Sonny warned him in a hoarse whisper.

He struggled for control of himself, then breathed out slowly, and gave a forced, shaky laugh. "I mean, what's done is done. We need to talk about your future, not your past. I can help you. I have connections. I can get you a faculty position, not tenured, of course, but a good job. You're a natural teacher."

A rare surge of anger flared in Bodhi's veins. He was being handled.

"No thanks."

"Now, don't be prideful. It's no trouble."

Bodhi exhaled and changed tack. "You know the Courtlands sued me personally?"

Sonny's eyes dimmed. "I do. You can't take that to heart. You didn't do anything wrong."

"I know." He sipped his wine. "But they allege I destroyed documents."

Sonny nodded, unsurprised. "I heard."

"Don't you wonder where they heard that? Aren't you worried it'll get out? The complaint's not filed under seal or whatever."

"Look, the City Attorney has already contacted the Courtland family. In exchange for their dropping the lawsuit against you and agreeing to keep all information confidential, the city will pay them a sum of money."

Bodhi blinked. "You're buying them off?"

"Now, come on, it's not like that. You were actin' in your official capacity when you did that autopsy. The City is obligated to defend you. The lawyers shoulda probably talked to you first, but no harm, no foul. You ought to be happy."

"Sonny, I'm feeling many emotions right now, but happiness isn't one of them."

Sonny drained his glass. Bodhi looked down and was surprised to see that his own was already empty.

27

"Get up."

Sasha bit down hard on her lower lip and tasted the tang of her blood.

She pushed herself off the sticky mat and stood to face her instructor again. She planted her feet in a wide stance and raised her hands.

Daniel looked at her and shook his head, a frown pulling at his mouth.

"You're going to get wrinkles, scowling like that."

"Stop joking around. What's wrong with you?"

His disappointment stung.

What *was* wrong with her? She knew she had to stay sharp. Even without Connelly

and Daniel's constant nagging, she intellectu-
ally understood she needed to be able to
protect herself. But she seemed to be unable
to maintain focus during their sparring
sessions.

"I don't know," she admitted.

He ran his hands through his wavy hair.

"Well, until you figure it out, we're just
wasting our time."

"So, what? You won't train with me?"

She couldn't believe he would kick her out of
the studio. She'd been Daniel's favorite pupil for
close to a decade.

"I don't know what to do with you. Your
mind's wandering. Are you thinking about your
wedding?"

"For crying out loud, Daniel, really? You
think I'm daydreaming about the big day?" her
embarrassment melted, replaced by indignation.
He knew her better than that.

"What is it then?"

"I said, I don't know," she snapped at him.

He exhaled slowly.

"So, let's figure it out." His voice was gentler,
conciliatory.

He lowered himself to the mat and arranged
himself into the crossed-legged lotus pose. He

rested the outsides of his wrists on his knees, his palms up and his fingertips touching.

"Really? We're going to meditate?"

"Get your butt on the mat, Sasha."

She huffed and sank down into the mat across from him, mirroring his pose.

He searched her face for a moment. "Close your eyes and clear your mind."

She complied.

She focused on her breath rising in and out, from her abdomen. Java popped into her mind—the kitten seemed to be a natural yogini. He was always belly breathing. She chased the thought from her mind. *Don't think.*

The sun streamed through the window behind her, heating the back of her head. Her ponytail tickled her neck.

She heard Daniel's even breathing. The ticking of the wall clock. The hum of the floor fan oscillating in the corner.

She smelled old sweat and the faint hint of lemon-scented floor cleaner.

Her mind was empty.

Then Bodhi's tranquil face floated through her thoughts. She pushed it away.

A moment later, she wished she hadn't. It was replaced by a very different face. One that had been destroyed by bullets, ripped apart and bloodied, unrecognizable. But she knew who it was. Deputy Gavin Russell, slaughtered by a crazed survivalist because she hadn't been quick enough to find him.

Her steady breathing faltered, and she wiped her mind.

Bodhi flitted back into view. Then Judge Paulson, dead on the floor of his chambers in the historic courthouse in Clear Brook County. Clarissa Costopolous. The side of her head bashed in with a hammer, blood and gray matter spraying her car window. Tim Warner, wrapped in a blood-stained comforter, staring up at her with sightless eyes from the inside of a Dumpster. Connelly, gray eyes soft and worried. Noah Peterson, her old boss and mentor, wrapped around the steering column of his car. Ellen Mortenson, her throat slashed in a wicked approximation of a grin, blood pooling. Naya, her head thrown back, mouth open, roaring in laughter. Her mother, cradling Julian against her chest. Larry, Daniel's father, crumpled on the floor of her office, his broken glasses out of reach.

She gasped, and her eyes flew open.

Daniel was watching her.

"What?"

She could feel her body trembling, as she drew a shaky breath and understanding flooded her.

"I'm afraid."

His cool eyes painted her with a disbelieving look.

"*You're* afraid?"

She nodded mutely.

He steepled his fingers and contemplated her like he'd never seen her before.

She tried not to squirm under his scrutiny while he weighed her admission.

After what seemed like hours, he said, "You're afraid of getting hurt?"

"No. I'm afraid I'm not going to be able to protect Bodhi. Or Naya. Connelly. Whoever. I'm afraid I'm going to fail."

Saying the words and having the truth hit her was like shedding a too-heavy backpack. She was unburdened. Lighter. Hopeful. Naming the fear meant she could overcome it. *Right?*

"Bodhi? This is the pacifist Buddhist who Leo wants to help?"

"Yes."

"And he's in danger?"

"Yes."

Daniel's eyes bore into her. "You know, Sasha, you're a lawyer."

"Uh-huh."

"Not a superhero."

"Pardon?"

"You don't have to save everyone. You don't have to save *anyone*. Krav Maga is a tool you can use when a situation spirals out of your control through no fault of your own. It's a last resort. Not a lifestyle."

She bristled. "I know all this. What's your point?"

He let out a long, loud breath. "My point is we live in a civilization. If your friend's in danger, call the police, you big dummy."

He leaned across the mat and gave her a playful shove, breaking the tension.

She feinted as if she were going to topple over and then charged him. They grappled. They were both fast, strong, agile. But she'd surprised him, and a moment later, he was on his back, pinned to the mat, her hand on his throat.

"Who's the big dummy now?"

He managed a smile.

~ ~ ~ ~ ~ ~ ~ ~ ~ ~ ~

DETECTIVE BURTON GILBERT, the senior detective on the elite Homicide Squad, which operated out of the Pittsburgh Police Bureau's central headquarters, was no more a friend of Sasha's than District Attorney Jeffries.

But, she told herself, as she loitered in front of the ugly square building, waiting for the shift to change, he was less of an idiot.

She'd taken Daniel's suggestion to heart. So here she was, skulking around in the parking lot at three o'clock, as a small blue tide drifted into the building, and another drifted out. The first wave of night shift officers were reporting for duty, laughing and calling greetings across the lot, and their counterparts on the day shift were beginning to fan out into their personal vehicles to head home, tired and quiet.

She stretched, loosening her tight muscles, still achy from the drubbing Daniel had handed her, and paced a small circle around the lot. For all she knew Gilbert was working another shift, staying late to catch up on paperwork, or had the day off and was chasing a golf ball around. She hadn't wanted to call and ask him to see her. She put a fair amount of stock into the element of surprise. He would be more likely to help her if she caught him unaware.

And, even if he blew her off, as she suspected he might, she'd be able to gauge his reaction in person. The phone was lousy for reading people. You had to sit across from them and watch their eyes. Diana Jeffries, for instance, had been scared. Of what, Sasha couldn't say. But for all the woman's practiced mannerisms, she'd given off a cloud of pure fear when Sasha had hinted that the highest levels of city government were corrupt. Sasha didn't get the sense that Diana was in on it, just that she was terrified to dig her teeth into the issue.

She could only hope the detective had a stronger appetite for the truth.

She checked her watch. She'd give him another ten minutes. If he didn't show, then she'd have to find something useful to do with her time. Like practice law.

The door opened again. Gilbert stepped out. He was alone. He paused on the walkway and blinked into the sunlight. Then he pulled a pair of aviator glasses from his breast pocket and jammed them on his face. His face gave no indication that he'd seen Sasha, but he beelined toward her.

"Counselor," he rumbled in his deep voice as he stopped in front of her.

"Detective Gilbert."

"I don't suppose you just happen to be in the neighborhood?"

"Not exactly."

"And it's too much to hope you're coming to report a stolen trash can?"

She smiled at the banter. Maybe she should have started with him instead of Diana. At least he had a sense of humor.

"Afraid not."

He nodded gravely. "Figures."

"I wanted to talk to you about some deaths."

"Thought you swore off criminal law," he observed.

"I thought so, too, and yet here I am."

"Here you are." He exhaled and snuck a peek at his watch. "Well, let's go inside."

"How about I buy you a cup of coffee instead?"

He smiled. "You're a big shot lawyer. I'll let you buy me breakfast."

"It's 3:15."

"If you try Dot's breakfast, you'll want to eat it three times a day."

"Lead the way."

"Where's your ride?"

Sasha pointed to her Passat, parked three rows back.

"I'll wait for you at the end of the lot."

She hurried to her car before the detective could change his mind.

28

Leo hunched over the lace-topped table with his knees jammed against the underside, feeling like an elephant. A ridiculous elephant.

A smiling waitress materialized.

"Good afternoon. My name's Cindy. Have you joined us for afternoon tea before?"

Leo threw her an *are you serious* look?

"Uh, no. Can't say I have."

"Well, you're in for a treat."

He suspected she had no idea how true that was.

"I look forward to it. But, I'm actually waiting for someone, Cindy. She'll be here shortly."

The waitress painted him with a look of her own. "Girlfriend?" she asked.

"Not exactly."

A light sparked in her eyes and her smile grew brighter.

Uh-oh.

"Future mother-in-law," he clarified.

"Oh. Oh, well, I'll just leave you with the menus, then."

He gave her a gentle smile and took the proffered menus.

How he ended up at the William Penn for high tea with Valentina while Sasha was skulking around some greasy spoon with a homicide detective, he couldn't say. But here he was.

He scanned the menu. Scones? Clotted cream? Cucumber sandwiches?

Based on her enthusiastic text message about a fried egg platter, Sasha seemed to have scored a better mid-afternoon meal. He took a swallow from the goblet of sweating ice water that Cindy had deposited in front of him. The beer he'd nursed while he'd been babysitting Bodhi at The Carlton lingered on his breath. The last thing he needed was for Valentina to think her unemployed future son-in-law spent his days drinking while her daughter busted her butt at the office.

He gulped another swallow at the thought and wished for a breath mint.

Valentina came gliding toward the table, trailing the hostess.

He stood and Valentina presented her cheek for a European kiss.

"I'm sorry I kept you waiting," she said, slightly out of breath.

"Don't be silly." He pulled out her chair and tried not to breathe on her.

"Julian woke up fussy after his nap, and I couldn't leave him with Grandpa like that," she explained.

"Of course not."

Leo was fairly certain Sasha's father knew his way around a cranky baby, having had four kids of his own, but he wasn't about to contradict her.

"I'm so glad you were able to meet me," she continued. "I'm sure you're very busy ... job hunting?"

He tamped down a smile. He'd figured she'd suggested this little get together so she could probe him about his financial situation. He figured it was a fair point for a parent to wonder about. Although Sasha would be livid if she knew Valentina was prying.

"I'm not really focused on looking for another position, to be honest. I'm enjoying spending time with Sasha too much to think about rejoining the daily grind."

The skin around her eyes tightened, and she plucked at the napkin in her lap.

"Well, that's ... nice, I guess."

He decided to cut her a break. He leaned across the table and pierced her worried eyes with his own. "Mrs. McCandless, I promise you, Sasha doesn't need me to take care of her, but I fully intend to."

The worry eased out of her face and she relaxed.

"That's comforting, Leo. But, I've told you, call me Val or Mom. And, I know Sasha thinks she doesn't need anyone—"

"She's right."

Valentina stiffened. "I'm not so sure about that."

"She doesn't *need* me, but she wants me around anyway. That's even better. You should be proud to have raised such a self-reliant woman, Val."

A pleased flush spread across her face.

"That's kind of you to say. She *is* very accomplished—if a little prickly."

He'd humor her to a point, but he was pretty sure it would be bad form to agree with her. The niceties of navigating Sasha's large family kept him on his toes. The only son of a single mother who moved around a lot for her job as a traveling nurse, he had no experience dealing with the dynamics of an extended family.

He dropped his eyes to the menu and changed the subject. "I've never had tea before. What should I order?"

He half-listened while she expounded with great enthusiasm on matching the different loose teas with the miniature foods.

"—of course, Russian teacakes would be a bit heartier, but we take what we can find," she finished with a smile.

He nodded.

A small silence fell over the table.

She looked around the opulent dining room and smiled at the Old World glamour.

"Have you and Sasha considered having your reception here?" she asked in a perfectly casual voice. Her face was the very picture of innocence.

He had to stop himself from laughing aloud.

He'd been snookered. Had. Suckered. He had stumbled right into a trap set by a Russian-American grandmother. This was all a move to get a say as to the reception venue.

Well played, Val. Well played, indeed.

29

Bodhi was sitting at the conference table meditating on Sonny's job offer when Naya banged into the room.

He had no intention of allowing Sonny to buy him off, but the idea of teaching had resonated with him, so he was sitting with the idea to see how it felt.

He opened his eyes warily.

Naya had been in a fierce mood when he'd returned from the meeting with Sonny. She'd received the news that Leo had gone off to have tea somewhere with a fair amount of grumbling and some unkind comparisons between Leo and Queen Elizabeth. Then Sasha called in to say she was headed to some diner with some homicide detective, and Bodhi had the unusual experience of watching a black woman turn red.

She'd been fuming ever since, so he'd made himself scarce—and quickly.

"Do you need something?" he asked mildly as he turned to look at her.

Instead of a face clouded with anger, he found himself looking into triumphant eyes and a victorious smile.

"I found it! Well, I *think* I found it," she said, shoving a sheaf of documents toward him with hands that trembled with excitement.

He recognized the exuberance in her eyes. She'd had a breakthrough.

"Show me."

She launched herself into the chair next to his and stacked the papers on the table.

"Let me walk you through it." Her voice was a half-octave higher than normal but steady.

He rolled his chair closer to peer over her shoulder as she grabbed the first document.

"See here, this is the agreement between Vita-Might and Greenway. After the contract renewal, Herbal Attitudes took over the account from Vita-Might, and agreed to provide the supplements pursuant to the terms of the existing contract."

"Okay."

"Now, while they were in the process of acquiring VitaMight's natural supplements business, they were also out drumming up new business. That same month, they signed a contract with Better Life Beverages. Problem was, it's also a requirements contract—"

"What does that mean, exactly, a requirements contract?"

"Okay, instead of a set amount of herbal ingredients, they agreed to supply all the herbals Better Life needed each month."

"Why would they do it that way? Isn't it more advantageous for both parties if Better Life places an order each month at the prevailing market rate? That way no one takes a big hit if the market price changes dramatically."

Naya's mouth twitched into a small smile and she nodded.

"Exactly, although in this case, Better Life traded nimble pricing for a guaranteed supply. They apparently had big plans—the bottling plant, the sport team sponsorships—they needed to know they'd get as much of the four herbal ingredients as they needed, as quickly as they needed it. They were streamlining operations."

"So, they chose efficiency over economy."

"Bingo."

"Okay, so?"

"So, everything was fine for a few months, but then they ran into trouble. They couldn't procure enough of the specific ingredients to fulfill Greenway's and Life Juice's orders and meet Better Life's needs."

She placed an internal memorandum on top of the contract. He skimmed the short memo. As she'd said, it indicated that the company was having trouble getting sufficient quantities of ginseng from its existing sources.

"Okay."

"The first thing Better Life did was to take over Life Juice. They bought the smaller company, siphoned off their herbals, and shuttered the smoothie joints."

"Ruthless."

"Efficient," she corrected. "But, it wasn't enough. They still needed more product—especially the wild red ginseng."

She leaned over and added a printout of an e-mail to the stack.

"The team responsible for the Better Life account went to management and pled their case that the beverage company account was more lucrative and more important than the Greenway account."

A quick scan of the email confirmed her summary.

"Let me guess? That's when Herbal Attitudes decided to just breach the contract with the pharmacy."

"Right. It was a business decision. They knew they'd make a lot more money from the Better Life Beverages contract than they would from Greenway. So, they weighed the costs of breaching and decided it was worth it. They probably also correctly guessed that if Greenway sued, it'd sue VitaMight first."

"Okay. So?"

A spiral-bound booklet landed on the table.

"So, that decision paid off. Get a load of these financials."

She flipped the booklet open to a page marked with a red sticky flag and pointed to a spreadsheet.

He gave a low whistle at the seven-figure income statement. "Wow, they're doing well."

"Right. And their biggest customer is none other than Better Life Beverages. It's not surprising, then, that the head of procurement fired off this nastygram to the guy in charge of buying the herbals." She shuffled some pages and handed him a one-page sheet.

Derek, I don't care if the wild red ginseng is harvested by child laborers working under the most horrific conditions this side of a Taiwanese sweatshop. I don't care if the growing methods don't comport with accepted practices and the product itself is crap. Get me more. I need as much as we can get our hands on, regardless of source, cost, or purity.

"Regardless of purity?" Bodhi read the last phrase aloud, and a chill tickled the back of his neck.

"Regardless of purity," Naya echoed.

They stared at each other for a long moment. Bodhi didn't know what was going through her head, but his was spooling images of four dead women in their twenties. He blinked, but the pictures remained.

"Uh, are there any documents that show what this Derek person did?" he asked, trying to drive the slack faces from his mind's eye.

She shook her head.

"But, you can connect the dots because two weeks later, according to the purchase order and invoice, they shipped Better Life Beverages a metric buttload of wild red ginseng."

He followed the pen she used as a pointer

and felt his eyes widen at the amount. Metric buttload, indeed.

"Any clues as to where they got so much, so fast?"

"Nope."

"But, it's clear they went outside their usual supply chain."

"Yep."

She gathered her documents into a stack and straightened them with a tap against the table.

"You think Better Life knows they're selling crap?"

Her only answer was a small shrug. "Does it matter? If they don't know, it's only because they're being willfully blind. That's no better."

She had a point.

"This is good work. You're going to make a great attorney."

Her smile faded and a cloud passed over her face but she didn't respond. She grabbed her documents and left the room without another word. She didn't exactly slam the door shut, but she didn't close it gently.

~ ~ ~ ~ ~ ~ ~ ~ ~ ~ ~

Sasha jumped when Naya stormed into the office with a bang.

"What's this?" Sasha asked, holding up a crumpled piece of paper.

Naya glared at her. "It's the summer reading list for incoming law students at Duquesne. Did you forget how to read?"

Sasha shot back, "What's it doing in your trash?"

"Isn't the better question what were *you* doing in my trash?"

Naya tossed her a furious look and threw a pile of papers on her desk. They landed with a thud.

Sasha took a moment to formulate a response. She'd faced down some evil people in the past—murderers, madmen, violent, abusive control freaks—but a pissed-off Naya was still a scary prospect.

Naya's highs were high, and her lows were low. And her temper was legend around Prescott & Talbott.

Sasha squared her shoulders.

"I was throwing away a tissue, and the paper

caught my eye. I'm sorry for snooping. Now, why'd you throw away your reading list?"

Naya clenched her jaw and gritted her teeth but didn't answer.

Sasha dropped her eyes to the paper. "I have some of these if you want to borrow them. *To Kill A Mockingbird*, *A Man for All Seasons*. I don't think I have *Inherit the Wind* anymore, but you could probably fudge it and watch the movie instead of reading the play."

Naya snatched the list out of her hand.

"I don't have time for leisure reading." She balled it up and threw it back into her wastebasket.

"It's not leisure reading. These books are designed to introduce all the bright-eyed idealists to the moral quandaries that go along with practicing law. I know you've had plenty of first-hand experience with the sticky decisions, but most of your classmates are going to be fresh out of college, Naya. Some of them have probably never held a job, *any* job—"

"Come off it, Mac. I'm not going to go back to Prescott. Not after Garrett's crap. And even if I did, I bet the scholarship would evaporate because I'm not a team player. Forget it. Law school was a stupid idea. It's over."

"Will won't do that to you. Don't sabotage yourself like this."

Naya put up a hand like a stop sign and fixed Sasha with a steely look. "I said it's over. Let's move on."

Sasha swallowed her response. A year or two earlier, she'd have dug in and argued with Naya, but instead she said, "I know you're trying to be strong here, but the strong move would be to fight for what you want, not to give up on a dream."

Naya narrowed her eyes. "What's with the touchy-feely crap? Where'd you get that from? Bodhi? Daniel? You're getting so *soft*."

Sasha burst into laughter. "Connelly, actually."

Naya waited with a face like stone while she wiped the tears from her eyes and tried to catch her breath.

"What's so funny?"

"Apparently hanging out with a guy who cuts open dead bodies, a self-defense expert, and an ex-federal agent is making me soft."

Naya ducked her head and covered her mouth with a hand, but a giggle escaped.

Sasha smiled and retrieved the reading list from the trashcan. She smoothed it flat and placed it on Naya's desk under the vaguely heart-shaped rock that Naya used as a paperweight.

Naya shot her a warning look, but the tension had left her face. She changed the subject.

"Is Detective Gilbert gonna help you?"

Sasha shrugged. "He agreed to look into it. Best I could do. Did you guys make any headway?"

"I don't know where your flyboy fiancé is. Bodhi said he thought Leo was going to tea. I assume he misheard him—or your guy has a very strange secret life. But, yeah, I think we found something. Let's go find Bodhi, and we'll walk you through it."

30

"Did you hear me? Do you think your office could help him?"

Mackenzie untangled the sweaty sheets from around her legs and combed her hair back from her face with her fingers. She ignored the question for a second time and crouched on the floor to hunt around under the bed for her shoes.

"Mackenzie?"

Saul walked over and stood behind her. When she rose from the disgusting hotel room carpet, her stilettos dangling from one hand, he caught her around her bare waist with his arm.

She beat back the chill of revulsion that crept up her spine. It wasn't his fault, after all. She hated being touched after sex. By anybody. But especially by somebody who smelled like formaldehyde.

She exhaled and turned to face him, keeping her expression gentle. Despite her post-coital physical reaction to his touch, she really was kind of fond of him.

"I know he's your friend, but I really can't help him. Personnel matters are internal. It was Sonny's decision to fire Bodhi King—the mayor can't interfere with something like that. And if he can't, I can't."

He pierced her with a look. His face was screwed up into a knot of panic or confusion. Maybe both.

"But something's going on. It doesn't make sense. Sonny loved Bodhi. No way would he fire him just for having the bad luck to get attacked. That's crazy."

"Trust me. Stay out of it. You don't have the stomach for intra-office politics, honey."

He shook his head, irritated. "This isn't just the usual dumb stuff. I think it has something to do—" he dropped his voice and scanned the room, as if someone could hear their conversation in this godforsaken suburban, business park motel, "—with the myocarditis deaths. I think Bodhi was close to finding a connection—"

She'd heard enough. It was time for a distraction. She stretched onto her toes and covered his mouth with a kiss.

He struggled against her lips in muffled protest.

She backed up a step, let her shoes fall to the floor, and crossed her arms over her bare chest. She was surprised to note that his rejection, such as it was, actually stung her.

Don't go getting attached, she warned herself. Especially not to this one, what with the doting wife and the gaggle of young children. Way too messy.

"I'm sorry. But this is serious. I was talking to a friend in the IT department about Bodhi's miss-" he stopped himself.

She tried not to smile. His discretion was cute, considering she'd figured out the password to his work computer (his wedding date) within an hour of their first tryst and had been logging into the system as him for months. He had no secrets from her. At least none that mattered.

"Go on? You were talking to the IT folks, and what, Saul?"

"Uh, well, there've been some ... irregularities with some records. And my friend told me in confidence that they'd been beta testing a secret program that would search records automatically to find connections between cases and all of a sudden the funding got pulled and all the stations were wiped clean of the program. That's convenient timing, don't you think?"

His brown eyes were liquid with concern.

She sighed.

"I'm sure it's just like your friend said. The funding dried up and the project got scrapped. It happens all the time, babe. Anyway, isn't that what *you're* supposed to be doing? Finding the connections between cases? You should be glad they didn't pursue the program. You wouldn't want to find yourself out of a job." She smiled broadly at him, willing him to let this go.

He didn't.

"Just like Bodhi."

"Saul—"

"No, Mackenzie. You're right. You can't get mixed up in this. I shouldn't have asked you to. It's inappropriate. I'll handle it myself." He squared his bony shoulder and puffed out his puny chest.

Great. From bad to worse.

She clasped both of his hands in hers. "Listen to me. You're a loyal friend. And a good man ..."

A shadow of pain darted across his eyes and

she knew he was thinking about his betrayal of his wife and his children, but she plowed ahead.

"You are, Saul. You're a good, kind, gentle man. But you don't want to get involved in this— whatever it is. Trust me. You owe it to Mona. And your kids. Stay out of it. I'll do some poking around and see what I can find out."

He opened his mouth to object.

She pressed another kiss on him. This time, his mouth yielded to hers. She felt his shoulders relax, and he leaned in toward her. Eager and warm, his heroic thoughts giving way to his lust.

She snuck a peek at the bracelet watch she refused to remove, even to make love. She could spare another thirty minutes to help him forget about Bodhi and the myocarditis deaths.

She nudged him backward, toward the rumpled bed.

Please stay out of it, Saul. I don't want you to get hurt. And if you get in my way, I'll have no choice but to hurt you myself.

The thought unspooled silently through her mind as they tumbled back onto the bed.

31

The condo was quiet. Java purred softly on the couch, Connelly was cleaning up the kitchen, and Sasha kept him company at the island, updating her invoices in the accounting program on her laptop. Bodhi sat at the dining room table, a mug of tea at his elbow, and Naya's papers spread out across the table. He was piecing together a rough timeline of wild red ginseng deliveries to Better Life Beverages.

Connelly paused in his rhythmic pattern of rinsing dishes and loading them into the dishwasher to refill Sasha's wine glass.

"Thanks." She tilted her mouth up for a kiss. He tasted a little bit salty, a little bit sweet—a hint of the caramel sauce he'd drizzled over their dessert.

He stroked the loose knot of hair she'd tied at the nape of her neck one-handed then returned to his dishes.

Sasha's ringing cell phone shattered the quiet domestic moment.

Java opened one eye to glare in the direction of the noise.

"Sasha McCandless," she answered on the second ring.

"Sasha, it's Detective Gilbert. Sorry to disturb you at home."

His voice held no hint of apology, but she did the dance anyway.

"It's no trouble, Detective."

The emphasis she placed on his title resonated with both Connelly and Bodhi. Both men swiveled their heads to focus on her.

"I ran your concerns up the flagpole."

She grabbed a pen and a sheet of paper in the unlikely event that she'd need to take notes.

"And?"

"No go. Headquarters' official stance is that the Department supports the ME's opinion. The deaths are all natural causes, no connection, nothing amiss."

Something about his tone made her ask the question. "Unofficially?"

"Unofficially, I've heard the Mayor's Office is driving the bus, not the ME."

"I already knew that. Come on, give me something."

He coughed. "Rumor also has it that the Mayor's breathing down the necks of the cops out at the Fox Chapel PD, looking over their shoulder in the Stone Fredericks homicide. I know a guy who knows a guy out there—they're pretty annoyed."

"Any suspects in that case?"

"Fox Chapel says no, dad's clean. Someone at Grant Street hinted that there were marital problems, maybe a mistress, but the wife is still darn near catatonic with grief."

"Or guilt," Sasha mused.

"Maybe. The lead on the case seems to think it's a pile of b.s."

"I guess we'll see. Well, thanks for hearing me out about the death cluster, Detective. I won't forget it." She worked to keep the disappointment out of her voice. She *did* appreciate his help —she had precious few friends in city government. It wouldn't do to alienate one of them.

"No problem. Oh, yeah," he added, like it was

an afterthought, "you're going to want to watch the ten o'clock news."

"I am?" she asked.

But he'd already ended the call. She was talking to herself.

She hit the button to hang up and looked up to see two sets of eyes staring back at her.

"Well?" Connelly demanded.

She shrugged.

"He said to watch the news."

It was the lead story. A somber anchorman with too-orange foundation but an impressive sweep of silver hair stared into the camera and informed viewers that yet another young woman had collapsed and been pronounced dead at the scene.

"Cherise Jordan, age twenty-two, of Homewood was found dead in her car. The Medical Examiner's Office has ruled out foul play, and a source tells us the preliminary cause of death has been identified as myocarditis," the silver-hair anchor intoned.

"Son of a—" Connelly began.

Bodhi held up a hand. "Shhh, it's Sonny."

The picture cut to the exterior of the building where Bodhi had worked. Sonny Jackson strode across the square, his head down, his gait just this side of a trot. A breathless reporter jogged alongside him, her cameraman doing his best to keep the shot steady.

"Dr. Jackson, sir, does your office have a statement on the latest dead girl?"

He pretended not to hear her and kept moving, beelining across the cobblestone to the City-County Building.

"Dr. Jackson, you're the Chief Medical Examiner, what do you have to say to the people who are worried about five dead women in less than two weeks? Is it true your office suspects yet another case of myocarditis?" She yelled the question at his back as he took the wide steps to the front of the building by twos.

Three-quarters of the way up, he paused and turned to face the camera. He cleared his throat and smoothed a hand over his hair. He squinted into the setting sun and said, "It remains our belief that these deaths are not connected. Now, if you'll excuse me, I have a meeting. I understand the Mayor's Office has scheduled a press conference for tomorrow morning to address this latest tragedy."

He turned and hurried into the building before the reporter could press him further.

"There you have it, Ryan. As it has all along,

Mayor Closky's Office is taking the lead on this issue. Unfortunately, they seem to have no more answers for why Pittsburgh's young women are dying at an alarming rate than Chief Medical Examiner Jackson has." She didn't bother to hide her annoyance.

Ryan's tight face filled the screen again. "That was filmed earlier out at the City-County Building. Now, for continuing coverage, we go live to Carson Bluth, who's live on the scene at the home of Cherise Jordan."

Carson smiled a toothy grin that was completely at odds with the cluster of wailing women who stood in a knot behind him. One woman, with tears running down her face, rocked a small boy, who looked to be about three, against her shoulder.

"Ryan, I'm here in Homewood with the friends and family of Cherise Jordan. They're obviously grief-stricken and in shock, but they're also angry and demanding answers from the City. Neighbors have been stopping by all night to honor Ms. Jordan's memory." He gestured to an impromptu memorial of hand-lettered signs, stuffed animals, and candles that lined the retaining wall in front of a tidy, well-maintained row house.

"Everyone I talked to had the same thing to say. Cherise Jordan was a devoted mother to her son, Micah, a hard working employee at her uncle's carpet business, and a good student in the part-time medical assistant program at CCAC. She still made time to sing in her church choir and had recently started a chapter of a nonprofit organization called Girls on the Run to help local girls develop strong self-esteem and good body images. Her loved ones want to know how many more women have to die before the City will take action."

He cut to an interview with the sobbing woman who held Cherise's young son. The captioning identified her as Doreen Jordan, Cherise's mother.

"She was always doing something. Always trying to make herself better. Burning the candle at both ends. She was a good girl, with so much life left in her." The woman's voice broke and she clutched her grandson tighter.

"Burning the candle at both ends," Bodhi muttered. He aimed the remote at the television and silenced Carson. The screen faded to black.

No doubt Cherise reached for Champion Fuel to keep herself going. Sasha felt her throat close.

"You okay?" Connelly asked, holding her arm.

She nodded her head and tried to swallow. She couldn't seem to draw a breath.

"Sasha?" he insisted.

She forced back her rising panic and exhaled. "I'm fine."

Bodhi interjected, "Well, I'm not. We have to do something. We have to stop this." His voice was firm, but his face was pale.

"Don't worry. We're going to," Sasha assured him. She turned to Connelly, "Will you do me a favor?"

"Of course."

"Call Hank and see if he can tell you anything about the Stone Fredericks murder investigation. He'll know if there've been any developments, right?"

"Probably. What are you going to do?"

"Bodhi and I have a complaint to draft."

Connelly tilted his head and scanned her face. She could feel her jaw tightening under his scrutiny.

"Okay."

He asked no more questions—just brushed her forehead with a gentle kiss and headed for the loft bedroom, already punching in the speed dial for Hank Richardson on his cell phone.

Bodhi turned to her with a question in his eyes. "We're filing a complaint?"

"Maybe. I don't know. Tonight, we're *drafting* a complaint."

"What's the difference?"

She smiled at him. "The difference is you don't have to file a complaint to leak a complaint. In fact, if an up-and-coming investigative reporter happens to be one of your bridesmaids, you don't even have to draft it to leak it. Come on."

She grabbed her phone from the island, slipped her feet into a pair of orange flip-flops, and headed out the door and across the hall with Bodhi a step behind her.

32

Maisy plunked down a mug of mint tea in front of Bodhi and a suspiciously watery-looking coffee in front of Sasha.

Sasha tried to sniff the contents of the mug without attracting Maisy's attention.

She failed.

Maisy threw back her cascade of long blonde curls and jabbed a deep red fingernail at Sasha.

"I saw that. I made that exactly the way you like it. Not one, but *two*, K-cups."

Sasha took a second sniff. "Is it—flavored?"

Maisy huffed. "You listen here, you drank all my dark roast already. Everybody else *likes* flavored coffees, you know."

Sasha wrinkled her nose but took a swig anyway to appease her friend and neighbor.

She turned to Bodhi. "So, in addition to being a horrible barista, Maisy is an investigative journalist."

Sorta.

She actually was a former weather girl, fill-in weekend anchor, and *aspiring* investigative journalist. But Maisy really was aspiring—she'd shed her Southern accent and picked up an entertainment agent. She had her eye on the national markets and had been working her perfectly rounded butt off to catch their attention.

Maisy raised one impeccably groomed brow but didn't contradict her.

"But enough about me," Maisy said sweetly, "let's talk about you. And why Sasha turned up with you on my doorstep just in time to ruin a promising date. Are you single, Dr. King?" She fluttered her eyelashes playfully.

Poor Bodhi, unfamiliar with Maisy's hyper-sexed Scarlett O'Hara routine, blushed a deep pink.

"Maisy, stop it. Until recently, Bodhi was a forensic pathologist with the Medical Examiner's Office."

Maisy widened her bright blue eyes and

made a little *moue* of shock with her mouth. "How deliciously creepy."

Sasha fixed her with a look that said *behave, already*. "In fact, Bodhi was the forensic pathologist who handled three of the autopsies of the women who died from myocarditis."

Maisy's Southern belle act vaporized at the hint of a juicy story.

"Oh?"

"Yes. And when he raised concerns that the deaths might be connected, he was suspended and ultimately fired. Since then, of course, there've been two more deaths."

"You mean one?"

"No, two. Wow, that must have been some date. *You* missed the late news?"

Maisy didn't even acknowledge the ribbing. She had shifted into hard-charging journalist mode and was furiously scribbling notes in a small notebook.

She focused on Bodhi. "And you want to go public with your suspicions?"

He turned to face Sasha. "Uh, do I?"

"I'm preparing a complaint alleging that he was terminated as part of an effort to cover-up the cause of the deaths. We believe someone in city government is being bought off by corporate

interests and is using his or her position to influence the medical examiner's office."

"And you'll give me an exclusive?"

"Of course."

"When will the complaint be done?"

"In the morning." Sasha ignored Bodhi's
stare. She'd pulled all-nighters for lesser causes.
This would be a snap, provided she upgraded
from the swill Maisy served to real coffee.

"I'm going to have to approach the chief
medical examiner for comment."

"Have at him. Just so you know; all press
inquiries are being directed to the Mayor's Office."

"Really?" Maisy's tone said what she thought
of that news.

"Yep. And, Maisy?"

"Yeah."

"Go big with this. Like CNN, Court TV, something beyond local news. I'm not positive the
local media isn't at least a little bit complicit.
They certainly haven't pushed the story."

"You let me worry about that. Dr. King, get
ready to make a splash."

~ ~ ~ ~ ~ ~ ~ ~ ~ ~ ~

SASHA AND CONNELLY walked hand-in-hand as they left the condo building. It was a clear night with a warm breeze. She tilted her head back to take in the few bright stars that fought their way through the city lights to shine in the sky.

She'd never lived anywhere outside city limits. In fact, until she'd been stuck in rural Clear Brook County for a case, she'd never realized a night sky could hold so many points of light.

"What are you thinking?" Connelly rubbed his thumb across the back of her palm.

"I'll be glad when this is over and Bodhi's back safe at home. He's the easiest house guest ever, but I miss having our space. And, truth be told, I'd much rather draft this complaint in my pajamas with Java on my lap than at the office."

Connelly's eyes crinkled. "I know. But I thought maybe we could … take advantage of the privacy your office affords?"

She shook her head at the innuendo in his voice. "Connelly, I have to work. That's the point. I'm going to be working on this brief most of the night and I don't want to keep anyone awake. I don't even know why you're tagging along. You could be home in bed."

"You can't blame a guy for trying."

She smiled at that.

They crossed the quiet street. The only sounds were their shoes hitting the pavement and the occasional siren drifting down from Fifth Avenue on the wind. Sasha began to silently run through the arguments she planned to make in the complaint.

They reached Shadyside's business district, and the residential hush gave way to a babble of voices, car engines, doors slamming, and snippets of music, as bar goers and late-night diners emptied out onto the sidewalks.

Sasha dropped Connelly's hand to veer around a college-aged girl who had stopped in the middle of the sidewalk to paw through her spangled purse in search of something. A cell phone, car keys, or maybe a pen to scrawl her number on the hand of the tattooed boy holding her elbow.

They swerved around the couple and came back to the center of the sidewalk together, Connelly's leg bumping gently against hers.

"What did Hank have to say?"

He scanned their surroundings and shook his head. "We'll talk inside."

Paranoid, she thought. No one was paying any attention to them. But she didn't bother to argue. They were only a couple yards from the front door of the office building anyway. It could wait.

They reached the building's front door. She unlocked the door and started through it to flip on the interior hall lights. Connelly brushed past her and got there first.

Once upon a time, she'd have been irritated by that move. But the truth was, she didn't much care for entering the building in the dark, having been attacked there on more than one occasion. It suddenly occurred to her that Connelly might have intuited as much, which explained his desire to tag along better than his lame innuendo had.

That thought was equal parts comforting and concerning, given Daniel's warning that she was getting soft. She pushed it out of her mind. At the moment, she needed to focus on cranking out a complaint, and nothing else.

She trailed Connelly through the hallway and up the stairs to her second floor offices.

Inside, while her computer booted up and the printer and copier hummed to life, she organized the documents and notes she'd ultimately need to create the draft complaint.

"So, Hank?" she prompted, as she rummaged through a drawer looking for a box of yellow highlighters. Yellow, as every trial attorney knew, was the one color of highlighting that didn't show up on copies, making it inherently superior to every other color.

"Okay, the short version is the borough police think the father's good for Stone Fredericks' death. He admits to being there the night Stone was killed and he has one heck of a motive."

"Motive being to stop Stone from digging into the connection between Champion Fuel and the myocarditis deaths?"

"Right. Well, we think that's his motive. I don't think the Fox Chapel police have drilled down quite so far. They generally believe there was a difference of opinion about how to run the business. They've interviewed some employees who said father and son were known to bump heads from time to time. Sometimes there were fireworks."

"Okay. Motive and opportunity. Means?"

Connelly gave her an amused look from the guest chair where he lounged, his long legs propped up on a side table.

"Well, detective, that is a sticking point. Fred has a registered weapon, but he handed it over for a ballistics test and it wasn't the gun used to kill Stone."

"So, now what?"

"According to Hank, the lead investigators are trying to establish that Fred had access to another gun. But, Allegheny County is whispering in their ear to look at Stone's widow."

Sasha tilted her head. "I assume you asked Hank what his take is?"

He confirmed she was right with a quick head bob.

"And?"

"And he asked me to pay Fred another visit, try to suss out a sense of whether the old man is truly grieving or if he's just playing a part. Apparently, though, Fred has kept the pressure on his political pals in D.C. to help him find his son's killer."

"So, what do you think? Is Fred just play-acting or does he want Washington to keep an eye on his cronies in Pittsburgh government because maybe he thinks they had something to do with Stone's death?"

He considered her for a moment. Then, "Well, that's the million dollar question, isn't it?"

"Yes. And your answer ...?"

"I don't know. He was an emotional mess when I saw him—understandable for a grieving father. Of course, if you murdered your son in a moment of rage, you might well be an emotional mess the next day."

"Your gut, Connelly. What's it telling you?"

He rose and crossed the room to stand beside her. With two fingers, he tipped her chin up and back so she'd meet his eyes.

"I don't know, Sasha. I'll go see him tomorrow. What I do know is somebody shot Stone Fredericks in the back. Somebody roughed up Bodhi. And when you and Bodhi go public tomorrow, you're likely to draw that somebody's ire. Is that your plan?"

"No."

His gray eyes searched her face. He waited.

"That's not the plan. The plan is to force those scumbags in the Mayor's Office, or the ME's Office—whoever's in charge—to do the right thing. To publicly say, you know, the city's spent a whole lot of money on tax breaks and public relations for the makers of Champion Fuel. And Champion Fuel supports all our beloved sports teams. But in case you haven't noticed, a lot of women are dying, and we think *maybe*, just maybe, they're dying because of something in the drink. So until we can investigate it, stop drinking the stuff. Is that really so outrageous?"

She realized she was shaking. Not from fear. From anger.

He dropped his arms to her shoulders and pulled her into his arms.

"No. That's not outrageous."

She allowed herself to relax into his solid chest. He stroked her hair, and she listened to his heartbeat through his soft gray shirt.

"Good."

"But it's probably not going to work."

She pulled back and stared up at him, stung by the matter-of-fact way he'd dismissed it.

"You have a better idea?"

"Nope. I just want to be realistic. Unlike most of your eleventh-hour legal machinations, I don't think this one's likely to save the day."

You don't know Maisy the way I do, she thought.

"We'll see. I have to try."

"I know. I just want you to understand that you're painting a bull's eye on your chest."

"I don't think I am. Once Bodhi goes public, there's no point in silencing him. It'll be too late. He should actually be safer after the interview."

"That's a gamble."

"Well, it's one I'm willing to take."

He gave her a long-suffering look but nodded. "And Bodhi? You're willing to let him gamble, too?"

Bodhi was a problem, she had to admit. She'd talked to him after they'd left Maisy's apartment and had satisfied herself that he understood the risk he was taking. But knowing that he wouldn't defend himself if he was attacked kept her stomach roiling. He was a very soft target—the softest. And she didn't know how to protect him.

She waved a hand, dismissing the problem she couldn't immediately solve to focus on the one she could.

"We'll figure it out tomorrow. I have a lot of work to do now."

He huffed out a breath but accepted defeat. He jammed his hands into his pockets and looked around the room.

"Let me at least make myself useful. What can I do?"

"You could go down to Jake's and brew us a pot of coffee." She shot him a hopeful smile.

He started for the door, shaking his head at her caffeine habit as he went.

"Make it strong," she called after him.

33

Mackenzie felt Saul's cell phone vibrating from somewhere deep within the sea of sheets, breaking the early morning silence that filled the motel room. She glanced over at him, but he just lay there, gazing at the room's popcorn ceiling with a stupefied, sated grin.

"Saul—your phone."

No reaction.

She gave him a jab with her elbow and was rewarded with a grunt.

"Sorry, what?"

"Your phone is ringing. You should get it. In case it's about your kids or something." It wasn't yet eight o'clock. Too early to be the office; it had to be his wife.

He dropped his eyes from her face, as he always did when she mentioned his family. He patted the bed linens blindly, feeling around for the phone.

She slid out of the bed, taking the top sheet with her. As she wrapped it around her body, the phone fell out of its folds and bounced to the floor.

She handed it to him.

"Here."

"Thanks."

He took it with his face averted and pressed the button to answer the call.

She swept into the bathroom with all the dignity she could muster, so she wouldn't have to listen to him lie to Mona about where he was and what he was doing.

She snapped the hotel-issued clear plastic bathing cap over her hair and showered quickly, running through her day's to-do list as she lathered and rinsed. The most recent myocarditis death would occupy most of her energy, she knew.

Barry was starting to crumble under the pressure. She could see it in the way he'd shrunk in on himself when she'd broken the news the night before. He felt trapped between the mounting death toll and the mountain of money pouring into the city's accounts thanks to Better Life's stellar sales.

To be honest, she was starting to feel some uneasiness, too. One death, a random event. Two, a coincidence. But five?

She resolved to add a meeting with Fred to her agenda. If nothing else, maybe the company could run some quiet internal tests to rule out any concerns.

What if the tests reveal a connection?

The thought fluttered, unbidden, to the top of her mind. She swatted it away like an insect. Negative thinking wouldn't help. Just focus on what you can control, she reminded herself. Starting with the public perception of Better Life Beverages and Champion Fuel.

She twisted the faucet to turn off the water and removed the shower cap.

She was naked, shaking her hair out, when Saul charged through the door.

She grabbed the cheap, scratchy scrap of terry that passed for a towel at this bargain motel and wrapped it around her midsection.

"What's wrong?"

Something was very clearly wrong. He was shaking, and the pink flush of contentment that she'd left on his face after their lovemaking was gone—replaced by a gray pallor.

He stammered, as though he couldn't find the words for whatever he had to tell her.

"Saul?" she prompted. A surge of concern pulsed through her. Her heart thudded in her still-damp chest.

"You should call your office," he managed.

She snatched her cell phone from the vanity and activated the display. Six missed calls.

"Another dead girl?"

He shook his head.

"Then what?"

"Apparently, Bodhi King hired a lawyer and plans to sue the city."

Her relief hit her like a wave. "So what? He has no case. You guys aren't unionized. He's an employee at will and can be fired for no reason."

"He's alleging that he was fired as part of a plan to cover up a connection between the myocarditis deaths and Champion Fuel, Mackenzie. Whether that proves true or not, the allegation alone is gonna mean a scandal for my boss. And for yours."

Another wave. This one was adrenalized panic, and it nearly knocked her legs out from under her.

"How do you know this? Did he call you to tell you his plans?"

If the City Attorney had been served with a complaint, she would have known about it before Saul. Unless King had sent a draft to Sonny, maybe in an effort to force Sonny's hand and get his job back?

Saul coughed and tugged at the neck of his tee-shirt.

"No, that was Wally calling. He, uh..."

"Spit it out, Saul."

"He said he was watching CNN at the gym this morning and the old Channel Four weather girl's face came on the screen. He thinks she's hot, so he started to pay attention. She had an exclusive interview with Bodhi about the complaint he plans to file." The words came out in a rush, one right on top of the next.

She stared at him. Time seemed to be moving slower than usual, and her mind was racing.

She speed dialed her assistant. Before Susan had a chance to speak, she started rattling off orders.

"Write this down. The Mayor's Office issued a statement today that it has not had an opportunity to see the complaint referenced by Dr. King and cannot comment at this time. The Mayor takes seriously Dr. King's allegations and intends to satisfy himself as to whether they have any credence. He expresses full confidence, however, in the Chief Medical Examiner and his office."

She paused and listened to Susan's keys clicking on the other end of the phone. When the clatter of the keys stopped, she continued, "Send that to Barry from my email with the subject line 'URGENT: RESPONSE TO MEDIA.' Do it now. I'll wait."

"Okay," Susan said. "It's gone."

"Send it to the press office, too. And then transfer me to Sonny Jackson."

"Will do. Are you going to be in later? There's a lot of people looking for you."

She could imagine. Barry was probably in a panic.

"I'll be in soon. Has Mr. Fredericks called?"

"Uh ... I don't think he did. I'm going through the messages now. No, doesn't look like it."

"Huh."

Maybe he was one of the missed calls on her cell phone. She could see him choosing not to leave a message about this particular topic.

"Hold on. I'll get Dr. Jackson on the line."

The line went silent while Susan transferred the call. Mackenzie glanced over at Saul. His color had returned but he wore a sickly look, like he was on the verge of vomiting.

She knew the feeling.

"Mackenzie?" Sonny's voice boomed, overly hearty, in her ear.

"Did you have any warning about this, Dr. Jackson?" she asked without preamble.

Saul's eyes, pinned on hers, widened as he heard the tone she took with his boss.

She didn't give a crap about the pecking order at the moment. Someone was going to pay for Bodhi King's stunt. And if she had her way, it'd be the chief medical examiner. Bodhi had been his guy, after all.

"By *this*, am I to infer you're referring to Dr. King's national television debut?"

Anger welled in her chest at the hint of amusement she thought she heard under the clipped question.

"Yes, Sonny. That's what I'm referring to," she forced out between clenched teeth.

"Well, let me tell you. I about choked on my cereal. It was news to me that there's a connection between Champion Fuel and the dead women who are piling up in my shop."

"He didn't contact you directly?"

"I *am* speaking English, aren't I?"

That was debatable, she thought bitterly, although she noted that his Pittsburgh accent hadn't made an appearance yet.

"Just confirming, sir. Have you checked with your press officer and the assistant city attorney assigned to matters involving your office—he didn't reach out to anyone?"

"I spoke to both of them. No one's heard a peep from Bodhi. We were all blindsided."

Blindsided. Ambushed. Trapped. They all summed up her feelings. She pushed her rage away and focused on controlling Sonny.

"I'll take care of Dr. King. You just make sure everyone in your office refers the media to my office. I'm sure neither of us wants to see your office under the microscope." The veiled remark was as close as she wanted to come to a reference to the Duquesne job in front of Saul.

"Of course not."

"Good. Then let me handle the press. We need to have a consistent message."

"We need a little more than that, don't you think?"

"Such as?"

"Such as a reaction, a response to his charges. I don't know if you saw his interview, but he made some pretty specific allegations about the quality of the herbal ingredients Better Life Beverages scrounged up to use in that Champion Fuel stuff. If he's right, and the drink caused the myocarditis in all five women, we have a real public health crisis on our hands."

"Wait, back up. When you say 'scrounging up,' do you mean he publicly accused Better Life of deliberately sourcing substandard herbal ingredients?"

"That's exactly what I mean."

"In that case, we won't have to take care of Dr. King. The civil lawyers are going to *destroy* him."

A weight lifted off her chest. Fred's attorneys would pounce on King.

She met Saul's gaze and gave him an encouraging smile. He still looked like he was about to puke.

34

Naya laughed and aimed a light punch at Leo's shoulder.

"One more time?"

He shook his head, but then a grin spread across his face.

"Okay, one more."

She hit the replay button and the conference room DVR obligingly restarted Maisy's interview with Bodhi and Sasha.

"Maisy's good," Leo observed, as the reporter's solemn blue eyes stared out from the screen and she advised viewers that a forensic pathologist who had recently worked for the City of Pittsburgh Medical Examiner's Office had some shocking revelations about a popular sports beverage and its connection to a slew of deaths in healthy young women.

"Mmm-hmm," Naya agreed. "Bodhi came off really good, too. He was very credible. He's so low key; it makes him seem more believable, somehow."

The camera cut to Bodhi. He sat next to Sasha and listened to Maisy's first question. His smooth, relaxed face was somber and calm. Like a placid lake, Leo thought.

Bodhi leaned forward and his eyes sparked with intensity as he carefully, step by step, walked the audience through the events that he and Sasha believed had led to the current public health crisis in Pittsburgh: Better Life's rapid expansion; its insatiable need for wild red ginseng; its suppliers' willingness to sacrifice quality to meet that need; and, most shocking of all, the medical examiner's refusal to conduct a field investigation when it appeared that Pittsburgh was the site of a cluster of unexplained myocarditis deaths.

"And you raised your suspicion that these young women formed a death cluster with the Chief Medical Examiner personally, isn't that correct, Dr. King?" Maisy asked.

"That's correct."

"Dr. Jackson didn't share your concerns?"

Bodhi's level gaze showed the barest hint of disdain for his former boss. "Dr. Jackson assured me that he did not believe the evidence showed the deaths were connected to one another."

"You weren't able to convince him?"

"Unfortunately, I was placed on leave and ultimately terminated within days of having raised the issue. I didn't really have a chance to bring him around to my view."

"The draft complaint that I had the opportunity to review is in response to your firing, isn't it?"

Sasha fielded this question, even though Maisy had directed it to Bodhi.

She stared directly into the camera, ire sparking in her deep green eyes. Her voice was strong but honeyed.

"As Dr. King's attorney, I'd like to respond to that."

Maisy smiled amiably and nodded her encouragement.

Sasha put a hand on Bodhi's forearm in a trial lawyer's show of support and continued. "Dr. King's complaint does arise out of the circumstances of his termination, but only tangentially. He's not interested in being reinstated to his position or even in being compensated. So, in that sense, this isn't a typical employment law issue. Dr. King simply couldn't sit by and watch more young women unwittingly sign their own death certificates by drinking a health drink."

She paused and let that little irony sink in.

"Dang, she's good," Naya remarked.

Leo felt his chest swell with pride. She *was* good. Collected, persuasive, smart—and, on top of it all, somehow, she looked perfectly rested and at ease despite the fact that she'd been awake for twenty-nine hours and counting when the interview had been taped.

"Yeah, she sure doesn't let her nerves—"

"—Shh, here it comes." Naya shushed him as, on the screen, Sasha moved in for the kill.

"Dr. King's lawsuit alleges that he was fired to cover up a pervasive, coordinated effort to improperly influence the work of Pittsburgh's medical examiners—in particular, the formal autopsy reports issued by forensic pathologists in their official capacity."

"That's quite an accusation, Ms. McCandless," Maisy said.

"Yes. It is. And we don't make it lightly. Not only do we believe that certain business interests are willing to do whatever it takes to keep a lid on the truth about the recent myocarditis deaths, we also believe that officials in the highest levels of City government are willing to use their offices to assist in covering up the truth."

Maisy and Sasha exchanged a long look.

"Do you believe the murder of Stone Fredericks, Vice President of Better Life Beverages last week in Fox Chapel, is related?"

Sasha's expression was unreadable, even to Leo.

Finally she said, "You'd have to ask the police about that. What Dr. King and I do know is that responsibility for the deaths of five young women rests with Mayor Closky. Dr. King intends to file his complaint so that the families of Nina Penrose, Christa Taylor, Jasmine Courtland, Mia Martinez, and Cherise Jordan get the answers they deserve. And, we hope, to prevent any more avoidable deaths."

Sasha said the names of the dead young women slowly, giving each the full measure of her attention. In a masterful touch, a file photo of each woman with her date of birth and date of death typed across the bottom filled the screen, one fading into the next.

The camera came back to the interview. Maisy, Sasha, and Bodhi sat motionless and silent for a long moment before Maisy broke the spell and did her wrap up.

He and Naya had watched the piece three times, and even on the third viewing, the hair on his arms stood up when Sasha listed the names of the dead women. It might have been the most effective closing argument she'd ever delivered, and she was nowhere near a courtroom.

Naya switched off the television.

"You want to grab some lunch? Or should we wait and see if Sasha and Bodhi turn up?" she asked.

He hoped Sasha was at the condo catching a nap. He checked his watch. He had time for a sandwich before he drove out to Better Life Beverages' headquarters to chat with Fred.

"Yeah, let's eat. I'm sure Sasha is crashed out. Jake's?"

She reached for her purse just as the telephone bleated.

She pulled it close and checked the display.

"That's the number for the Prescott switchboard," she said, raising an eyebrow.

"It could be Will calling to congratulate Sasha."

"We'll see." She depressed the speaker

button. "Law Offices of Sasha McCandless. May I help you?"

"Naya—is that you?" an agitated male voice boomed from the speaker.

"Yes. Who's this?"

"This is Garrett English. Get me Sasha."

"I'm afraid Sasha isn't in, Mr. English. May I take a message or offer you voicemail?" Naya rolled her eyes vigorously at his brusque tone, but Leo was impressed to see that her voice stayed pleasant.

"You tell her she should be proud of herself. Her little television appearance just put your legal career in the crapper before it even started. Is she crazy? Herbal Attitudes is livid. She'll be lucky if we don't sue her and that cracked-out Buddhist for slander!"

Leo didn't know what Garrett English looked like, but based on the strained shouting coming from the telephone, he pictured a red-faced man, veins bulging in his neck, spittle flying.

Naya just smiled slyly.

"Okay, got it. Do you want me to read that back to you, Mr. English?"

"You think this is funny? You're as delusional as she is. I'm going to ... going to ..." he sputtered.

"Going to barf? Better make sure you don't hit

any partners' shoes this time, Garrett. I don't think *your* career could take the hit."

She ended the call before he could respond and grabbed the purse she'd abandoned to answer the phone.

"Come on. Let's go get some food."

35

Maisy was still buzzing from the interview and the rush of attention that had been pouring in ever since CNN had aired it. Her agent had sent her a bottle of champagne, and she was trying valiantly to get Sasha and Bodhi to pop the cork with her.

"Come *on*, y'all! We need to celebrate." She bounced around Sasha's kitchen on her bare feet, shaking the bottle as she did so.

Bodhi watched her with a bemused smile. Sasha clutched her coffee mug with both hands and stifled a yawn.

"Maisy, honey, I'm really excited for you. Honest. But it's only noon. At some point I probably need to actually file the complaint. And I've been awake forever. Let me catch a nap and then I'll come find you."

Maisy waved a hand, dismissing Sasha.

"Fine. You're a party pooper. How 'bout you, Bodhi?"

"You know, the way you're dancing around with that, it's going to explode when you open it. And, to be honest, I don't share your sense of victory."

That earned him a steely glare from Maisy.

He hurried to add, "Yet."

"What is wrong with you two? Stores all over town are already pulling Champion Fuel from their shelves. Bars and restaurants are refusing to serve it. Nobody's waiting for the city to take care of the problem—they're taking their own precautions. Isn't that what you wanted?"

"Of course. And I'm grateful, very grateful, to you for helping me get the word out. I just can't find it within me to feel festive, thinking of the lives that have already been lost."

Maisy's face fell. Sasha could tell her friend felt reproached. But she tended to agree with Bodhi on this one. Plus, she was exhausted.

"Maisy, you did good. I love you. Why don't you call up the date we ruined last night and ask him to share the bubbly with you to make up?"

That idea seemed to appeal to Maisy, and her megawatt smile returned.

"Oh, be that way. I'll see you later."

She leaned in and enveloped Sasha in a perfumed hug then waggled her fingers in a goodbye to Bodhi. She let herself out, and the condo fell quiet.

Sasha and Bodhi looked at each other for a silent moment. He spoke first.

"She has a good heart."

"I know."

"I just ... this isn't over, right?"

She nodded. "Not by a long shot."

She wasn't sure what the city's next move would be, but she doubted it would be to capitulate. Human nature being what it was, whoever was behind the attacks on Bodhi and the cover up wasn't going to just give up. His personal safety might no longer be an issue, but a countersuit was a strong possibility. Better Life Beverages, Herbal Attitudes, or both were likely busy preparing defamation or commercial disparagements actions at the moment.

Yay, more briefs.

He cocked his head and gave her a puzzled look. "Do you think I'm still in danger? Doesn't having gone public serve to protect me?

Someone was trying to keep me from piecing together the full picture and telling people. But, it's too late. The damage, from their perspective, is already done."

"It's true they can't silence you now. But it's a little early to assume that they—whoever they are—are going to be sanguine about that. Doesn't Buddhism recognize the human capacity for revenge?"

"Of course. But a Buddhist would never seek revenge. Karma will take care of it."

Right. Karma. Of course.

She nodded and slowly dug around in her overtired brain for a way to make him understand. "Okay, I'm pretty sure that it's almost over, one way or another. But, for now, out of an abundance of caution, it would probably be a good idea if you don't go back to your house just yet."

His shoulders fell. "Okay."

"How about some lunch? I'm no Connelly, but I can throw together a salad or something."

"You're very kind, but you must be running on fumes by now. Why don't you get some sleep and I'll make us lunch. It'll be ready when you wake up."

He didn't have to ask twice.

"That'd be great. I could use a power nap."

She scooped up Java and started for the stairs.

Her advice to Bodhi applied equally to herself, she realized. She needed to stay sharp until the drama played out. Connelly was fond of telling her sleep was a weapon. And she could use all the weapons at her disposal right about now.

She flopped onto the bed and closed her dry, burning eyes. She listened to the cat's rhythmic breathing and tried to drive out the thoughts of what might happen next. She fell asleep within minutes.

~ ~ ~ ~ ~ ~ ~ ~ ~ ~

BODHI'S CELL phone chimed softly. He marked his place in his book and hurried to grab the phone before the noise woke Sasha.

He knew she must be sleeping. The apartment had a stillness to it.

The phone displayed a familiar number, but he couldn't place it. He hesitated with his forefinger over the screen. He'd been sending most of his calls to voicemail. He'd been amazed by how quickly his private cell phone number had made its way into the hands of the media. Within minutes of the interview airing, he'd been bombarded by calls from journalists, talk show hosts, even a literary agent who just knew there was a bestseller lurking inside him.

After the fourth call, he'd stopped answering calls from numbers he didn't recognize. But this one was a local call.

He exhaled.

"Hello?"

"Bodhi?" a shaky female voice replied.

Cora Willham.

"Yes. Mrs. Willham, is everything okay?"

The uncertainty vanished from her voice, replaced by mild indignation.

"I should be the one asking you that. You've disappeared. I haven't seen you in days, young man. Then this morning, I'm having my hair done at Jean's and whose face pops up on the television? You've lost your job? And, Bodhi, you need a haircut."

He laughed. It felt good to laugh, to be on the receiving end of his neighbor's concern over something mundane and normal.

"Duly noted. Did you need something?"

Her voice dropped. "You've had some visitors.

I didn't think anything of it, of course, since you didn't see fit to tell me what's been going on. But, given all the news ... well, wherever you are, you might want to stay there for a spell."

The illusion of normalcy was gone.

"No one's bothered you, have they?"

"Aside from tramping through my garden to try and peek through your windows, you mean?" she sniffed. "I should have called the police. I didn't realize, not until I came home today and saw a man trying to pry open your kitchen window."

"I'm sure it was just—a friend, that's all."

A heavy silence passed between them, as they both considered his lie.

"Well, some friend he is. I rattled my trashcan lid near the door and he lit off like a rabbit."

He continued, "Please don't answer your door, though, if any more friends come around looking for me. Okay?"

"I can take care of myself, Bodhi. Any of your *friends* give me a problem, and they'll find themselves on the business end of Bud's old Smith & Wesson."

He didn't care for the image of his elderly neighbor wielding a gun.

"Mrs. Willham—"

"Oh, pipe down. I'm not going to go looking for any trouble. But, you keep your head on a swivel, you hear me?"

Bodhi reflected that Sasha would love Mrs. Willham.

"Yes, ma'am. I will."

"Good. Now I have to go. The Ladies' Auxiliary is meeting. But, one more thing."

"Yes?"

Her voice softened. "I'm proud of you."

She ended the call before he could respond. He was surprised to find that his eyes were damp.

He lowered himself to the floor, in lotus position, sat with that feeling for a long while. And then he turned his mind to the reason for Mrs. Willham's call.

Sasha was right. This wasn't over yet.

A chill tickled his spine, and the fine hairs on his arms prickled. He opened his mind to the cold fear that grabbed him then closed his eyes and focused on his breathing.

36

Leo followed the grim-faced secretary from the reception area past a maze of cloth-sided cubicles to Fred's office. Judging from her curt greeting and the funereal silence that hung over the building, he assumed Bodhi's interview hadn't been a hit around the offices of Better Life Beverages. Coupled with the death of their vice president and the heir apparent, it had probably been a tense week for the staff.

The woman stopped and knocked stiffly on a frosted glass door. She didn't wait for an answer.

"Fred, you have another visitor," she said, swinging the door open and gesturing for Leo to walk into the office.

Another visitor? Leo hesitated in the doorway.

He hadn't called to arrange a meeting, mainly because he hadn't wanted to give Fred the chance to put him off. He should have expected that the man would be in some sort of executive session, though—given the news coverage about Champion Fuel.

At a public company, he knew, the Board of Directors would have scrambled to arrange an emergency meeting to deal with the fallout. But Better Life was family-owned, and Fred didn't strike him as the sort of CEO who answered to a board made of up cousins and uncles.

Maybe Fred had called in a crisis management consultant to help him figure out how to spin the public relations nightmare that Sasha and Bodhi had brought down on his head? Or a lawyer.

The secretary was waiting for him to enter the room. He smiled at her and walked in.

"Mr. Fredericks, I'm sorry to interrupt. I can wait outside until you're free," he announced as he strode across the room to the desk in the corner.

Fred was on his feet, a befuddled expression on his face.

The secretary pulled the door closed and returned to her station.

Fred's eyes flashed from Leo to the striking blonde who sat on a small couch against the far wall. She appraised Leo with naked curiosity.

"Uh, don't be silly, Agent Connelly. Ms. Lane and I were just finishing up."

He beamed and hurried around the desk to pump Leo's hand. He seemed almost giddy at the notion of getting rid of his visitor.

"Mackenzie Lane? I thought I recognized you," Leo lied, turning to the woman. "You're the mayor's economic development czar, right?"

She quirked her mouth up into a slow smile. "Deputy Director, actually. But czar works, too. And what is that you're an *agent* of, Mr. Connelly?"

He sidestepped the question. "I'm not here in an official capacity, Ms. Lane—"

"It's Mackenzie, please."

"Mackenzie. I was asked by a friend of a friend of Mr. Fredericks' to offer whatever unofficial assistance I could on behalf of his friends in federal law enforcement."

She looked suitably impressed by the hinted-at backscratching, which, as far as he could tell, had an effect like catnip on politicians.

"I see," she drawled, her voice like honey.

Leo had dealt with his share of powerful,

attractive women. Some of them both more powerful and more attractive than this one. But Mackenzie oozed a very obvious, almost feline, sensuality.

He imagined it was intended to lull males into a trusting, lustful state. Instead, he found himself on high alert.

A glance at Fred confirmed that she had a similar effect on him—although he couldn't determine if it was the sex kitten routine or something else that had Fred on edge.

Fred cleared his throat. "Mackenzie, I'd like to talk to Agent Connelly here about the status of the investigation into S.J.'s death. So, if you don't mind, let's continue our little pow wow later?"

Mackenzie flushed and her eyes flashed. "This is no small matter, Fred. You need to get out in front of these accusations if you want to preserve your relationship with the City of Pittsburgh. Letting some disgruntled coroner with an ax to grind destroy Champion Fuel's reputation isn't going to bring Stone back."

Leo checked Fred's reaction. He seemed less drunk than he'd been the day after his son had died, but no one would describe the man as sober. His voice held a hint of boozy bluster, and Leo would be willing to wager that one of Fred's desk drawers held a flask that he dipped into on an as-needed basis throughout his work day. Leo would further wager that the need had been near-constant in the days since Stone's death.

Fred's jowls trembled and he clenched and unclenched his fist.

"You've got some nerve."

Leo casually moved a step closer to the couch, ready to spring between them if Fred lunged at her. He judged the likelihood of Fred doing exactly that at better than fifty percent.

"I'm sorry if I overstepped, Fred. I didn't mean any disrespect. I hope you believe that," Mackenzie hurried to say, apparently reading the odds the same way Leo had.

Fred didn't respond.

"Fred, I'll come back. I don't mind."

Leo turned to shake the old man's hand, but Fred clutched his arm.

"No, tell me. Do you have any information about S.J.'s murder?"

Leo cut his eyes toward Mackenzie, who had settled back into the couch now that the immediate danger seemed to have past.

"Not exactly," he said in a low tone. "The Fox Chapel Police thought you were a strong suspect, but they're getting pressure from the city to look elsewhere."

He watched the man's face carefully to gauge his reaction. For a brief instant, Fred telegraphed sadness and anger, but not surprise.

He nodded sorrowfully. "I figured they had me at the top of the list. Hell, wouldn't you? I was the last person to see him alive."

He continued to address Leo but turned toward Mackenzie, who was studying her manicure and pretending not to listen. "Now, why anyone in the Pittsburgh Police Department would be mucking around, whispering in the borough's ear, I can't say. I know *some* people seem to think the quicker we sweep S.J.'s death under the rug, the better it'll be for business. I'm his father first and a businessman second, as it turns out. If I find out that someone's interfering in the investigation into his murder, I'm not going to react well."

There was a long silence.

Leo waited while Mackenzie calculated her response to the veiled threat. When she looked up at Fred, her eyes blazed with anger.

"For the sake of argument if anyone did call in any favors with the Pittsburgh police, she probably did so in an effort to protect you, you old fool."

"Protect me? More like protect your own backside, you mean."

She grabbed her tan leather shoulder bag from the floor beside the couch and stood. She stormed across the room, closing the space between them and jutted her chin up into Fred's face.

"Really? What was it you said to me the night Stone died? Oh, that's right, I think it was 'he's a problem, but he's my problem. I'll take care of it.' You sure took care of it, didn't you? Now, unless you want him to have died in vain, I suggest you pull your head out of your rear and take care of these new problems."

She cut her eyes toward Leo. "A pleasure to have met you."

And with that, she walked out of the room, closing the door behind her with a bang.

Fred rubbed a shaking palm over his eyes and forehead.

"Can you believe her? I've been in business a long time, and I admit I may be calloused. But what kind of monster kills his own son over profit?"

All kinds, Leo thought. Most murders were

committed by family members. Many of them involved financial disputes. But he just nodded sympathetically and clasped an understanding hand on Fred's shoulder.

"Now, Ms. Lane, she looks like she's got balls of steel, if you'll excuse the phrase. You don't think ...?" he trailed off, and left the question linger unasked.

Fred thought about it, then gave his head a quick shake.

"There's not much I'd put past Mackenzie Lane. She's ruthless, that's for sure. But, a killer? No. If she had taken care of it, I think her play would have been to seduce S.J. and then blackmail him into keeping his trap shut. That's how she greased the wheels for the bottling plant and the Champion Fuel City of Champions sponsorship."

"Blackmail?"

"Some blackmail. Some bribes. Some sexual favors, from what I heard. She's just an old-school, backroom deal-maker in a shiny new feminine wrapper."

Leo studied Fred's face while he considered this character assessment. Finally, he nodded. It felt right. A nakedly ambitious political hack wouldn't get her hands any dirtier than required to raise funds and close deals. Shooting a businessman in the back on his front porch would be outside her comfort zone.

~ ~ ~ ~ ~ ~ ~ ~ ~ ~

LEO WAS PRETTY sure neither Mackenzie nor Fred killed Stone. But when he left Better Life Beverages' parking lot, he continued down the road about fifty yards and pulled off on the shoulder. He killed the engine and fixed his eyes on the parking lot exit.

If he was wrong about Fred, he expected the man would make a few frantic phone calls and then hurry out of the office to meet whomever he'd hired to murder his son.

Leo was confident Fred couldn't have pulled the trigger himself. His hands had trembled both of the times Leo'd been with him. Even if that shakiness was the result of temporary emotion, and not a permanent condition, his hands would almost certainly have shaken too hard to get a bead on Stone.

He'd seen it again and again during new

agent training. A trainee who couldn't keep a lid on his emotions would never pass marksmanship testing. Whoever killed Stone Fredericks had done so with a single, clean, well-aimed shot. The shooter was likely a professional. Or a sociopath.

Or an experienced meditator, he considered.

He had aced his marksmanship training because he was adept at clearing his mind. He had friends who served as SWAT team snipers. To a person, they meditated before setting up, narrowing the world to a scope and a target and blocking out the rest.

"Do you really think Bodhi killed Stone?" he asked himself the question aloud and immediately laughed.

There was no way the man who had rescued a stinkbug from torture at the paws of a house cat had executed a husband and father on his front porch.

No. It was a hired gun or a remorseless antisocial stranger.

That settled, he pulled out his cell phone and called Bodhi's number.

Bodhi answered on the first ring.

"Hi, Leo," he said in a slightly breathless whisper.

"Hi. Is everything okay? You sound out of breath."

"Sasha's upstairs sleeping. I didn't want the phone to wake her."

Good girl, Leo thought.

"Ah, of course. You're at the apartment?"

"Yes. She thought it was better if I didn't go back to my house yet," Bodhi said, a hint of petulance creeping into his voice.

"She's probably right. I just left Fred. I'm pretty sure he didn't kill his son."

"That's good."

"It's good for Fred. I wouldn't say it's good for you. Somewhere out there, someone's really pissed off that their efforts to conceal the connection between Champion Fuel and myocarditis failed. If they're looking to blame someone, they'll fixate on you."

And Sasha, he added silently.

Bodhi was quiet for a long moment, then he said, "You sound just like Sasha. Don't worry, I get it. I'll abuse your hospitality a little longer."

"It's probably just another day or two, man. I'm sure your interview will shake everything loose pretty quickly. To be honest, it's probably overkill, but we like having you around."

Bodhi laughed at that.

Leo squinted through the windshield as a maroon Civic pulled out from the parking lot and glided down the road toward him. Not Fred.

"Do me a favor, okay? Tell Sasha I'll be home in a couple hours. I'll stop and pick up groceries for dinner, but I have a few errands to run first."

"Okay."

"Do you need anything?" Leo asked.

"I could really use a small container of almond milk."

"You got it."

"Thanks. And, Leo, thank you. I don't know how I can ever repay you and Sasha for your kindness."

"Don't even think about, Bodhi. Really. We're glad to help."

Leo ended the call. He and Sasha were glad to help, and he was even gladder that, for once, they may have helped someone without risking their own lives. He considered that evidence of personal growth for both of them.

37

Mackenzie's pulse thudded in her ears as she sped toward Downtown and the City-County Building. She blew through the light at the end of the bridge and zipped along Grant Street, ignoring the driver who laid on his horn, and she assumed, flipped her the bird.

She didn't have time for red lights. She didn't have time for anything.

Fred hadn't killed his son. She'd known from looking into his eyes that he was telling the truth. And if it hadn't been Fred, then she thought she knew who'd pulled the trigger.

Now some tall, dark, and brooding agent of something or other was lurking around, and it was going to come back to her. All her work, cultivating relationships, forging alliances, and discrediting challengers would be destroyed.

The good she'd done for the city would be forgotten. The stronger tax base, higher employment rates, civic engagement, public-private partnerships she was responsible for would fade in Pittsburgh's collective memory, replaced by a sordid story about covering up a health risk at any cost, even murder.

She twisted the steering wheel and jerked her BMW into the right lane, cutting off a black Saab and making a careening turn around the corner and into the parking lot behind the Medical Examiner's Office.

She grabbed her purse and slammed the car door shut then took off running across the parking lot in her heels, her hair streaming behind her. She ignored the shouts from the blue-jacketed hearse driver having a smoke break and raced through the steel door marked "EMPLOYEES ONLY."

She pounded down the metal stairs to the bottom floor, where the forensic pathologists had their offices and their creepy stainless steel lab rooms.

She skidded to a stop in front of a closed office door and caught her breath. She tucked in her blouse, which had worked itself out of the waistband of her skirt during her run, and combed her fingers through her hair.

Then she pulled the door open without knocking and barreled into Bodhi King's former office.

The new occupant looked up, startled, then smoothed his expression into a smile.

"Hi, Mackenzie. What do you think of the new digs?"

She strode across the small office and put her face close to Wally Stewart's.

"What have you done?" She spat the words in barely controlled fury.

He pulled back.

"What are you talking about?"

"Don't be coy. I don't have time for games. I told you to keep an eye on Bodhi King."

"And I did."

"What else did you do, Wally?"

"Don't get indignant with me. You said to make sure he didn't go poking around in the files. You told me to delete his records. I killed the software trial for you." He crossed his arms and pouted.

She resisted the urge to strangle him.

"I know, Wally. What else did you do?"

"I thought you didn't want to know any details. Plausible deniability, isn't that what you said?"

He glared at her as she struggled to keep her temper.

She took a deep breath in through her nose and let it out through her mouth. Wally let his eyes travel to her chest, which was heaving with anger and worry.

You lie down with dogs, you get up with fleas, her father's voice echoed in her mind.

She forced herself to speak in a neutral voice. "You're right. I did say that. But, unfortunately, we're well past that now that Bodhi's face and story are plastered all over the news. Can you please tell me everything you did, so I can try to control the damage?"

She smiled at his thin, rodent face, and let her tongue flick across her lips.

He smiled back and his posture loosened.

"Okay, since you asked nicely. I followed him a few times. Put a sniffer on his computer. Hired a crackhead to steal his laptops. You owe me two hundred bucks, by the way."

She massaged her temple. "Is that all?"

"Isn't that enough? Seems like you should be a little more grateful."

He trailed a finger along her clavicle. She swallowed her disgust and kept her face an emotionless mask.

"The person I'm really grateful to is whoever offed Stone Fredericks. I'm hoping I can convince him to take care of Dr. King, as well," she lied smoothly, purring the words near his ear.

Wally put a hand around her waist and pulled her closer.

"Really?"

"Really." She stared into his eyes, willing him to tell her what she already suspected.

After Fred had told her Stone was trying to run down a connection to the death, she'd gone looking for Saul in his office, hoping to work off her anxiety with a quickie.

But he'd already left for the night. Wally, that prick, had taken great pleasure in letting her know Saul's kid had a baseball game.

She'd let him buy her dinner. After all, he was one of her cultivated sources. He was well-placed because he volunteered for every committee that could garner him attention from his higher ups. As a result, he knew what was going on in nearly every department of the Medical Examiner's Office.

He'd alerted her when the software linked

the women's deaths to a common ingredient. And he'd readily agreed to keep an eye on Bodhi. So, she figured it was a logical extension to ask him to make sure Stone didn't do anything stupid.

Although he was a thoroughly unpleasant person, he was an excellent resource. Motivated by a desire for promotion and a diffuse hatred and jealousy of his fellow pathologists, he never held her up for more money. He took whatever cash she offered. She periodically rewarded him with vague promises of career advancement and even vaguer suggestions of sex.

A smile spread across his face.

"That could be arranged," he said, his breath tickling her ear.

Her stomach lurched with the realization that he really had killed Stone. She swallowed hard, and her mouth went dry.

He bent his head to kiss her, and his door opened.

Saul stood in the doorway. A sheaf of papers fell from his hand to the floor, and he stared wide eyed and pale faced at the two of them.

"Oh, my God." His hand flew to his mouth.

Beside her Wally laughed softly, cruelly.

She closed her eyes for a moment, willing the

scene to dissolve. It didn't. She opened her eyes and stared hard at Saul.

"It's not how it looks," she said, pleading with her eyes for him to understand.

He jerked his head and bent to gather his papers with shaking hands.

"What a fool I've been," he said to the floor.

She wrenched herself free of Wally's grasp and knelt beside Saul, helping him pick up his printouts.

"Saul, look at me, please."

He shook his head.

She put her hand on his forearm and he froze.

"Please don't touch me."

She dropped her hand, stung.

"Saul, we're not involved. Wally's been helping me with ... a project."

He looked at her sideways through lidded, cautious eyes. "What kind of project?"

She threw Wally a look. He just watched them with open amusement splashed across his face.

She hesitated. If she told Saul the truth, she was risking her career. If she lied, it meant the end of their affair. It should have been a no-brainer. She hadn't gotten as far as she had by sacrificing professional ambition for her personal life.

But to her surprise, her chest squeezed at the thought of losing him.

She looked at him for a long moment. A disheveled, prematurely balding, married father of four who smelled of formaldehyde.

"I asked Wally to keep an eye on Bodhi."

"Why?"

"I was afraid he'd start digging and decide that the myocarditis deaths were related to Champion Fuel. It would cause a scandal, undo all the hard work the mayor has done."

"You *knew*?"

If anything, he looked more horrified than he had at the sight of her in Wally's arms.

"No, no. We *suspected*. Saul, I promise you, the company was looking into it. If they had reached the conclusion that there definitely was a connection, we would have gone public immediately."

He didn't respond.

"Baby, look at me? I would have insisted."

He clenched his papers in his fist and stood stiff-legged. He turned without a word and walked down the hallway.

She felt tears stinging behind her eyes.

Pull it together.

She blinked rapidly and chased the tears back. Then she looked at Wally and weighed her options.

It was over with Saul. But she could still save her project. She folded her heartbreak into a tiny square and crammed it away. Then she exhaled slowly and cast her lot with the psychopath standing across the room.

"He's probably going to tell Bodhi. Do you know where Bodhi is?" she asked.

"I might."

"Fix this. Please."

38

Bodhi assembled the ingredients for a hearty lunch in the slow cooker he found in the cabinet under the sink and settled in with his sketchpad to draw the sparrow perched on the tree outside the living room window. He tried to capture the way each feather nestled against the next in a soft, downy coat. He turned his charcoal pencil on its side to shade the bird's belly.

For the third time since Sasha had gone upstairs, his ringing phone shattered the quiet. He put aside his sketch pad and pencil and hurried to answer it.

"Yes?"

"Bodhi?" said an unfamiliar voice.

"Yes?" he repeated.

"It's Saul. I need to talk to you."

It *was* Saul, he realized. He hadn't recognized Saul's voice because it was high, tight, and squeaky.

"Is something wrong?"

"Yes. Can you meet me?"

"Can't we just talk over the phone?"

"I really need to see you. It's about this myocarditis stuff ... and some other stuff."

"I'm trying to keep a low profile, Saul. I've got reporters hounding me."

"Yeah, tell me about it. They're crawling all over the building. I'll come to your place then. This is really important."

"Actually, I'm staying with a friend."

Bodhi was about to rattle off Sasha's address, but he stopped himself.

He was safe at Sasha's because no one could find him here. While Sasha and Leo were still worried about an ambush by some random stranger, he didn't think that was a real danger anymore. His more pressing concern was trying to preserve some sliver of privacy in the wake of the interview with Maisy. If Saul came to the condo, he'd no doubt lead a pack of journalists right to Bodhi. He weighed the two risks.

"Tell you what, I'll meet you at the Reservoir. I'm leaving now."

"Thanks."

He ended the call and searched around for his sandals. After he strapped them onto his feet, he ripped a sheet of paper from the sketch pad and jotted a note to Sasha.

He hoped to keep the meeting with Saul short. With luck, he'd get back before she woke.

He dropped his phone into his front pocket and unlocked the front door as quietly as he could. He slipped silently out into the hallway and eased the door shut.

~ ~ ~ ~ ~ ~ ~ ~ ~ ~

A SOFT CLICK jolted Sasha from sleep to full wakefulness.

She opened her eyes, lifted the cat from her chest, and deposited him on the bed in a protesting ball of fur. Then she raised herself to her elbows.

"Bodhi? Is everything okay?" she called.

Silence.

She sat for several more seconds and listened hard. Nothing.

She threw back the blankets and slipped out of the bed. She smoothed her sleep-tangled hair into place as she hurried down the stairs.

Her kitchen was empty. She scanned the rest of the first floor. He was gone.

She pushed back a wave of irritation. It was possible he'd left with Connelly, although she doubted it. She'd have heard Connelly coming in.

Connelly's slow cooker sat on the counter. She peered through the condensation that fogged the glass lid. She could make out quinoa, black beans, and tomatoes. Maybe Bodhi had run out to the store to pick up an avocado. For some reason the dish looked like it called for an avocado.

She'd asked him not to go anywhere, but he wasn't under house arrest. She told herself that a quick trip to Trader Joe's was almost certainly safe at this point.

She poured cold coffee from the carafe into an enormous mug and popped it in the microwave. While the coffee heated, she stretched her back and rolled her neck, trying to wake up.

The microwave beeped. She removed the mug of muddy, reheated coffee and leaned against the counter to sip it.

She looked around for her Blackberry. Might as well listen to the pile of voicemails that had no doubt materialized while she'd slept. The phone sat on the small shelf in the foyer, nestled in the charging station Connelly had created for their small electronics. It was anchoring a sheet of paper.

She pocketed the phone and picked up the paper. Bodhi had left her a note.

Went to meet Saul. He said it's urgent. Didn't want to wake you. Don't worry.

She stared at the slanted letters for a long time, willing them to change, to spell out words that weren't so willfully stupid. They didn't.

She rested her mug on the counter with a bang and pulled up Bodhi's cell phone number.

He answered on the third ring, slightly out of breath.

"Hello?"

"I'm just curious, what does 'don't go anywhere alone' mean to you?"

"Hi, Sasha."

"Well?"

"Listen, I'm on my bike. It's kind of hard to

pedal and talk at the same time. Maybe you could yell at me when I get back?"

"Where are you?"

"I'm on Highland Avenue. I'm meeting Saul at the Highland Park Reservoir."

"I'll be there in fifteen minutes."

"It's really not necessary. It's just Saul. He's the definition of harmless."

She didn't bother to respond. She chugged the coffee and found her running shoes and a baseball cap.

She tried Connelly's number but he didn't answer. She hung up without leaving a voicemail and tapped out a quick text message instead.

Bodhi went to meet Saul in HP. I'm going to get him. No worries if we aren't here when you get back, xoxoxo.

She grabbed her keys and headed out the door. Bodhi was probably right. In all likelihood, Saul was harmless. But that didn't necessarily mean that meeting him was a low-risk activity. Saul could lead someone else—someone who wasn't harmless—straight to Bodhi, either intentionally or unknowingly.

She jogged down the stairwell wondering if she would ever, in her entire career as a lawyer, run across a client who actually listened to her advice. She doubted it.

39

Bodhi chained his bike to the rack and then settled on one of the wire-backed benches ringing the fountain and admired the spray of water in the center of the riotously blooming garden and, beyond it, the gentle, sloping hill and the city skyline. It was a view carefully designed to create a sense of tranquility and relaxation within the hectic noise of urban life.

But he felt neither.

He wanted to jump on his bike and pedal until he had to rest. Then get up and do it again.

Maybe that's what he would do, he thought. He'd make a fresh start somewhere new after he'd seen this mess through to whatever ending it held.

He stared blankly at the foaming water until he heard a car approach the entry to Reservoir Drive. He glanced up and saw Saul, his pale face clenched, easing his Prius between two stone eagles that perched on high columns like majestic, twin guards to the park.

Saul parked under the shade of a tall maple tree and paced across the entry garden toward Bodhi. His head was bent and his hands were jammed in his pockets. Bodhi thought he looked like a man weighted down with regret.

He stood and raised a hand in greeting as Saul drew closer. Saul nodded a hello and then twisted to look over his shoulder. Bodhi followed his gaze. There was no one behind him.

"Are you okay, buddy?"

Saul shook his head. "No. I've screwed up. Big time." He bounced from one foot to the other and then craned neck to look backward again. "Mind if we walk and talk?"

Between Saul's nerves and his restlessness, Bodhi suspected they could probably sprint and talk, but he just nodded his agreement.

They mounted the wide stairs to the walkway ringing the reservoir and fell into a fast rhythm. They walked in silence for several paces.

"I saw your interview."

Bodhi'd figured as much. He was fairly certain everyone at the Medical Examiner's Office had seen it by now. He made a noncommittal *hmm* noise.

Saul continued, "You just do the right thing, huh? No internal struggle for you."

"I'm not sure how to respond to that."

"It's not a jab. I guess I envy you."

"I'm unemployed, possibly unemployable. And basically trapped indoors. Your jealousy is a bit misplaced."

"But I bet you can sleep at night, can't you? You don't toss and turn until morning, wracked with guilt."

And with that, Bodhi had a sinking feeling that Saul was about to confess his affair. *Great.*

"I'll sleep better once Champion Fuel's off the market," he said in an effort to keep the focus on public, not private, issues.

Saul wasn't dissuaded. "I've been cheating on Mona."

He stopped walking and turned to face Bodhi.

"Um ..."

"No, please just listen. I don't know what I was thinking. I *wasn't* thinking. I couldn't believe it when she came on to me. I mean, what's a hot blonde in her twenties want with a married middle-aged lab rat? And her career's attached to a rocket. She's a deputy to the mayor. It all seemed so unbelievable, so unreal—like a dream. It didn't seem like it was really happening. I know that's not an excuse," he hurried to add.

Bodhi waved it off. "Your mistress, or girlfriend, whatever, is a deputy to the mayor?"

"Deputy director of economic development." Saul spat out the words like they tasted sour.

"You've been sleeping with Mackenzie Lane?"

Saul's eyes widened. "You know her?"

"I know of her. She's been instrumental in keeping everyone in the dark about the connection between Champion Fuel and the deaths."

"That's her. And, I guess she's been using me to do it. How could I have been so stupid?"

"Saul—"

"Don't try to make me feel better. I deserve to feel like crap. I betrayed Mona, our kids, our entire life. For what?"

"I don't know, Saul. I'm sure you can make things right with Mona."

His encouragement sounded lame and empty even to him, but Bodhi didn't know what else to say. If Saul had dragged him out here for counseling, he'd chosen his emotional support person poorly. The inner workings of a marriage were as foreign to him as the legal theories Sasha talked about. He didn't know how to help Saul salvage his marriage.

"I hope so. It's over with Mackenzie. That should count for something, right?"

Bodhi shrugged and didn't even try to answer the unanswerable question. "C'mon, let's walk."

He matched his stride to Saul's. They continued on in silence for several moments before Saul said, "Mackenzie was spying on you."

"Spying on me how?"

"She was worried that you were going to do exactly what you did—make a connection between the deaths and Champion Fuel and then go public. So she had Wally, freaking Wally, follow you."

"Wally?"

"I think she's sleeping with him, too."

Saul fixed his gaze on the ground. Bodhi didn't press him for details about the love triangle. He was trying to reason his way through the news that Wally had been tailing him.

"But that means she knew there was a connection before I did? That's why my files went missing, right?"

Saul threw his hands open in a frustrated *beats me* gesture. "I don't know. Mackenzie had a finger in everything. She had sources all over, in every department. Somehow, she knew. I swear I didn't tell her. I didn't know anything about it until you and I talked after your laptop was stolen."

"That was her? My laptop?"

"Well, Wally."

They fell silent again, lost in their respective unpleasant thoughts about Wally.

"She told you that Wally was following me?"

"I walked in on them in a ... um ... compromising position. She was trying to tell me it wasn't how it looked—that it was all business between them—that business being you."

"You don't believe her?"

Saul shrugged. "I don't know. I don't think it matters. I've been feeling worse and worse as our affair or whatever went on. This is just the final straw. She actively interfered in the medical examiner's ability to investigate those deaths. If she hadn't, maybe at least one of those girls might be alive. I'll have to come to terms with my adultery and what it means for my marriage, but I can't stand by silently knowing what I now know."

"Why'd you come to me and not Sonny?"

Saul screwed his face into an expression of disgust and disdain, and Bodhi knew he was about to spout off about Sonny's cowardice.

He never got the chance. As they rounded the bend and passed by the old stone public restroom, Wally stepped out from behind the far wall. He walked directly in their path and then stopped. His posture was that of a man looking for a fight. He leaned forward, straining toward them, and bounced on the balls of his feet.

"Fellas. Nice day for a walk."

Bodhi glanced sideways at Saul, who seemed to be vibrating with emotion.

"Wally. I guess it's too much to hope that this is just a coincidence, huh?" Bodhi said slowly, calculating how much longer it would take for Sasha to show up.

Wally flashed a cold smile.

Saul, his face gray, said, "What do you want, Wally? You still carrying your girlfriend's water?"

"Good one, Saul. Mackenzie's not my girlfriend. *Yet.* But once I show her what it's like to be with a real man, I'm sure she'll stick around." Wally's smile faded and he jerked his head toward the grassy hill that sloped away from the walkway, down into the park. "Let's talk some-where more private."

"No thanks. Come on, Saul," Bodhi said in a firm voice.

He moved to the side to skirt Wally, and Saul followed him. Wally snaked out an arm and grabbed Saul's collar as he passed.

"Want to reconsider, Dr. King?" Wally asked. He hauled Saul upright with his left hand. His right arm emerged from his pocket fisted around a glinting scalpel. He flicked the blade cover to the ground in a one-handed motion and pressed the metal against Saul's ear.

The world began to spin more slowly. A sour tang of fear filled Bodhi's mouth, and his throat closed.

Saul was frozen, his eyes pinned on Bodhi, urgent and pleading.

Where was Sasha?

Bodhi swallowed hard and raised both hands in front of his chest, pushing against the air as though it would somehow calm Wally. "Okay, Wally. Take it easy. Sure, we can talk. That's a great idea."

Wally grinned and tightened his grip on Saul's neck. "I thought you'd see the light. Down there. In the grove." He nodded toward the covered picnic area at the bottom of the hill.

He eased the scalpel off Saul's ear and pushed him toward the hill. Bodhi followed, craning his neck in a futile search for a small, dark-haired woman making her way around the reservoir. He saw no one but a pair of middle-aged matrons walking their dogs, lost in conversation.

He trudged behind Saul and Wally, his despair mounting with every step.

Wally hurried Saul across the lawn and on to the covered wood pavilion. He pushed Saul backward onto a picnic table bench and gestured for Bodhi to sit next to him. Bodhi stepped up onto the concrete pad and joined Saul on the bench.

He was encouraged that although the pavilion was tucked away behind a copse of trees, it was still public. He judged the likelihood that Wally would harm them here, where anyone could wander across them, as remote. Given the sickly grimace pasted on Saul's face, his friend didn't share his optimism.

He gave Saul an encouraging pat on the shoulder.

"Don't do that," Wally ordered, pointing the scalpel at Bodhi for emphasis.

He let his hand drop to his thigh, and his hopeful outlook leaked away.

"Sorry."

"Quiet." Another jab at the air with the scalpel. Wally took a step closer to the picnic table and then paused as if gathering his thoughts.

Saul and Bodhi watched him in silence.

"So," he finally said, "we appear to have a problem."

Bodhi cocked his head. "Saul and I have a problem, that's for sure," he agreed.

"Aren't you clever? But, then that cleverness is what landed us all here, isn't it?"

"Wally, I really don't understand what's going on. Why don't you just tell us."

Wally exhaled through his nose. It was something short of a snort, but just barely. "You always have to be the big man, don't you? You've stirred a hornet's nest with your media debut, Bodhi. The office was taking appropriate measures to handle the myocarditis issue in a reasoned, calm manner. Now, we have to quell a panic. And it's going to cost the city a lot of money. But, you're such a glory hound, you don't care. Anything for attention."

Bodhi stared at the man, searching for the

humanity he assumed must be buried somewhere within. "Wally, people are *dying*. We're
charged with protecting the public health and
welfare. We can't assist in—or even turn a blind
eye to—a political cover up."

"It's not your decision to make, hotshot. Just
because those first cases fell in your lap, you
think someone appointed you to make that call
and hog the limelight? You really think you're
special, don't you?"

Bodhi watched him silently. Wally's face was
twisted in an ugly sneer.

"Let's talk about you, not me. You've always
wanted advancement, adulation. This is your
chance to get it. Help us. It's over, Wally. I did go
public with my concerns. There's going to be an
investigation and it'll show a link between Champion Fuel and the death cluster. You can't stop it,
but you can get on the right side of it."

"You really are that naive. You thought airing
your suspicions would protect you? Mackenzie
needs someone to do damage control. Saul here
proved himself to be incompetent—probably
impotent, too, I'm guessing. She's going to be
grateful to the person who minimizes the fallout.
And you know who won't be giving a lot of

follow-up interviews? A dead coroner, that's who."

The giant gaps in his logic were lost on Wally. His face was twisted with passion and triumph. Somehow he genuinely believed he'd be rewarded for murdering two of his coworkers.

It was pointless to try to reason with him in the face of his unhinged conviction. Bodhi changed tacks.

"If that's true, then so be it." He paused and let his words penetrate Wally's fervor.

Wally looked at him, unsure if this was a ruse.

Bodhi raised both hands. "Kill me. If you think it helps your cause, go ahead. But, let Saul go."

Wally smiled coldly. "Oh, of course, the self-sacrificing Bodhi King wants to die a hero." The smile vanished. "No."

"Wally—"

"I said no." He stepped closer, slashing the air with the scalpel. "Poor, hapless Saul. Always the innocent victim. No. He made his bed, rather literally, when he started banging Mackenzie. Besides, do you really think I'm going to leave a witness, Bodhi? Don't be stupid. I'll have to do you first, I think. Then him. Cleanup will be a challenge, but if I drag you into the woods, it'll take a while for anyone to find you. By then, Mackenzie will have appointed me Chief Medical Examiner. I will, of course, issue a heartfelt public statement and vow not to rest until your killer is apprehended."

Saul blanched and pitched forward as if he were going to vomit.

Wally cut his fevered eyes away from Bodhi and watched to make sure Saul wasn't about to charge him. Once he was satisfied, he looked back at Bodhi. "That's about enough chitchat." His voice was unnaturally flat.

Where the devil was Sasha already?

Wally walked toward him and stopped just a foot or so away. "Stand up."

Bodhi hesitated. "Did you kill Stone Fredericks?"

"Shut up and stand up, Bodhi."

Bodhi inhaled slowly, deeply, focusing only on the breath entering his body. Then he exhaled through his nose, letting go of his attachment to life. He didn't fear death. He would accept it as the natural progression.

He stood and locked eyes with Wally.

~ ~ ~ ~ ~ ~ ~ ~ ~ ~ ~

Sasha parked her Passat behind a dusty Prius and jogged across the entry gardens. As she passed by the fountain, out of the corner of her eye, she registered Bodhi's bicycle chained to a bike rack. She raced up the stairs to the walkway that ringed the reservoir, hurrying, but not frantic.

Saul probably did just want to talk to Bodhi, she reminded herself, as she slowed her pace to a fast walk. *Probably.*

But she couldn't deny that Bodhi's exposure made her uneasy. He was a soft target under the best of circumstances. And a clandestine meeting in the park was sub-optimal. She scanned the benches that lined the walk as she strode by. One older gentleman sat reading a paperback. Several yards away, a teenage couple occupied another bench, making out, wrapped around each other in an oblivious windmill of arms and legs.

She raised a hand to shield her eyes against the late afternoon sun and searched the concourse for a pair of men. Her pulse thrummed as she realized they weren't there.

She broke into a trot and fumbled with her cell phone. As she neared the stone structure that housed the bathroom, she slowed to avoid crashing into two dog-walking women in coordinated track suits. Sisters, if she had to guess. As she pulled up Bodhi's number, she watched the women with one eye.

One was crouched next to her dog, a long-eared hound, trying to wrest a small piece of plastic from its mouth.

"Bliss, give!" she tugged on the plastic.

The dog, shook its head and tugged back, amused at the game.

"Dirty. Drop it!"

The dog continued to tug.

"Oh, for Pete's sake. Here," the woman's sister said, reaching into her pocket and removing two small treats.

She tossed one treat at Bliss's nose, and the dog dropped the plastic. She fed the other to her own dog, complimenting it on its good behavior.

"What is it, anyway?" she asked.

Her sister straightened, holding the mangled plastic between two fingers. "Who knows."

She started toward the trash barrel that sat alongside the bathroom and then froze.

"Tessie? What's wrong."

She pointed down the hill. "Look at that, Betts."

Her sister followed her finger and so did Sasha. She squinted to make out three figures under a pavilion. Men. One was advancing toward a bench where the other two sat. His posture screamed menace. One of the seated men rose to his feet slowly, with a finality that worried her. Sasha noted his lanky figure and unruly curls. Bodhi.

The phone in her hand connected her call.

In the pavilion, Bodhi looked down at his pocket, at his own ringing phone.

The standing man raised an arm and shouted at him. Sunlight glinted off something metal that he brandished in his hand.

Sasha disconnected the call and pressed her phone into the closer woman's hand.

"Call 911. Hurry!" she shouted over her shoulder as she sprinted down the hill toward the grove.

She filled her lungs with air and exploded across the grass. A cold wave of adrenaline rushed through her body.

Her mind frantically worked to analyze the scene before it as she drew near.

Three men. A white-faced man, seated, a look of horror pasted across his face. Saul.

Bodhi, standing bolt upright and somehow

defiant, staring at a red-haired man who was wielding a scalpel.

Red-hair. Cruel, thin face. Holding a surgical instrument.

The tumblers in her brain clicked into place. Wally.

She ran flat out until she reached the grove. Bodhi and Saul turned their heads to look at her. Wally kept his eyes pinned on Bodhi.

"I wondered if you were ever going to get here," Bodhi said with a gentle smile.

Saul gaped, open-mouthed.

Wally let one eye travel toward her and then returned his attention to Bodhi. "Ah, it's your little lawyer friend. Well, the more, the merrier, I guess. Now, of course, the question becomes who goes first. You or her? Saul, you're still last in line, buddy."

Saul snapped his mouth closed but didn't respond.

"It's not too late to rethink this," Bodhi said.

"Shut up." Wally jabbed the scalpel into Bodhi's cheek.

A thin line of blood immediately bloomed. Bodhi didn't react.

Wally turned toward Sasha, his mouth set in an angry slash. "Ladies first, I think."

He strode toward her.

Daniel's voice echoed in her ears. *Evade. Strike. Attack. Disarm.*

As he closed the gap between them, she eyed the scalpel and calculated her options. She didn't like them.

She'd rather face a gun than a bladed weapon any day. An attacker with a firearm generally followed a fairly straightforward process to use it. He was unlikely to get too close. He'd aim and fire. An unpleasant prospect, but predictable.

But an assailant with a knife was unpredictable. He might charge her, fast and clean, and drive the blade into a vulnerable area. He might take a more circuitous route.

If he plunged straight toward her, committed to cutting her, her defense would be relatively straightforward.

Burst toward him. Plow into his right arm, ideally, with enough force to cause him to drop the scalpel, while at the same time punching him in the neck or throat. The goal would be to overwhelm, immobilize, and then disarm him.

If, instead, he danced around from side to side, waving the scalpel as he advanced, it would be a trickier, and more dangerous, prospect to attempt to charge him and take the scalpel.

Come and get me, Wally, she thought. She stood stock still, willing him to come right for her.

He didn't.

He weaved from side to side, swinging the scalpel in wild loops as he moved.

Great.

She bobbed and dodged, staying in constant motion, as he neared her.

He swiped at her chest with the scalpel. She pulled back and he caught nothing but air.

He came at her again and sliced the air closer to her head. She ducked. Bounced back up and danced to the side.

She indulged in a quick scan of the pavilion, hoping to spot something she could use as a weapon. A brick to throw. A nice, thick stick to use as a baton. Nothing.

Bodhi and Saul were frozen in place, identical looks of horror on their faces.

That was good, at least. The last thing she needed was well-intentioned help from an amateur.

She snapped her attention back to Wally as he circled toward her. His nostrils flared with anger and effort. He was losing control now, slashing randomly.

She gritted her teeth. Less than ideal, but likely to be the best shot she'd get at taking him down.

She watched as he wheeled toward her. She pulled her torso to the left as he grazed her side.

Now.

As he was pulling his arm back, she lunged forward and drove her fist into his nose. Small bones crackled and popped as they shattered. Blood gushed down over her hand.

Instinctively, he brought both hands up to his face to staunch the flow.

She assumed he'd drop the scalpel first.

He didn't.

As his right hand flew up and she twisted toward him to lock his arms, the scalpel slashed down through her left triceps.

A hot, searing pain took her breath away. Her arm burned and sticky blood spurted, mixing with the blood already flowing from his nose.

She clamped her right hand around his wrist and squeezed. His left hand was busy pinching his nose. As he brought it down to try to pull her off, she threw her right elbow up and smashed it into his already crushed nasal passage.

Wally gasped. She forced the scalpel out of his hand and heard it clatter to the ground. It was the sweetest sound she'd ever heard. Like a harp. Or a child singing.

Wally looked like he was shimmering.

She was getting dizzy. Her arm was numb.

Time to put this to bed.

She drove a knee up and into his ribs, pushing him back over a picnic table and landed on top of him with a thud.

Her left arm hung useless and weak, a fountain of blood pouring from it. She crawled to her knees and gripped his throat with her right forearm. She applied as much pressure as she could, hoping he'd choke out before she passed out. Sweat dripped into her eyes. She shook with effort. Her vision dimmed at the edges.

This was it. This was how she was going to die. In a puddle of blood in a picnic pavilion.

Arms were tugging at her waist, gently pulling her away from Wally.

"No."

"Sasha, it's okay. It's over." Bodhi's voice, soft and concerned, in her ear.

"No." She struggled against him but she was so cold.

"Sasha, listen to me. Saul has Wally. Let go. I have to get some pressure on your brachial artery or you're going to bleed out."

Bodhi sounded like he was talking underwater.

She released Wally's throat and slumped back against Bodhi's chest.

The pain in her arm screamed as he pressed down on the wound. She was on fire.

And then her world turned black and blessedly quiet.

40

Leo hurried down the stairs from Sasha's parents' house to his SUV, cursing the time. He'd needed to stop to finalize plans with Valentina, but he hadn't realized how much time he'd spent there.

He blamed Julian. The cooing baby had fallen asleep in his arms and he hadn't had the heart to disturb him. But now he needed to rush to the grocery store and get home. Sasha and Bodhi were probably starving—if they'd even waited for him.

And, of course, he'd left his phone in the car.

As soon as he was settled behind the wheel, he reached across the console and grabbed his phone to call and let them know he was on his way.

A text message from Sasha scrolled across the screen. He checked the time of the message. She'd sent it more than an hour and a half earlier.

He also had a missed call from Naya. He tapped in his voicemail password and listened to her message. The words chilled him.

He froze. Go back in and tell Sasha's parents their daughter had been stabbed or get to the hospital faster?

He swallowed and jabbed the key into the ignition. The engine roared to life and he raced toward the city with a lump in his throat and a pit in his stomach.

He connected the phone through his Bluetooth and listened to a series of frantic messages—from Bodhi, Maisy, Naya, and finally Detective Gilbert—-all the way to Shadyside Hospital. Not one of his callers bothered to sugarcoat the news: Sasha had lost a lot of blood. She was in surgery, and it was touch and go.

He called and broke the news to Sasha's father. He waited silently on the line while her dad relayed the message to her mother. Valentina's wail of anguish tore through his chest.

After what felt like hours, he pulled the SUV

crookedly into a parking spot and ran through the emergency room entrance.

An empty black and white squad car was parked at an angle in the turnaround, its lights still flashing. Behind it, near the ambulance bays, was an unmarked car with a light affixed to the dash. It was also unoccupied.

He skidded to a stop in front of an information kiosk. A young couple leaned over the counter and followed the volunteer's painted fingernail as she traced a path along a map. She patiently explained how to get to the man's mother's room in a slow cadence. Then she repeated the information.

Leo forced himself to remain calm. He focused on slowing his breathing while he waited.

At last, the couple thanked the woman and shuffled off with the map, clutching one another's hands.

"May I help you?" she asked as Leo stepped forward.

"Sasha McCandless. I think she's in surgery. She was stabbed." He forced the words out against the rising tide of panic in his throat.

She smiled impersonally and consulted an electronic database on her monitor.

"She's out, actually. She's in recovery. You'll want to take one of those elevators back there," she said pointing to her right. "Fourth floor. East wing. Would you like a map?"

He was already walking toward the elevator bank. His feet moved of their own volition.

He pushed the button to call the elevator. He waited years. Finally, a car groaned to a stop and slowly, impossibly slowly, opened its doors.

He almost barreled into a preteen on crutches as she made her way off the elevator.

"Sorry," he mumbled.

His brain was wrapped in cotton as he tried to make sense of the numbers on the panel. At last, he recognized the four and pressed it.

A man holding a baby followed him into the car and pushed two.

"You okay, buddy?"

Leo nodded numbly and stared at the doors, willing them to close.

The elevator jittered to life and inched its way upward. At the second floor it slowed and then stopped. Seconds passed. Finally the doors opened. The man and the baby got off. Another eternity passed before the doors closed and the car lurched upward to the fourth floor.

At last he burst off the elevator and raced

along a maze of hallways and signs to the East wing.

Finally, a sign announced he'd reached the recovery waiting area. Leo steadied his breathing and pushed the door open. He walked right into the chest of a very large uniformed police officer, who reached out and stiff-armed him back a step.

"It's okay," Maisy said from the couch. "He's her fiancé."

She gave him a shaky smile. Bodhi sat beside her, his expression unreadable.

"Let him pass," a second voice ordered.

Leo looked past the officer and recognized Burton Gilbert, the homicide detective who Sasha knew from the Lady Lawyer Killers case.

The officer stepped aside. "Sir."

Leo nodded to him and headed for the couch.

"She's lost a lot of blood," Maisy said as he approached. "But Bodhi applied compression until they got here. He saved her life."

He exhaled shakily. "She's going to be okay?"

"She's going to be okay."

He turned to Bodhi with wet eyes. "Thank you."

"Wally." Bodhi's voice came out in a dry croak.

"Wally? Wally Stewart?"

Detective Gilbert cleared his throat, "According to Dr. King and Dr. David, Mackenzie Lane was using Wally Stewart to gather information on Dr. King's investigation into the dead women. She seems to have had her hooks deep in the medical examiner's office."

That squared with what Fred had said.

"Okay."

"Dr. Stewart got a bit ambitious and decided to go above the call of duty. He's the one who was following Bodhi, and he arranged for Bodhi's laptops to be stolen. He went after Bodhi and Saul with a scalpel and Sasha tackled him," Maisy explained.

"He caught her across the brachial artery but, somehow, she managed to get the knife away from him," Bodhi added, his voice stronger.

That sounded like Sasha.

"He would have killed her—just like Stone Fredericks," Bodhi said.

Leo turned to Detective Gilbert, who confirmed the news with a short nod.

"Dr. Stewart's in custody for the attack on Sasha, but he hasn't confessed to killing Mr. Fredericks. Saul David corroborates everything

Dr. King has told us. And I'm told Ms. Lane is also talking. Of course, Stewart's having some trouble talking about anything, seeing as how Sasha busted his nose and knocked out his front teeth," Gilbert said with a small chuckle.

Leo felt a grin crease his mouth.

"Can I see her? Sasha?" he asked Maisy.

"She's not alert. You should wait," Maisy said in a soft voice.

He shook his head.

"I want to see her now."

Gilbert nodded, and the uniformed officer stepped to the side. Until that moment, Leo hadn't noticed that he'd been blocking a doorway.

He steeled himself and pushed the door inward.

The room was antiseptic and quiet. Sasha lay in a bed on the far side of the room under a large window. The fading light streamed in and fell across her face.

She looked like she was sleeping peacefully. Her face was whiter than the rough sheet tucked under her armpits. Her left arm was outside the sheet, wrapped in gauze and blood-stained bandages.

He stared at her for a long moment. At her

dark eyelashes brushing her cheekbones. The curve of her neck. The tangle of her hair. He reached out and stroked her forehead. She didn't move.

Then he sank into the chair beside her bed, placed his head on her stomach, and cried.

41

Sasha, Connelly, Bodhi, and Naya stood behind and slightly apart from the small cluster of reporters crowded around the mayor and Detective Gilbert.

"I'm going to say just a few words about the myocarditis situation and then will turn you over to Detective Burton Gilbert of the Homicide Squad, who will answer questions about Dr. Stewart's involvement in the murder of Stone Fredericks," Mayor Barry Closky said with a nod toward Burton.

He ignored the murmur from the assembled press and continued, "I personally want to apologize to the people of Pittsburgh, who trusted me and the Chief Medical Examiner to protect them. My investigation reveals that we've failed to do that in light of the evidence that the recent spate of myocarditis-related deaths all trace back to a single batch of contaminated Champion Fuel. Dr. Jackson has submitted his resignation, effective immediately, to spend more time with his family. I asked Dr. Bodhi King, who first raised concerns regarding Champion Fuel to serve as interim Chief Medical Examiner while a search is conducted for a permanent replacement for Dr. Jackson, but I regret to say, he declined."

Sasha turned to Bodhi.

"Is that true?"

"Yes."

"When did that happen?" she whispered.

"This morning, while you were haranguing every medical professional within fifty yards to release you."

She ignored that. "Why'd you say no?"

He gave her a long look. "I think it's pretty clear that power corrupts."

"Not you."

"Power corrupts everyone."

He turned his attention back to the mayor.

"However, Dr. Saul David has agreed to fill that role. He has already convened a committee to examine the policies and procedures of the Medical Examiner's Office with an eye to avoiding any future repeats of this tragic failure to safeguard the public health," the mayor said.

"Is Better Life Beverages going to be charged with a crime?" a dark-haired reporter yelled from the middle of the pack.

"No. Better Life and its CEO, Stone Fredericks, Senior, immediately cooperated earlier today when we asked them to halt operations at the bottling plant. The company has also issued a recall of Champion Fuel and has agreed to test its entire supply of wild red ginseng. In addition, Mr. Fredericks has committed one million dollars to the University of Pittsburgh to fund research into myocarditis and has established a one-million-dollar scholarship fund in memory of the victims of the myocarditis deaths. He is as shaken by these events as we all are."

"Nice touch," Connelly whispered.

"Finally, I want to announce that, pending the outcome of an investigation into what role, if any, my deputy director of economic development may have played in suppressing information regarding these events, I have disbanded that office. Although Mackenzie Lane has not been charged with any wrongdoing, she and I agreed that because her department no longer exists, she should move on to greener pastures with my blessing."

He checked a stack of index cards and then looked back up at the press. "That's it for me. I'll turn this over to Detective Gilbert now."

Sasha slipped her hand into Connelly's and turned to leave. "He's not going to say anything publicly that he hasn't already told us. Stewart's good for the murder. Let's go."

Bodhi and Naya fell into step beside them.

"So," Connelly said to Bodhi, "what are you going to do now?"

Bodhi considered the question.

"I'm not sure. I might look for a teaching position. But, first I'm going to travel some."

"Where are you headed?" Naya asked.

"Costa Rica, first. There's a sustainable banana plantation there that does interesting work. I'm going to travel around the countryside and then see if I can intern there."

"You turned down a position as the Chief Medical Examiner for an internship at a banana plantation?" Naya asked.

"Potential internship," Bodhi corrected her with a gentle smile.

Sasha threw back her head and laughed. It

felt good to laugh. Scratch that. It felt good to breathe.

Just then, a striking blonde woman stepped out from the brick alley leading away from the courtyard.

"Sasha McCandless?" she asked.

"Yes," Sasha answered, turning toward the woman's voice.

At the same moment that Connelly was forming the words 'Mackenzie Lane,' the woman hauled off and caught Sasha squarely on the cheekbone with a solid punch.

Sasha's vision exploded into a million stars and her head snapped back. Connelly caught her around her waist as she stumbled.

The next thing she saw was Bodhi holding a struggling Naya, who seemed intent on going after the woman.

Mackenzie smiled and sauntered off in the direction of the City-County Building without another word.

~ ~ ~ ~ ~ ~ ~ ~ ~ ~ ~

THE KNUCKLES on Mackenzie's right hand ached. Sasha McCandless apparently had a very hard face because a row of bruises had blossomed across Mackenzie's hand shortly after she had punched the attorney.

Mackenzie had gone to the press conference intending to watch from a distance while Barry spun his web of lies. But when Sasha and her entourage walked past the alley, laughing and joking, all of Mackenzie's anger and disappointment welled to the surface and she reacted.

Still, though, she didn't regret landing the punch. Although she supposed she might have, if McCandless hadn't refused to press charges—or if Bodhi King hadn't restrained that very angry paralegal.

It might be the *only* thing she didn't regret, she mused, as she tossed framed pictures haphazardly into a cardboard carton.

Barry had been decent enough to agree to let her clear out her office after hours—although not so decent that he hadn't also sent along a security officer to lurk around her doorway and watch her like some kind of criminal.

And she was *not* a criminal.

The district attorney herself had told Barry that prosecuting Mackenzie would likely prove to be a waste of resources. So, he'd settled for tossing her out without so much as a reference or recommendation.

It hardly mattered. She had a wealth of contacts, many of whom would view what she'd done as understandable, even admirable. She was protecting her project. She'd land on her feet. Eventually.

There was a city manager position open in Sacramento. She'd work her virtual Rolodex until she got herself an interview. And once the powers-that-be met Mackenzie Lane in person, their reservations would evaporate. All concerns about whispered rumors of her past would fade once she captivated her new boss with her determination, dedication, and bold vision. Just like always.

She threw a pile of bound deal documents—mementos of the impressive results she'd garnered—into the box then dumped the contents of her pen drawer on top. She jammed the lid down on the carton and dusted her hands on her jeans.

"All set, ma'am?" the security guard asked.

"Give me a minute."

She walked over to her floor to ceiling window and looked out at the city, *her* city, lit up in the dark. She scanned the skyline from the illuminated fountain at Point State Park to the fireworks going off over PNC Park, to the blinking lights atop the downtown skyscrapers.

She'd miss Pittsburgh. Maybe even more than she'd miss Saul, who refused to take her calls.

She pressed her head against the glass and whispered a goodbye.

Then she hefted her box and walked out of the office.

ap, tap, tap.

Sasha massaged her cheekbone and checked the time. She couldn't take another ibuprofen until three o'clock, but now the dull throbbing pain had been augmented by a persistent noise.

Great, she thought, *it's probably my brain rattling.*

Mackenzie Lane had packed a real wallop. Her cheek ached almost as much as her arm. Almost. She regretted her decision to toss out the painkillers the doctors had forced her to take with her when she'd finally convinced them to let her go home.

Tap. Tap.

She tried to ignore the noise and focus,

through the cottony feeling in her mind, on the invoices spread out in front of her. She couldn't cover Naya's law school tuition, but she thought she could swing a raise to help out with the costs. She squinted at the numbers through her puffy eye as if she could will a few extra zeroes into the rows.

Tap.

"Sasha? Are you in there?"

Only when she heard Will's voice calling from the hallway did she finally put it all together and figure out that he'd been knocking on her door.

She eased herself out of her chair and walked stiffly to the door. She'd have to convince Connelly to give her a massage when she got home. She suspected it wouldn't be a hard sell.

"Coming, Will," she said as she unlocked the door.

"I apologize for not calling first. May I come in?" he asked. He held a mug of coffee from Jake's in each hand and wore a contrite, uncertain expression.

"Sure. Sorry. I'm not used to the door being locked and I was concentrating on something."

She took the proffered mug from his left hand and inhaled deeply. He'd either guessed correctly or Ocean had chosen for him—it was definitely Jake's dark roast.

"How are you feeling?" His voice was threaded with concern.

"I'll live."

"Was the door locked for any particular reason?"

"To keep out the blasted reporters. Same reason my phone's off the hook." She gestured to the handset on her desk. Once they'd filled her voicemail box, she'd had no choice but to meet the incessant calls from the media with a busy signal.

She led Will to her guest chairs and sunk into the nearest one. She could see he was eying her shiner with some alarm. She was glad she'd thrown a cardigan over her shoulders. The bandaged wound on her triceps might have done him in.

"Are you sure you should be working today?"

"It looks worse than it is. I'm not doing any heavy lifting, just some administrative stuff. You know how that is, I'm sure."

"I do, indeed." He sipped his cafe Americano.

She watched his face as he considered his next words. He wanted something.

"Is Naya around?" he asked.

"No. She's up at the law school looking into whether she can pull together any kind of financial aid package this late."

Will flinched. "I'm so sorry, Sasha. I did tell her if she would just give me a few weeks, I could surely straighten out this morass with the scholarship committee."

"I know. She told me. She'll figure something out. To be perfectly honest, I think it's better this way."

"Better?"

"Come on, Naya's never going to allow Prescott to mold her into a Prescott and Talbott-approved lawyer. You know it as well as I do." She sipped her coffee and watched his face.

He merely nodded. "Perhaps."

"So, if you came here to talk her into changing her mind, she's not here and, frankly, you should reconsider."

"I'm not here about Naya. I came to talk to you."

"Will, I give you points for perseverance, but I'm not going to come back to Prescott. I probably never would have, but after this ... experience ... I'm really and truly happy to be free of the big firm life. So, please stop trying to convince me."

"I have no intention of asking you again to rejoin Prescott & Talbott."

"Oh."

Her face burned. Now she felt crappy *and* stupidly arrogant. Awesome.

"In fact, I have a very different proposal for you to consider."

His tone was unusually hesitant.

She took a long drink of coffee, wondering what he was driving at.

"What's that?"

He cleared his throat. "I'd like to join your firm."

"Pardon?"

"I don't enjoy managing a large law firm. I enjoy practicing law. Specifically, I enjoy practicing law with colleagues whom I can respect and trust. Although that's true of some of my partners at Prescott & Talbott, it is, sadly, not true of a substantial number. The longer I'm there, the more unappealing the dark underbelly of that particular institution becomes."

She arched a brow. "Dark underbelly's a bit much, don't you think?"

"No, I don't, actually. As it turns out, the reason Greenway dropped its lawsuit against your client was that Garrett English approached their counsel personally and wrote him a check to do it."

"He bribed Chip?"

"Yes," Will said with a sad smile. "I've just filed disciplinary complaints against both of them."

"Wow."

"But let's not pretend Garrett is an outlier. The firm's behavior, as a whole, in this Champion Fuel business is repugnant. Coming on the heels of the mess that Cinco created, it's just taken the joy out of practicing there. I don't want to work with people who could participate in such ugliness. I want to work with someone like you. And like Naya."

Will smoothed a hand over his tie and watched her face.

She'd never considered bringing on a partner. But Will was a talented lawyer. And, even better, a decent human being.

"What're you suggesting—a 50/50 partnership?"

"If you'd be amenable. But it's your firm. I'd certainly understand if you wanted to have a majority stake."

"So The Law Offices of Sasha McCandless would become McCandless & Volmer?"

"Again, if you're willing. You can, as they say, call the shots."

She tilted her head and considered. "It has some appeal," she admitted. "Would Caroline come with you?"

"Possibly. Probably. I would cover her salary for at least the first year. And provided Naya was willing to work for both of us, between the two of us, you and I could likely provide her with a salary increase that might help with her tuition," he pointed out.

"But no associates, right?" She didn't want him bringing any junior lawyers over from Prescott.

"Certainly not." He paused. "Does this mean you're interested?"

To her surprise, she was. "I am. On one condition."

"Which is?"

"Presumably you're going to continue to do white collar criminal defense, right?"

"I'd like to. It seems that your civil clients might have a need for some criminal law representation from time to time. Or at least, *you* could."

Leave it to Will to make the understatement of the ... year? Century?

"No Prescott clients. I don't want to poach their clients and, truth be told, I'd rather have an office full of violent felons than have this firm represent the type of business and industry leaders Prescott manages to attract."

"Trust me. I want to cut all ties with Prescott & Talbott."

She nodded, satisfied. "Well, then, as long as Naya has no objection, I guess we have a deal."

Naya would be thrilled, she knew, but it was only fair to let her weigh in. She'd taken a risk leaving Prescott to join Sasha; she deserved a say.

Will extended his hand. She put down her mug and gave him a firm, warm handshake.

"Excellent, Partner."

"Welcome aboard, Partner." She smiled.

There would be partnership papers to draw up. And she was sure Prescott & Talbott would make Will's departure as painful and unpleasant as possible, but those were just details. She had just moved her fledgling firm into the next phase of its development. It felt exhilarating and frightening all at once.

He smiled back at her. "Do I get the benefit of your free coffee arrangement with Jake?"

43

After begging off with a rain check for Will's offer to celebrate the formation of their new partnership when she was slightly less battered, Sasha decided to make it an early evening.

She packed up her laptop, her billing files, and her headache and trudged down the stairs to the street. The warm spring breeze lifted her spirits. By the time she'd walked through the neighborhood to her condo, she was feeling almost human—despite the sidelong stares her battered face seemed to be drawing from her fellow pedestrians.

Even the black and gold streamers and signs littering the street—a reminder that the Penguins had been busy losing to the Bruins while she'd been facing off with Wally Stewart—didn't dampen her mood too much.

She climbed the stairs to the condo, ready to collapse into a pile of pillows and blankets, nestled in Connelly's arms with Java curled into a ball of fur between them.

But before she'd removed her key from the door, she knew that plan wasn't about to happen.

A platter of mango, pineapple, and starfruit rested on the counter under a glass dome to keep the cat out. A pitcher of margaritas and two salt-rimmed glasses sat beside it. Upbeat music—her music, not the classic rock that Connelly favored —played softly.

Connelly rounded the corner and came into view with a vase full of some fragrant-smelling, vaguely tropical-looking flowers. He placed them on the dining room table and gathered her into a tight hug. He was wearing a white linen shirt and rumpled khaki shorts.

He smelled like ... coconut?

"Are you wearing sunscreen?"

"Not exactly."

He brushed her lips with a soft kiss and led her to the table. While she freed her feet from their high-heeled prison, he poured two margaritas.

Then he returned to the table and handed her one.

"Cheers," she said, still not entirely sure what he was up to.

He rubbed a thumb gently over her bruised and swollen cheek. She smiled up at him and sipped the drink.

It was the perfect combination of cold, salty, sweet, and citrusy. She could tell he'd made it from scratch. No pre-made mixes for her resident mixologist.

He traced his hand along her injured arm and gave her a serious, searching look. She imagined he was picturing the scalpel attack.

"To our wedding," he said.

"Excuse me?" she sputtered.

He smiled, and his gray eyes crinkled.

He produced a box wrapped in cheerful paper from beneath the table.

"What's the occasion?"

"Open it and see."

Java materialized and draped himself around her ankle, stretching to bat at the lemon yellow silk ribbon as she slipped it from the package.

She lifted the lid from the box to reveal a wrinkled and creased junk mail pamphlet addressed to her; a bottle of sunscreen; what appeared to be her mother's ridiculous, oversized beach hat; and a barely-there bikini in baby blue.

"I don't understand."

Connelly clucked his tongue and reached into the box.

"Something old." He smoothed the pamphlet with his hand and laid it on the table.

"Something new." The sunscreen was next.

"Something borrowed." Out came the hat.

"And something blue," he finished, removing the bikini and shooting her a suggestive look.

Sasha wondered if it was possible to sustain brain damage from a black eye, because she still wasn't following.

"Is this my mother's hat?"

She turned the floppy white hat with its black-and-white striped ribbon in one hand. She couldn't fathom why he had her mom's hat, but it was a distinctive hat. It had to be Valentina's.

"Yes."

"And she's lending it to me because ...?"

He took the hat from her hands and drilled her with a look.

"Because I haven't been listening to you. You've been trying to tell me for months that you don't want the wedding your mother and I have been planning."

She opened her mouth to protest, but he cut her off.

"I know, you agreed to it. But it isn't what you want."

"Connelly, it's important to you—"

"No. *You're* important to me. Standing before God, and your family, and our friends and declaring myself bound to you forever is important to me. The rest of it is just pageantry."

Tears flooded her eyes and fireworks of happiness exploded in her chest.

She smiled up at him and he pulled her close.

"You want to elope?" she asked, snugging into his chest.

He leaned back and looked down at her with a bemused, mildly horrified expression. "Do you really think your mom lent me that hat so we could elope?"

Point taken.

"Uh, I'm guessing no," she said, confused again.

"We're going to this island and getting

married," he grabbed the pamphlet. "And we're bringing everyone who matters to witness it."

She just smiled and reached over to scratch Java's chin.

"Okay?" he said.

"My mother agreed to this?" She couldn't imagine how he'd gotten Valentina on board.

"Your mother agreed that this is our wedding."

She'd have to get the details about *that* conversation. Maybe after a few drinks.

"Okay, then."

"Good."

"I love you, Leo Connelly. Thank you."

He traced her cheek with a finger and handed her glass back to her.

"No, thank you."

She leaned forward and covered his mouth with hers, breathing in the scent of coconut and Connelly. Hers. Forever.

"To our wedding," she said, touching her glass to his.

"To our wedding. Screw the cookie table," he proclaimed.

She lowered her glass and gaped at him owl-eyed. "Wait. What? No, no, we *have* to have a cookie table."

I HOPE you enjoyed *Improper Influence*. Turn the page to read an excerpt of *Dark Path*, the first book in a series of forensic thrillers featuring Bodhi King!

AUTHOR'S NOTE

AUTHOR'S NOTE

Readers who've been lucky enough to attend a wedding held in Pittsburgh (or elsewhere in Western Pennsylvania), or one where the bride, the groom, or both had ties to Pittsburgh, are probably nodding sagely right about now. For those who haven't had the experience, it's traditional at a Pittsburgh wedding to have a cookie table. For weeks, or months, before the wedding, the family and friends of the bride (and sometimes the groom) make dozens upon dozens of cookies of every imaginable kind—all from scratch. The cookies are frozen, if need be, until the big day, when they are plated and carefully transported to the reception site. There will probably also be a wedding cake, but no one will eat it—because, oh, the cookies. So many delicious cookies. This all true. No less venerable an institution than *The New York Times* has reported on it. http://nyti.ms/11uTHWq.

ALSO BY MELISSA F. MILLER

Want to know when I release a new book?

Go to www.melissafmiller.com to sign up for my email newsletter.

Prefer text alerts? Text BOOKS to 636-303-1088 to receive new release alerts and updates.

The Sasha McCandless Legal Thriller Series

Irreparable Harm

Inadvertent Disclosure

Irretrievably Broken

Indispensable Party

Lovers and Madmen (Novella)

Improper Influence

A Marriage of True Minds (Novella)

Irrevocable Trust

Irrefutable Evidence

A Mingled Yarn (Novella)

Informed Consent

International Incident

Imminent Peril

The Humble Salve (Novella)

Intentional Acts

In Absentia

Inevitable Discovery

Full Fathom Five (Novella)

The Aroostine Higgins Novels

Critical Vulnerability

Chilling Effect

Calculated Risk

Called Home

Crossfire Creek

Clingmans Dome

The Bodhi King Novels

Dark Path

Lonely Path

Hidden Path

Twisted Path

Cold Path

The We Sisters Three Romantic Comedic Mysteries

ABOUT THE AUTHOR

USA Today bestselling author Melissa F. Miller was born in Pittsburgh, Pennsylvania. Although life and love led her to Philadelphia, Baltimore, Washington, D.C., and, ultimately, South Central Pennsylvania, she secretly still considers Pittsburgh home.

In college, she majored in English literature with concentrations in creative writing poetry and medieval literature and was stunned, upon graduation, to learn that there's not exactly a job market for such a degree. After working as an editor for several years, she returned to school to earn a law degree. She was that annoying girl who loved class and always raised her hand. She practiced law for fifteen years, including a stint as a clerk for a federal judge, nearly a decade as an attorney at major international law firms, and several years running a two-person law firm with her lawyer husband.

Now, powered by coffee, she writes legal thrillers and homeschools her three children. When she's not writing, and sometimes when she is, Melissa travels around the country in an RV with her husband, her kids, and her cat.

Connect with me:
www.melissafmiller.com

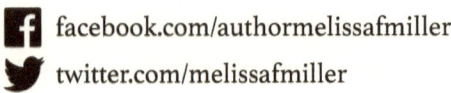 facebook.com/authormelissafmiller
twitter.com/melissafmiller

ACKNOWLEDGMENTS

Sincere thanks and appreciation to my editing and proofreading team, especially Curt Akin and Lou Maconi. As always, any mistakes or errors that remain are mine and mine alone. Five novels in, there's not much left to say to my amazing husband and children, other than thank you so much for supporting my writing and for bringing me food when I am holed up in the office. Special thanks to Sasha's Associates for their sustained cheerleading, excitement, and support.